We Almost Had Forever

Some Bonds Defy Time, Distance and Memory

Written by

Simon Mennell

Dedication

To Winan

My Love. My Inspiration

Copyright

Disclaimer

This book is a work of fiction. Names, characters, businesses, places, events, and incidents are either the products of the author's imagination or used in a fictitious manner. Any resemblance to actual persons, living or dead, or actual events is purely coincidental.

The views and opinions expressed in this book are those of the characters and do not necessarily reflect the views or opinions of the author or the publisher. This book is intended purely for entertainment purposes, and the author and publisher assume no responsibility for any actions taken as a result of reading this fiction.

Reader discretion is advised as this story may include themes or portrayals that some readers might find sensitive or triggering.

Table of Contents

1

City in Bloom – Monsoon Season 1957 (Singapore)

Our story begins in Singapore, October 1957. The island woke gently—still marked by the scars of war and occupation, yet filled with hope for a future rising from its wounds. The streets hummed with life—a lively mix of cultures, histories, and dreams. Old shophouses, their paint peeling in spots, stood side by side with new buildings. Their different fronts told of a city caught between past and future.

The air was heavy with humidity, carrying the smell of rain-soaked earth, spices from street stalls, and the sweet scent of kaya toast. As the sun sank low, painting the sky with shades of orange and purple, vendors shouted their specials—their voices weaving through the sounds of modern cars, trishaws, and rustling leaves. Lanterns came alive, casting a warm, golden glow over the bustle. The city, full of movement, stood ready for change.

Tucked within this lively mix was a modest shophouse in Emerald Hill, just off Orchard Road—a peaceful haven where Daniel and Mei Lin's life unfolded in soft rhythms. They were young—dreamers, lovers—but their roots went deep. Daniel's father, a British colonial officer, had come to Singapore decades before. His mother, a proud Singaporean, had met him in the chaotic years after the war. Their love stood as a quiet symbol of the city's complex past: a blend of empire and strength.

Daniel was a man of quiet passions. As a skilled radio engineer, he spent his evenings hunched over his workbench, soldering delicate circuits and drawing distant voices from his ham radio. Each faint crackle was more than noise—it was a lifeline, a whisper from another world. His eyes sparkled with wonder at every broadcast, caught up in tales of adventurers and explorers who mapped the edges of human experience. To Daniel, the radio was more than a device—it was a bridge between worlds, linking far-off places through a gentle mix of sound and static. Mei Lin often sat nearby, reading or sketching, her presence steadying him. She understood his quiet moments, just as he loved her soft laughter. In their small home, their days turned like pages in a diary—filled with moments both simple and meaningful.

Mei Lin, kind and caring, was a teacher—her heart set on guiding young minds in a world that changed by the minute. She often sat by the window of their modest Emerald Hill home, her hands resting on her belly, feeling the gentle flutter of life inside. The love she held for Daniel and their unborn child was a steady, quiet rhythm—a heartbeat running through her every thought. She pictured the days ahead, their future unfolding like the tropical rain outside: unpredictable yet full of promise.

Each night, as rain drew silver lines down the window, Mei Lin sat quietly, her hand resting softly on her growing belly. Every flutter of the child inside her was a reminder—a promise of new life and hope. She pictured calm afternoons by the sea, gentle walks under starry skies, and bedtime stories told in the dark. In her heart, their child would grow wrapped in love and learning, free from the shadows of the past. Yet, sometimes, when the wind howled fiercely or the clouds hung too low, a hint of worry crept into her dreams. Light as a butterfly's wings, but there all the same.

Outside, the world buzzed with life and sound. But inside Mei Lin, a world was taking shape—fragile, hidden, and full of gentle promise.

The coming arrival of their child sparked a wave of feelings: joy, nervousness, and a love so deep it took her breath away. Together, she and Daniel were building a new start in a city that carried its past scars yet still leant, boldly, toward the future.

In that small room—where rain pattered gently on the windows and electric lanterns cast soft glows—Mei Lin felt a yearning almost too gentle to name. It warmed her heart with joy and worry: the wish to protect what was coming, to guide a life not yet born, and to cherish a love that had already changed her in ways she hadn't expected. Deep down, a quiet question stayed: Would this delicate peace last long enough for their child to grow in it?

"How was work today, Pip?" Mei Lin's voice floated softly through the room, light as the rain pattering at the windows.

Daniel sat hunched over their messy table, surrounded by tangled wires, notepads, and the warm light of vacuum tubes. His hands stopped mid-task, her familiar voice breaking through his thoughts.

"Pip"—her playful nickname for him—came from pipsqueak, a cheeky tease from their school days, when he'd been smaller than most of their mates. He'd grown taller since, but the name had stayed, worn now like a favourite jumper, worn but cosy.

Daniel's eyes lifted, glancing briefly at the small gecko perched on the wall behind him—his quiet companion through many late nights with the radio. Some said geckos brought luck, guarding the home. He liked to think this one was looking out for them.

His gaze met hers—bright, familiar, steadying. The noise of the world faded for a moment. "It was good," Daniel said, a soft smile spreading. "During lunch, I caught a transmission—from Sputnik, that satellite the Soviets launched. Even picked up a signal from Jakarta before sunset."

Mei Lin raised an eyebrow. "Sputnik? Sounds like a name for a cat."

Daniel laughed, his eyes sparkling. "Maybe. But think about it—this is just the start. One day, they could send radio signals from the Moon… or even Mars!" His excitement was boyish, catching. Mei Lin leaned closer, drawn to the happiness shining in his eyes. "Do you think we'll ever go there?" she asked, half-teasing, half-curious. "Picture it—our little one, hopping about on the Moon. An adventure among the stars." Daniel shook his head, chuckling quietly.

Mei Lin watched him a moment longer. He always looked like that when he spoke of distant places—like a lad with dreams stuffed in his pockets. Though her feet stayed firmly on the ground, her heart reached upward too, wondering how far love and science might take them.

"For now, we're explorers in our own backyard," Daniel replied, chuckling. "But who knows? Maybe one day we'll take a family trip to Mars."

Daniel burst into laughter, a boyish joy shining from him, filling the room with warmth. Mei Lin smiled, letting his optimism wrap around her like a cosy blanket.

As the evening settled into its usual rhythm, Daniel leant toward the radio and turned the dial, fingers moving with natural ease. Static filled the room—a soft hiss and crackle—before a voice came through, calm and steady, laced with a warm Southern drawl.

"Hey Buddy, how's it going over there?"

It was Billy—Daniel's technician friend from Florida. His voice brought a grin to Daniel's face, the way old friends do when their words cross oceans to reach you.

The evening was filled with soft talk about the life ahead—a new start, a fresh beginning. Joy sparkled in Daniel's voice, every word filled with excitement, showing he couldn't wait for it all to start. With a gentle, careful motion, he reached out and took Mei Lin's hand, placing it on his chest. His heartbeat thudded steady and strong beneath her fingers—constant, full of hope.

"Okay, Billy, I've got to go," Daniel said quietly at last. "Catch you later."

The radio crackled once more, then fell silent—only static lingered.

He looked at Mei Lin, his eyes shining with love and promise.

"Listen," he whispered, wonder laced through every word. "This—this wide universe—is what we're part of. And soon, we'll have our own little star with us."

Mei Lin smiled, her heart swelling with a love so strong it almost ached.

"What shall we name them?" she asked softly, her voice quivering with excitement. "I suppose it depends on whether they're a boy or a girl when they arrive."

Her eyes glowed with hope, excitement, and a longing that reached far into the future. Daniel's face broke into a grin, and he chuckled warmly.

"If it's a girl, how about Sputnik-Ava?" he suggested, laughing, his voice warm with feeling. "For that amazing feat—the first satellite in space—and because it sounds bold, full of promise. I want her to feel she can do anything, just by being herself."

Mei Lin's smile grew as she savoured his words, her fingers softly tracing the curve of her growing belly.

"I want her to feel her Thai roots too," she said, her voice gentle but filled with certainty. "If it's a girl, how about Na Khing? It's simple and special, like her grandmother Po's name. And if it's a boy, I'd like his middle name to be Sirawat, after his grandfather. Either way, I want them to carry that bond—a piece of Thailand's heart in their name."

She paused, then added with a quiet laugh,

"And no Sputnik, alright?"

She glanced at Daniel with playful affection, then turned and walked to the kitchen, joy rising inside her like a tune she couldn't help but hum.

"Whatever makes you happy, my love," Daniel replied, turning from the radio to meet her eyes. "I just want to see you smile. And I love that she'll have that special tie to Thailand—her roots, her heart. That means the world to me too."

As night settled in, their home brimmed with plans and dreams—visions of the future dancing between the stars and the earth.

Mei Lin spoke of teaching their child the beauty of nature, the arts, and the small wonders in life that often go unnoticed. Daniel pictured countless evenings gazing at the sky, pointing out constellations, and sharing tales of far-off galaxies—his voice gentle, like a bedtime lullaby sprinkled with stardust.

The warm glow of their lamp cast a soft light across the room, mixing with the quiet rustle of leaves outside and the faint buzz of insects near the window—like a night-time melody humming in tune with their dreams.

Their words wrapped a cocoon of hope and excitement around them, as if time had slowed—each heartbeat pulsing with eagerness for the great adventure of parenthood ahead.

Suddenly, a gentle realisation swept over Mei Lin. The thought of soon carrying the weight of motherhood—of holding a new life in her arms—felt as thrilling as it was daunting. A hint of uncertainty flickered in her eyes.

"What if I'm not ready?" she whispered, her voice shaking with openness.

Daniel, noticing her change, gently put his work aside and took her hands, holding them in his warm palms.

"We'll work it out together," he said, his voice a calm comfort. "Every step, every challenge—we'll learn as we go. As long as we fill our child's life with love, that's what counts most."

He paused, then smiled softly.

"Like those Soviets in space—no guidebook, just courage and hope. We'll face whatever comes, hand in hand. No rules—just our love to light the way."

Hearing his words, Mei Lin leant closer, resting her head on his shoulder. For a moment, she closed her eyes, embracing the unknown—with faith in their love and trust in the path ahead.

Outside their shophouse, Singapore buzzed with life—lively streets, busy markets, and the endless hopes of a nation nearing independence. It was a world full of change and promise. But inside their home, there was peace—a haven built on love and shared dreams.

In that quiet moment, they felt ready. Ready to open their hearts and welcome the life growing between them. The world outside could shift and grow, but in their hearts, they had all they needed to start anew.

And as they sat wrapped in the warmth of their hopes, Daniel and Mei Lin knew: their greatest adventure had already begun.

The next morning, Daniel and Mei Lin woke early, a spark of excitement mixed with quiet nerves. The air was lighter than it had been for days—a welcome relief from the usual humidity, especially for Mei Lin. Still, they knew the day ahead would be warm.

Mei Lin had been up for a while, quietly lost in her thoughts as she made Daniel's favourite morning drink—teh tarik. It was a simple habit, but one that brought her gentle joy each day. She poured the tea from cup to cup, letting the amber stream flow and swirl, forming a frothy top that glowed in the soft morning light.

Even in the smallest acts, she found a way to show her love. And to her, that meant everything.

Daniel sat in the kitchen, watching her with quiet affection. He loved the care she put into these mornings—even when she was tired from the heat and the slow walk downstairs. His smile was gentle but true, the love clear in his eyes.

Taking a long sip of the rich, sweet tea, he looked at Mei Lin—her face glowing with warmth and kindness.

"This is wonderful, Mei Lin," he said softly, a small smile playing on his lips. "So… what shall we do today? We're meeting Khian-Seng for lunch, but the morning's ours."

Mei Lin paused, her eyes sparkling with an idea.

Khian-Seng, Daniel's older brother, had always been a steady guide in his life.

"I'd love to visit Sungei Road," Mei Lin said softly, her voice warm with quiet excitement. "The market there has lovely baby clothes, and it's near where we're meeting Khian-Seng. We could choose a couple of outfits—one for a boy, one for a girl. I want everything to be just right for the baby, prepared with love."

Stepping outside, the city welcomed them with bright colours and sounds. The smell of street food and the noise of morning life filled the air—vendors shouting their wares, children giggling as they ran past, carts rattling over uneven cobbles. The scent of fresh herbs, fried fish, and sizzling satay drifted on the breeze, rich and familiar.

Above, the sky was a clear blue. The tropical sun was already climbing, shining down with its usual warmth.

They moved through the busy market, weaving between stalls brimming with colourful fabrics—red, blue, and gold—tiny shoes, handmade treasures, and heaps of fresh produce. The air hummed with chatter, bargaining, and the lively clatter of life in motion.

Mei Lin's eyes sparkled at the sight of tiny rompers and dainty lace dresses. She wandered from stall to stall with quiet joy, her fingers gliding over soft cotton and neat embroidery, picking only the gentlest, most lovely pieces she pictured her baby wearing.

She held up a bright pink outfit, smiling broadly.

"Oh, Daniel—look at this! Isn't it gorgeous? I love the colour—it'll look smashing!"

Daniel chuckled, a playful grin on his face.

"Not if it's a boy, it won't!" he teased, his laughter rising above the buzz of the crowd.

"Alright," Mei Lin said, her voice carrying a hint of tiredness. "We're a bit late. Khian-Seng will be waiting… and I could use a rest."

Daniel nodded gently, spotting the fatigue in her eyes.

"You're right. You've done plenty today," he said kindly, placing a comforting hand on her arm.

A short stroll later, they reached their favourite laksa stall just down the road. The warm, spicy scent of broth filled the air, rich and soothing. Daniel saw Khian-Seng and waved, his smile growing wider.

"You're late—again," Khian-Seng called out with a playful grin as they approached.

"Come, Mei Lin. Sit here," he said, standing slightly to offer his seat. "You look warm and knackered. Rest your feet while Daniel grabs us some food. You seem like you need it."

Mei Lin gave a tired smile, grateful for her brother-in-law's kindness. She sank onto the shaded bench, savouring the brief rest amid the morning's hustle. Daniel gave her shoulder a gentle pat before heading off to order their meal, his touch and the warm presence of family easing the day's weight.

"How are you holding up, Mei Lin? You doing alright?" Khian-Seng asked, his voice soft with concern as he watched her catch her breath.

A faint, weary smile crossed her lips. She lightly dabbed her forehead, then smoothed the damp fabric of her dress, the heat sticking to her skin.

"I'm okay," she said quietly, though a hint of tiredness lingered in her voice. "Thanks for asking. It's just the heat— nothing I can't manage."

She closed her eyes for a moment and took a slow, deep breath. The air was rich—filled with the scent of rain on dry earth, spices from nearby stalls, and the gentle buzz of the market carried on the breeze. Her shoulders relaxed, the tension in her body fading as the morning's strain quietly slipped away.

"I'm really fine," Mei Lin said, opening her eyes again. "You two don't need to fret. It's just the sun—a bit rough today, that's all." Her voice was softer now, tinged with quiet relief. "This little rest... I reckon I needed it more than I thought."

She looked at Daniel, giving him a weary but grateful smile. "Could you fetch me some water, please?"

Daniel's smile warmed, his eyes full of quiet fondness. Watching her, he felt a familiar glow—her steady strength calming him in their ever-changing world. He waved to the waitress for a cold glass of water, then turned back to Mei Lin, his eyes fixed on her.

"You've done plenty today," he said softly, gently squeezing her hand. "Rest now, my darling. We've still got time to sort things for the baby."

He paused, his thumb gently brushing her knuckles. "After lunch, we'll head home. This is just the start, Mei Lin. Whatever's coming, we'll tackle it—like always—side by side."

Mei Lin nodded slowly, leaning back on the bench, letting Daniel's words wash over her like a comfort. Her shoulders eased off, shedding the tension that had gripped her all morning. A gentle smile curved her lips as she held Daniel's hand, finding quiet strength in his warm touch. Despite the heat and her tiredness, there was a deep calm between them—a silent vow that whatever lay ahead, they'd tackle it together.

Soon, three steaming bowls of laksa arrived, their tasty spices swirling in warm curls. The rich scent—coconut, chilli, lemongrass—filled the air, wrapping them in a familiar, cosy feeling.

They ate in easy silence, the spicy broth warming their bodies and hearts. Each spoonful carried a bit of hope—simple and nourishing. A reminder that even in a chaotic world, love and small joys could steady them and light the way.

When they finished, Mei Lin glanced at Daniel across the table, now chatting with Khian-Seng. Her eyes lingered, shining with gratitude and love.

"Thanks, Pip," Mei Lin said softly, her voice just above a whisper. "For everything. For today, and all the days ahead. I've never been this happy…" She paused, then gave a light chuckle. "Even if I'm roasting in this heat."

The tiredness in her body faded, just for a moment, as quiet joy grew in her heart.

Daniel turned to her, his hand reaching across the table to gently squeeze hers. "We're in this together," he said, his voice soft but steady. "Whatever comes, we'll tackle it side by side. With love. That's what counts. One step at a time, we're building something proper. Something that'll last."

Just then, Khian-Seng cut in with a cheeky grin. "Alright, enough of this mushy stuff for one day," he said, laughing. "I'll leave you two lovebirds to it. Catch you next weekend—let me know if anything exciting pops up."

Daniel stood to shake his brother's hand, smiling warmly. "Cheers, Khian-Seng," he said.

As Khian-Seng walked off, he tossed a wave over his shoulder. "Keep me in the loop, yeah?"

Mei Lin and Daniel got up from the stall, their bodies tired, but their hearts light. They strolled side by side through the bustling streets, the city alive around them with its usual buzz—laughter ringing from alleys, the clatter of carts, the lively hum of chatter, and the rich scent of spices floating in the warm air.

The world outside was full of life—noisy, unpredictable, and always changing. But in their quiet bond, there was something lasting. A love strong enough to handle any change. A hope ready for what came next.

As the days went by, Daniel threw himself into getting ready for their baby. He spent hours painting bright murals on the nursery walls—stars and blooming flowers that seemed to dance under his brush. He carefully hung little pictures and keepsakes, each one a sign of love and hope, turning the room into a cosy haven full of warmth and excitement.

Mei Lin often sat close by, her hands resting gently on her belly as she watched Daniel work. She gave quiet cheers, her eyes shining with pride. Though exhausted from the heat and the strain of pregnancy, she found strength in just being there—sharing his happiness, a calm and steady mate beside him as they built their future, one loving touch at a time.

In those quiet moments, with the soft buzz of the radio in the background and the cosy glow of evening settling around them, they felt it: a love deep and strong. Ready to care for the little life waiting to join them.

Their simple home hummed with hope, wrapped in the quiet sureness that whatever lay ahead, they'd tackle it hand in hand—building their life, step by step, side by side.

One evening, as Bill Hayley tunes crackled through the radio's soft static, Daniel shared an idea that had been quietly brewing in his head.

"What if we start a family tradition?" Daniel said, staring at the ceiling as if spotting stars. "Something that ties us to the universe, and to our kid."

Mei Lin tilted her head, her curiosity sparked. Wonder what he's on about, she thought, a gentle smile forming. "What's your idea?"

Daniel turned to her, his face glowing with quiet excitement. "Every night, before bed, we pick a star to wish on. One day, we'll share stories about those stars—tales, dreams, old myths. Let our baby grow up knowing there's a big, beautiful world out there waiting."

His eyes shone with hope, a spark of possibility dancing between them.

"That's proper lovely," Mei Lin said, her heart full at the thought. "It'll be our little tradition—something they can pass on, maybe to their own children one day."

And so their nightly ritual kicked off. Each evening, they stepped into the back garden, looking up at the endless sky. Daniel pointed out stars and spun yarns of ancient tales woven around the lights above. With every story, they planted seeds of wonder and adventure—gifts to light their children's path through the world one day.

As December rolled in, Singapore's festive season wrapped the city in a burst of colours and cheery decorations. The smell of baked treats drifted from nearby street stalls, mixing with the cool evening breeze. The air seemed to buzz with joy and hope, matching Mei Lin's growing excitement for the baby's arrival soon.

On a warm evening, with the city glowing softly around them, Mei Lin turned to Daniel, her voice full of wonder. "Pip, can you believe it's nearly time? The baby will be here in just a few weeks."

Daniel grinned, his heart full of pride and excitement. "It's like waiting for a new signal on the radio," he said, eyes sparkling. "Or picking up a beep from an old Soviet space launch. We've done the prep, got everything ready—and soon she'll be here, ready to join the world."

Mei Lin chuckled, gently shaking her head. "Oh, Pip... it's a baby, not a radio signal."

In those final days before the birth, the couple treasured the simple, everyday moments. They celebrated the smallest steps—Mei Lin checking baby clothes with a keen eye, Daniel painting the nursery walls in soft, calming colours, then tussling with the crib while she gave playful natter from nearby.

Laughter filled their home, blending with the smell of fresh paint and the buzz of far-off traffic. Love wrapped them like the warm glow of the Singapore sun—steady, bright, and full of hope.

Then, one big night, with the air thick with excitement and nerves, Mei Lin felt the first pains of labour. It hit like a wave—sudden, strong, impossible to miss.

"Daniel!" she called, her voice shaky with both worry and excitement.

He dashed to her side, eyes wide, heart thumping. "Is it time?" he asked, catching his breath as he looked at her.

"Yes… I reckon so. We need to go—now!"

Together, they jumped into action. Daniel grabbed the overnight bag Mei Lin had packed weeks before and placed above the wardrobe. Their hearts beat as one as they hurried downstairs, out into the courtyard, and into the car.

The streets of Singapore shone around them, lights twinkling on the pavement like stars on water. The city, their constant backdrop, now felt alive—buzzing with the hope of something new, something proper special. As they headed to Kandang Kerbau Hospital near Little India, the night itself seemed to hum with excitement.

Daniel held Mei Lin's hand tight, offering steady words of comfort as they moved through the hospital's bustle. This was more than just a building—it was a step into a new life, where their dreams would soon become their little one.

With each contraction, Mei Lin felt their hopes tied to the raw, strong force of life. Her breath came in waves, her body shaking with the effort, but Daniel stayed close, solid and caring. He leaned in, his voice soft but firm.

"You're doing brilliant, Mei Lin. Soon, we'll be holding our little star."

As they reached the hospital entrance, Daniel stopped the car. Mei Lin stepped out carefully, leaning into the growing pain.

"It'll be two minutes, Mei Lin," Daniel said, pointing to a nearby parking spot, trying to hide the rush in his voice with calm. "I'll be right back, love."

At that moment, as night turned to dawn, they stepped into the unknown—hearts full of love and courage—ready to take on their biggest adventure yet.

As they entered the hospital's maternity ward, the lively buzz of the city faded, replaced by the clean, sharp air of the emergency room. The strong smell of antiseptic mixed with a hint of incense and the gentle warmth of people. Bright lights hummed overhead, casting a stark glow on nurses and doctors moving quickly through the halls, each focused and steady.

The reception area was full of noise—the rustle of papers, the soft ping of call buttons, the quiet natter of voices. For a moment, it was a bit much. Daniel held Mei Lin's hand tighter, his heart thumping as the rush of the moment hit hard.

"Mei Lin, you alright?" Daniel asked, his voice tight with worry, eyes locked on her as another wave of pain crossed her face.

Mei Lin turned to him, her gaze steady. In that moment, she twigged something surprising—Daniel was more afraid of what was about to come, more than she was.

With each contraction, she breathed deep, finding her calm in the rhythm of her breath. Despite the noise and rush around her, she stayed focused on the one thing that mattered: the little life they were about to bring into the world.

"I'm okay, just—just a bit sore. I'll be fine!" Mei Lin said, her voice strained but strong, determination and excitement shining in her eyes.

Daniel, though, was starting to fret. The bustle around them rushed like a tidal wave—flashing lights, quick footsteps, sharp chatter—everything felt too loud, too fast. Worry crept into his thoughts like a shadow.

"What if something goes wrong?" Daniel blurted, eyes darting between the nurses, the monitors, and Mei Lin's tight grip. His heart thumped hard, like it was searching for something solid to cling to.

Mei Lin winced, then gave him a sharp look. "That's not helping, Daniel," she said through gritted teeth, a flash of pain crossing her face.

Before his worry could grow worse, a nurse stepped calmly in front of them, her presence like a steady hand in a storm.

"Sir," she said softly but firmly, "everything's going to be alright. Your wife's strong—and we're here to help you both. Let's get to the delivery room."

Her calm was a lifeline in the storm of Daniel's fears. He took a deep breath and managed a small smile, letting her kind words wash over him like a comfort. She led them through the maze of corridors, her voice a steady guide.

"Just keep focusing on Mei Lin," she said gently. "Support her with every breath. You're in good hands, mate."

As they got close to the delivery room, Daniel felt the walls close in a bit, sharpening his focus. The room was bright and clean, softened by pale colours meant to calm. Machines buzzed softly in the background, and cheerful posters lined the walls, their words fading as his eyes stayed on Mei Lin.

"Here we are, right in here," the nurse said, guiding them inside.

Mei Lin climbed onto the hospital bed, gripping the rails as another contraction hit hard. Daniel stood by her side, their fingers locked—his grip firm but gentle. A bit of worry still buzzed in his chest, but a stronger sense of strength started to grow.

Seeing her there— strong, yet open—something clicked in him. He leaned in, voice calm but steady. "Breathe, Mei Lin. Like we practiced," he whispered, matching his breaths to hers. "In and out, yeah?"

Her eyes met his, wide but sure. She nodded slowly, and in that shared look, her fear eased. His presence steadied her; her courage lifted him.

The nurse checked Mei Lin's signs, her voice a steady comfort in the rising storm. "You're doing brilliant, Mei Lin. Keep those deep breaths going. Just a bit longer, and you'll meet your baby, my darling."

The mood in the room started to change. Each minute brought a new spark of energy—calm, focused, but buzzing with excitement. More staff came in quietly, moving with the ease of long practice. Their soft natter and teamwork created a steady rhythm, a comforting balance to the growing tension.

Then, the doctor walked in, his presence sure but kind. He gave a warm smile that instantly settled them. "Morning! We're ready to welcome your baby," he said brightly, resting a steady hand on Mei Lin's shoulder. "Let's get going. Mei Lin, when you're ready, just give us a shout."

Daniel felt the tightness in his shoulders ease a bit. Surrounded by skill and care, his worries faded, replaced by wonder. He turned all his focus to Mei Lin—her face glowing with quiet strength, eyes sharp, body braced but calm. She looked proper special, not despite the pain, but somehow through it.

He squeezed her hand gently, quietly amazed at the strength and grace she showed in this moment. "You've got this," he whispered, his voice full of wonder and steady love.

The minutes melted into a blur of deep breaths, soft voices, and growing excitement. Each contraction hit like a crashing wave, stretching time and squashing it all at once. Yet through the blur, Daniel held tight to Mei Lin, feeling the beat of their shared hope—steady, rising, unstoppable.

"We're nearly there," he murmured, gently brushing damp hair from her face. "You're amazing. Just a few more pushes, and we'll meet our little star."

A quiet fire sparked in Mei Lin. Drawing strength from Daniel's voice, the steady hands around her, and the love holding them together, she gave everything to the moment. Pain turned to purpose. The noise, the bustle, even her fear— all faded. There was only this: the step from one world to the next.

And then, like the first light of dawn, a sound rang out.

A cry—sharp, bright, and utterly beautiful—rang through the room. A newborn's first wail, clear as the sky after a downpour, cut through the noise and settled in their hearts like a cherished hymn.

Their baby was here.

The room filled with the stunning sound of the newborn's cry—sharp, piercing, yet wonderfully beautiful. It wasn't just a sound; it was a melody of life, the peak of all their hopes and dreams. Daniel's heart swelled as he gazed at Mei Lin, her face glowing despite her exhaustion, a radiant smile spreading across her lips, lighting up the whole room.

"Congratulations! You've got a beautiful baby girl," the doctor said, gently placing the tiny bundle into Mei Lin's waiting arms.

In that moment, the world around them faded. Time stood still. Nothing mattered but the warmth of their new little family.

Mei Lin cradled the baby against her chest, the softness of her daughter's skin sparking a wave of love so strong it stole her breath. Tears welled in her eyes as she looked down at the delicate, rosy face nestled in the blanket's folds.

"She's perfect," Mei Lin whispered, her voice heavy with emotion. "Our little Ava."

Daniel edged closer, his heart beating in time with their daughter's cries. As he gazed at Ava for the first time, it felt as if all the stars from their nightly rituals had come together in one tiny, perfect being. Awe enveloped him like a warm blanket, and when he spoke, his voice was little more than a whisper.

"Hello, my darling little Ava. Welcome to the world."

Ava's cries softened, as if she sensed the love surrounding her. Nestled against her mother's chest, she seemed to feel the safety that enveloped her. Daniel reached out and gently touched her hand, his breath catching as her tiny fingers curled tightly around his thumb—small, yet with a grip that anchored him completely.

"Look at her," Mei Lin whispered, tears rolling down her cheeks. "She's so calm now."

The nurse, watching the quiet miracle unfold, gave a warm smile.

"It's wonderful how newborns respond to their parents' voices and touch. You're both doing brilliantly."

They sat in quiet awe, enchanted by the soft coos coming from the tiny bundle in Mei Lin's arms. Ava blinked slowly, her dark eyes wide and curious as she gazed up at them—her look unsteady but searching, as if trying to learn the faces of the two people who would be her whole world.

"Can we name her Ava Na Khing?" Mei Lin asked, looking up at Daniel, her eyes seeking his approval.

"Yes, Ava Na Khing," he said gently, a smile spreading across his face. "Ava, for the adventures to come."

They shared a soft chuckle, their joy easing the weight of the moment. In that bubble of love, where tiredness met excitement, the intensity of birth softened into something deep—a bond warm and glowing, like the stars they often wished upon.

"Have you thought about your first adventure together?" the nurse asked, skilfully cleaning Ava and wrapping her snugly in a fresh blanket. "How about a first family photo?"

Daniel and Mei Lin shared a glance, their hearts brimming with unspoken excitement.

"Yes! Let's take one now," Daniel said, stepping beside Mei Lin, still smiling. He handed the nurse the camera and leaned in close, his arm gently around Mei Lin's shoulder.

"Hang on, let me dry my eyes first. I don't want to ruin the photo." Mei Lin said, as she wiped her eyes with a tissue.

The camera clicked softly, capturing the tender moment—Daniel's tearful smile, Mei Lin's quiet joy, and the delicate beauty of Ava nestled between them. Just as the shutter clicked again, Ava's tiny fingers reached out and brushed Daniel's hand.

He looked at Mei Lin, emotion catching in his throat as tears rolled down his cheeks.

"She's already reaching for the world," he whispered.

Daniel knew this was just the start—an adventure that would unfold in ways they couldn't yet imagine. Ava, so tiny and perfect, lay between them like a promise of all the paths yet to come.

"Okay, smile," the nurse said, camera ready. "I'll take a few more to make sure we get a good one."

After the photos, the nurse gently lifted Ava for her first check-up, leaving Daniel and Mei Lin in a hush of quiet wonder.

"Can you believe she's ours?" Mei Lin whispered, her voice filled with awe.

Daniel nodded slowly, his eyes fixed where their daughter had been moments before.

"It's amazing," he said, his voice heavy with emotion. "Ava is our dream come true. We'll show her the world—just like we always promised."

"We'll make sure she knows the stories of the stars and explores every possibility," Mei Lin said, a bright smile lighting up her face.

Just then, the nurse returned, cradling Ava gently in her arms.

"She's healthy and perfect! You've both done a brilliant job."

The room seemed to shimmer, as if wrapped in a warm embrace—joy settling around them like a gentle cocoon.

"You must be hungry," the nurse said.

"I am," Mei Lin admitted with a soft chuckle.

"Your favourite is what you need now—fish ball noodles," Daniel said, heading for the door. "There's a hawker stall across the street. I'll grab some for you. And I need to call our parents—they'll be eager to hear the news."

Mei Lin smiled after him, her heart brimming, shouting "Don't forget to tell our parents, and Khian- Seng" as he slipped through the doorway.

Daniel reached the main reception area, where the family had gathered in anticipation. Waiting eagerly were his parents, David and Mei Lian, his brother Khian Seng, and Mei Lin's parents, Somsri and Wei Ming—all desperate for news.

"I'm thrilled to tell you all that Ava has arrived," Daniel announced, his chest swelling with pride. "Mother and baby are both doing well and resting now. You'll be able to visit later, and when they come home, we'll have a gathering at the house—everyone's welcome."

"Oh, that's wonderful news!" Somsri exclaimed. "A girl! Can you believe it? Our first grandchild—and she's a girl!"

Cheers erupted from the group as they leapt up, showering Daniel with congratulations and joy.

"I'm off to get Mei Lin some fish ball noodles," Daniel added with a grin. "Anyone fancy joining me?"

"Can't we go see them?" Wei Ming asked.

"No, they're resting now, you can see them tomorrow. Let's goget some food, I'm starving" Daniel replied.

The whole family followed him eagerly down the road to the nearby hawker market, ensuring Daniel brought back plenty to keep Mei Lin well-fed.

Hours passed, and a new rhythm slowly settled into place—the start of their life as a family. The worries and chaos of the past faded into the background, overtaken by the quiet simplicity of shared moments. New stories were beginning. Dreams, once distant, were now coming true.

Visitors came and went, their arms laden with gifts and kind wishes, the room glowing with warmth and celebration for the new arrival.

Through the thin fabric walls of the hospital room, Daniel could still hear the hum of Singapore outside—a city alive, bustling with its own tales. Yet in that calm, precious moment, nothing mattered more than the soft sighs of Mei Lin and the gentle whimpers of Ava, safely nestled in her mother's arms.

As night fell and they settled into the hospital bed together, wrapped in warmth and new beginnings, Daniel leaned down and kissed his daughter's forehead. His voice was a whisper, but his words carried a promise that would last a lifetime.

"We're going to explore the universe as a family—together."

And with that vow wrapped around them like a lullaby, they drifted into peaceful sleep—hearts entwined, dreams quietly blossoming, ready for all the adventures waiting just beyond tomorrow.

2

The Baby Years
(Singapore)

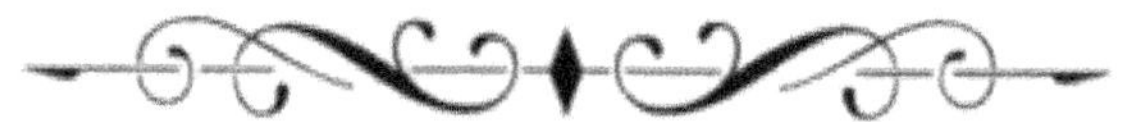

As the joyful new parents brought their precious bundle home, waiting at the house was Nur—the maid Daniel had carefully chosen to help care for little Ava. He had interviewed many candidates, seeking not just someone skilled, but someone who would look after Ava with the tenderness and devotion of a mother. From the moment he met her, Nur felt like the perfect fit—as if she were destined to be part of their story.

When the car pulled up, the whole family was already gathered outside, their faces glowing with joy and anticipation. As Daniel stepped out, Nur moved forward and gently took Ava into her arms, cradling her with practised ease. Meanwhile, Daniel and Mei Lin were swept into a flurry of hugs, cheers, and warm congratulations from their excited relatives.

"Welcome home, little Ava!" they all chimed, their voices brimming with love and laughter. The warmth of their welcome wrapped around the new family like a gentle blanket.

Inside, the air hummed with celebration. The comforting aroma of traditional dishes drifted from the kitchen, promising a night of feasting, storytelling, and the start of a new chapter—together.

In traditional Singaporean families, it was customary to wait a full month before celebrating a newborn's arrival—a time for the mother's recovery and the baby's early growth. But Daniel's father, being British, saw things differently.

He believed every precious moment deserved immediate celebration.

"Why wait?" he had said to Mei Lin, his enthusiastic grin hard to resist. "We have a beautiful daughter, and it's a day for joy! Let's cherish every moment!"

Daniel's father came from a family with deep roots in Asia, especially Singapore. Their connection stretched back generations. His grandfather had arrived as a senior manager with the British East India Shipping Company. When the company was taken over by the British government in 1874, he made a life-changing decision: to stay in Singapore and build a future in the vibrant, growing city.

It was during this time that he met Daniel's grandmother—a striking German woman from a wealthy family whose father owned a shipping company of his own. What began as a chance meeting blossomed into a love that crossed cultural and national boundaries, uniting two very different worlds.

When his role with the East India Company ended, he stayed on. Instead, he joined forces with his father-in-law, continuing his career in Singapore through the family shipping business.

Their son—Daniel's father—was later sent to England to study at Cambridge. After graduating, he returned to Singapore and began working for the British colonial government. It was there, among colonial officials and traders, that he met Daniel's mother, adding another chapter to the family's rich and lasting legacy in the region.

As the family gathered around the dining table, the room hummed with laughter and lively chatter. Plates of chicken rice, spring rolls, and other tasty dishes adorned the table— a vibrant feast that beautifully blended their cultures.

Daniel raised a glass of ginger tea, the traditional drink for new parents, and smiled warmly.

"To family," Daniel said, his voice brimming with joy. "To love—and to our precious little Ava. May she bring endless happiness to our lives!"

A chorus of cheers followed, glasses clinking in celebration. The evening unfolded with stories, laughter, and quiet, heartfelt moments shared between generations. Ava's soft coos joined the harmony, her gentle sounds blending seamlessly into the music of the evening—a symphony of love that filled every corner of their home.

Nearby, Nur tended to Ava with quiet devotion. As she watched the celebration unfold, she felt a deep sense of belonging and pride. In her heart, she made a silent promise—to care for Ava with love and to support this family on their beautiful new journey ahead.

As the sun dipped low in the sky, casting golden hues across the room, Daniel and Mei Lin sat in quiet awe. They had embarked on a wonderful journey—one that not only bound them to their daughter but also wove them deeper into the rich tapestry of love and culture that surrounded them.

Every moment shared that day became a thread in the fabric of their new life—building cherished memories and lasting bonds. In their hearts, they could already feel the promise of adventures yet to come.

In the weeks that followed, life settled into a rhythm of care and discovery. Mei Lin, Daniel, and Nur embraced parenthood with open hearts, nurturing Ava with gentle care.

They chose not to follow the expectations of a typical middle-class family. Instead, they carved their own path— hands-on, fully present, and deeply committed to building a bond with their little girl.

Each day brought something new—a shared wonder, a quiet victory, a deeper love—turning even the simplest moments into precious treasures.

They often strolled to the nearby beaches, where the soft sand squished gently under their feet and the sea breeze carried the scent of salt and freedom. Mei Lin would cradle Ava close, pointing out seashells scattered like gems, crabs scuttling sideways, and the vast sky blending into the endless blue of the ocean.

Daniel led their little outings with enthusiasm, turning each trip into an adventure. He'd spin tales of pirates and explorers, his voice brimming with wonder, and just as often, he'd share his passion for his ham radio.

Back at home, as weeks turned into months, he would show Ava how it worked, carefully threading wires and turning dials. Her eyes would sparkle with curiosity as the screen glowed and strange crackling sounds filled the room—faint echoes of far-off voices crossing the airwaves.

In their shared courtyard, centred around a charming fountain that bubbled gently, Ava would play among the shimmering streams, her tiny hands splashing in the cool, flowing water. The soft sound of the fountain became her lullaby, blending with her delighted giggles and the faint crackle of a nearby radio.

Daniel often joined her on a blanket spread across the grass, bringing along a small, child-friendly radio. Together, they'd sit under the open sky, and he would guide her through the curious world of sound—teaching her to listen for distant signals and to spot the difference between static and the rare clarity of a voice breaking through.

As evening fell, the courtyard became a place of quiet wonder. They collected colourful stones, chased fluttering butterflies, or sat watching the sky turn vibrant shades of orange and pink. Sometimes, Daniel would set up an old antenna, carefully adjusting its angle, explaining to Ava how invisible radio waves danced through the air—threads of energy carrying voices and music from distant lands.

They would sit close, listening to faint broadcasts crackling through the receiver, imagining they were tuned into secret chats or forgotten messages from the other side of the world.

Back at their cosy shop house—a blend of home and workshop—Daniel continued welcoming Ava into his world of radio and communication. He built simple radio kits for her to explore, turning everyday objects into small gateways of discovery.

Mei Lin wove their shared experiences into lessons, teaching Ava about nature, curiosity, and the joy of asking questions. Her encouragement nurtured Ava's inquisitive spirit, turning even small moments into chances to learn.

Daniel often sat with Ava on his lap during his chats with Billy over the radio. "Hello there, little Ava," Billy's cheerful voice would crackle through the speaker. "I'm honoured to talk with you—how was your day? "Daniel and Billy would ask. Ava, would simply reply "Dolly" holding her toy up to the microphone. Billy simply replied "I sure would like to meet your dolly one day"

Every milestone—her first taste of sweet mango, her first giggle, her wobbly first steps—was celebrated like a tiny miracle. Daniel watched with pride as Ava copied him, twiddling radio dials with her small fingers, pressing buttons with focused care. He'd kneel beside her, gently guiding her hands, chuffed to share the magic of how invisible signals could zip through the air to reach someone miles away.

"Look at you go, Ava!" Daniel cheered, his claps filling the small room. Ava beamed back, her joy as bright and catching as sunlight pouring through the window.

As the seasons changed, so did their adventures—each one a new page in their growing story. One sunny Saturday morning, Daniel decided it was the perfect day for a family trip to Seletar, eager to show his little girl the wonders of wildlife.

With her tiny hand gripping his tightly, Ava's eyes sparkled with excitement as they stepped into the lush greenery. Daniel felt her wonder ripple through him—her awe bringing fresh life to familiar sights.

"Look, Daddy! Monkeys!" Ava cried, pointing excitedly at the nimble creatures swinging through the treetops. Daniel knelt beside her, smiling at Mei Lin before looking up. "Yes, clever little things," he said softly. "They use their wits to find food—but we mustn't get too close. They can be a bit naughty sometimes." Ava nodded seriously, her wide eyes glued to the monkeys, soaking up every word.

"Do you see how they splash?" Daniel asked, as a monitor lizard darted into the water, sending ripples across the surface. Ava's joyful giggles mixed with the chatter of monkeys overhead, their lively antics sparking a flurry of questions. She tugged at Daniel's shirt, her face glowing with wonder.

He loved these moments of curiosity—each question a window into her growing mind. Every answer he gave seemed to light a new spark, sending her imagination flying. To Daniel, the world was transformed when they were together—a bright tapestry of colour and sound, full of endless possibilities.

After their adventure at Seletar, the family headed to a nearby beach. The golden sands stretched out before them, tempting Ava to kick off her shoes and race toward the sparkling waves, her small hand held tight in Mei Lin's.

Daniel stood back, watching them with a quiet smile as their laughter rang through the salty air. Ava was still but a slip of a child, yet within her dwelt a spirit as vast and free as the sea itself.

"Catch me, Daddy!" Ava squealed, her hair whipping in the ocean breeze, light as the sea foam cresting the incoming tide. Without hesitation, Daniel leapt to his feet and chased after her, laughter swelling in his chest. Alongside Mei Lin, they plunged into the cool surf, water splashing every which way as their joyous shrieks filled the air. The sun danced upon the ocean's surface, casting a sparkling reflection that mirrored the radiant bond they shared.

Yet their joy wasn't confined to weekends alone. Even in the quiet in-between moments, Daniel discovered magic. On rainy afternoons, they crafted blanket forts in the sitting room, transforming ordinary spaces into extraordinary adventures—a spaceship voyaging through galaxies or a castle besieged by fire-breathing dragons.

"We are fearless explorers, Ava," Daniel proclaimed, instilling in her the courage to dream boldly. Each imaginary expedition formed a new chapter in the stories he spun— tales of distant planets, enchanted realms, and valiant adventurers. "And when we land, we'll discover new worlds brimming with adventure!" he'd say, his eyes alight with enthusiasm.

These moments didn't merely entertain Ava—they shaped her. Her imagination blossomed, vibrant with colour and possibility, enabling her to see the world not only as it was, but as it could be.

On other days, they danced in puddles beneath their umbrellas, giggling as rainwater splashed about their ankles. Daniel and Mei Lin were determined to create as many cherished memories as possible—small moments woven into a vivid tapestry of family life.

Each evening, Daniel would sit at his ham radio, tuning in to connect with old friends. Billy, always the warm voice on the other end, never failed to make time for Ava.

"Hello there, little Ava!" he'd always say cheerfully. "How was your dolly today?"

Ava would smile and shout "Good"

Daniel patiently showed her how to operate the dials, explaining each step with care. It became their cherished ritual. Sometimes, when he was at work, Ava would wander to the radio and call excitedly for Nur.

"Let's call Daddy at work—I want to talk to him!" Ava would exclaim, her little face alight with excitement. Nur would smile gently and divert her with a new game, guiding her imagination elsewhere until it was time for their next adventure.

Their explorations extended far beyond the familiar shores of Singapore. Together, they journeyed across nearby parts of Asia—Malaysia, Thailand, and Indonesia—where each destination opened a doorway to a new world of discovery.

Thailand held a special place in their hearts. They often travelled to Isaan to visit Mei Lin's family, where Ava could run freely with her cousins. The children would splash through the rice fields or gather for family festivities, enveloped in laughter and the aroma of home-cooked meals. The entire village would turn out to greet them, eager to see Ava. There, she was lovingly called by her Thai name, Na Khing, a nod to her heritage and a way to keep her rooted in her mother's family traditions. Ava loved every moment and wasn't confused at all by being called Na Khing; she even tried to learn some Thai words.

Each journey nurtured Ava's boundless curiosity. One summer in Malaysia, they hiked through dense jungles, with Ava often perched on Daniel's back as he pressed forward, marvelling at cascading waterfalls and vibrant, exotic plants. Daniel seized every opportunity to teach her the importance of respecting and preserving the natural world, gently fostering her awareness of how interconnected everything in nature truly is.

"These trees are home to many creatures—and they help us breathe," Daniel would explain, watching Ava's face light up with wonder and understanding.

Mei Lin, always there with a smile, would often call out, "Hey, you two, wait for me!" she would cry with a laugh as they forged ahead.

In every new place they explored, he encouraged her to engage fully with the world—to touch, see, and taste the diverse textures of life. At bustling street markets, he'd gently nudge her towards new experiences. The father-daughter bond was unbreakable; they were like two peas in a pod.

"Let's try some traditional noodles, Ava. These people have been cooking them for generations," he'd say with a smile, his eyes gleaming with anticipation. He'd watch as she took her first bite, her expression shifting from curiosity to sheer delight. Each cultural encounter introduced Ava to new flavours, stories, and friendships. Daniel ensured she appreciated the richness of the world around her and the beauty in every difference.

Their international adventures reached a pinnacle with a dream trip to Australia. The moment their plane touched down, it felt like stepping into another world. Together, they traversed the wild landscapes—from the vast outback, where a journey led them to the awe-inspiring majesty of Uluru, to the open bushlands dotted with bounding kangaroos, and concluding the trip with a visit to the Great Barrier Reef. Daniel had promised Ava a glimpse of marine magic, and he kept his word. Holding her in his arms, with Ava wearing her goggles, he encouraged her to dip her head underwater. They marvelled at the vibrant corals, surrounded by schools of rainbow-coloured fish. Ava's reaction was striking; her wide eyes shone behind her goggles, and Daniel knew this moment would linger in her memory for years to come.

"Just like in the books, Daddy!" Ava exclaimed, her eyes sparkling in the sunlight. Daniel's heart swelled as he shared her wonder, filled with a profound sense of fulfilment. They spent hours swimming through the crystal-clear waters, marvelling at sea turtles gliding gracefully past and vibrant coral gardens that shimmered with life. Every splash, every laugh, formed a symphony of discovery. Daniel seized every opportunity to capture these precious moments, snapping photographs he knew would become cherished memories long after the trip had ended.

That evening, as the sun dipped below the horizon, painting the sky in warm hues of orange and pink, Mei Lin laid out a modest picnic on the beach. They sat together on the soft sand, nibbling on treats they'd packed earlier. Ava leaned against him, her heart still brimming with the day's excitement.

"Can we come back to Australia again, Daddy? There's so much more to see," she asked, her voice filled with hope and wonder.

"Absolutely," he replied, wrapping his arms around Ava and Mei Lin. "There are always new adventures awaiting us, and we'll explore them together."

A profound warmth settled in his chest as he watched the vibrant hues of the sunset reflected in Ava's eyes. In that serene moment—enveloped by the gentle lapping of waves and the embrace of his family—Daniel knew they were weaving a tapestry of memories, stories that would resonate through their lives for years to come.

Back home, as the seasons shifted in Singapore, Daniel remained steadfast in his devotion to showing Ava how deeply she was loved. He transformed ordinary days into celebrations of wonder, laughter, and discovery. In their cosy apartment, he'd switch on the radio and sit beside her, pointing to the stars through the window, explaining the constellations and planets in his calm, patient voice. The night sky became a classroom, each twinkling light a gateway to dreams.

"Every star has a story," he would say, gesturing at the twinkling lights above. "And, like us, they shine brighter together."

Whenever Ava grazed her knee or faced a small disappointment—like failing to climb the tallest tree—Daniel was always there, patient and encouraging.

"It's alright to fall, sweetheart. What matters is that you get back up and try again," he'd say, kneeling to examine the scrape, his heart aching slightly but brimming with pride at her resilience.

These quiet, tender moments strengthened their bond, weaving a foundation of trust and understanding that would sustain them through the years.

As Ava grew into a curious and intelligent young girl, her questions became more thoughtful, revealing a blossoming, inquisitive mind.

"Daddy, do you think girls will truly be able to go into space? Can I explore space like them?" she asked one evening, her face radiant with determination.

Daniel smiled, touched by her ambitious spirit.

"Of course," he said warmly. "Girls can do anything they set their minds to. You could be an astronaut, a scientist… even a superhero. Just believe in yourself, and you can reach for the stars."

These conversations were vital—grounding Ava's dreams and ambitions while fostering her understanding of equality and empowerment. Daniel made it his mission to ensure she always felt strong and capable, reminding her that her dreams were valid, no matter how grand or modest.

On weekends, their routine continued to evolve. Daniel would often bring home art supplies from local markets, creating a vibrant space at the dining table where Mei Lin and Ava could paint and craft together. He'd eagerly join in, offering help or simply watching with admiration.

"Let's create our own galaxy!" he suggested one Sunday afternoon, laughter swirling through the air as they painted swirling dark blues and purples, scattering glitter like distant stars.

These creative sessions became some of their most cherished memories. Each artwork captured a fragment of their shared adventures—an elephant from a zoo visit, a kangaroo from

Australia, or a dazzling interpretation of the stars they loved to admire. As their home gradually filled with Ava's creations, the walls became a living storybook—a vibrant diary of love, laughter, and learning.

Daniel cherished every moment—each memory another stitch in the vibrant tapestry of their lives, woven tightly with love and laughter. Under his and Mei Lin's gentle guidance, Ava thrived. Her intelligence sparkled, her creativity blossomed, and her compassion for others deepened daily. To Daniel, Ava was more than his daughter—she was his closest friend, his fellow adventurer, and the light that brightened his every day.

One early Saturday morning, while Ava played in the backyard, a sudden crash was followed by loud cries. Daniel and Mei Lin rushed outside, hearts racing.

They found Ava in tears, cradled by Nur. She had tripped while playing and grazed her knee. Without hesitation, Daniel scooped her into his arms, holding her close as tears streamed down her cheeks. Gently, he kissed her injured knee and offered a comforting smile.

"There, Ava, see? It's all better now, isn't it?"

Ava looked up at Daniel, her cheeks still wet with tears, and gave a small, brave nod.

"I'll always be here to care for you, my darling girl. You're my little princess," he whispered, pressing another kiss to her forehead.

In every grazed knee, every new word spoken, and each tiny discovery, Daniel felt a restless energy stirring within him—a blend of awe, pride, and the profound responsibility of fatherhood. With each passing day, he was reminded that parenting was not only about teaching but also about learning. The journey offered endless lessons in patience, love, and wonder, which he embraced wholeheartedly.

Their lives were interwoven—each shared moment a thread in a vibrant tapestry of joy, imagination, and unconditional love. As they faced each new day, Daniel knew they were building something enduring. Together, they were shaping a future as boundless as Ava's dreams and as limitless as the stars.

3

A Passport to Possibility, Winter 1963

The gentle hum of morning seeped into the house, curling into corners and drifting through open windows like a whisper. Outside, the city stirred languidly—oblivious to the weight today held within the modest home Daniel shared with Mei Lin and their daughter, Ava.

For months, Daniel had devoted every spare hour to his invention—a breakthrough in radio communication that, if realised, could redefine connections across vast distances. He had penned countless letters, sketched blueprints by lamplight, and made phone calls that often led nowhere. Yet, he persevered. He had to believe—because if he didn't, no one else would.

Then, just days ago, a glimmer of hope appeared. A promising manufacturing company in Korea had contacted him, intrigued by his design. They wished to meet him—to hear his idea in person. It was sudden. Unexpected. But it was an opportunity—perhaps the only one he'd get.

The night before his flight, Daniel sat with Mei Lin in their small kitchen, the overhead light flickering above them as if uncertain of its role in the moment.

"I know I'll be away for a few weeks," Daniel said softly, his fingers tracing the rim of his mug. "But this trip… it could truly change our lives if I secure their investment. Do you understand?"

Mei Lin nodded, her eyes steady and warm. "Don't fret, we'll be fine while you're gone. You'll be back before we know it."

The next morning, as the first light of dawn slipped through the bedroom curtains, it cast a soft glow across the room. Ava perched on the edge of the bed, watching her father with wide, curious eyes. Daniel moved quietly, methodically packing his belongings into the suitcase, each fold and zip imbued with quiet purpose.

The rustle of fabric and the soft click of the case filled the silence—a familiar sound, yet today it carried a heavier weight, laced with the promise of change. Even at just six years old, Ava seemed to sense something momentous was afoot. She couldn't yet grasp its magnitude, but she felt the shift in the air, the unspoken anticipation.

"Daddy, what are you packing in there?" Ava asked, her small figure standing by the bed, delicate fingers tracing the seams of his travel bag.

"Just a few things I'll need for my trip, sweetheart," Daniel replied, kneeling to meet her gaze. His smile radiated a warmth that enveloped her like a cherished blanket. "You'll help me remember everything, won't you?"

Ava tilted her head, pondering, her eyes wide and thoughtful. "Can I give you something for your trip, Daddy?"

"Of course," he said, amusement glimmering in his eyes. "What do you have in mind?"

Without another word, she scampered to the window, where pots brimmed with flowers blooming in the soft morning light. Her fingers hovered before carefully plucking a small, delicate blossom—its petals a gentle lavender hue that seemed to shimmer in her hand.

Clutching it with pride, she hurried back and presented it with quiet significance.

"Here! This will watch over you and ensure you come back soon," Ava declared, offering the flower with both hands.

Daniel's heart softened at the gesture.

"That's perfect, Ava," Daniel said, taking the delicate bloom from her fingertips and gently tucking it into the breast pocket of his suit jacket. He could almost feel her innocence and love enveloping him like a quiet shield against the unknown. "Whenever I see it, I'll think of you."

Ava beamed, her eyes sparkling with pride. "Now you'll always have me with you!"

Daniel smiled, the weight of her love grounding him in that moment. "Always," he murmured, his voice thick with emotion.

Her simple, unwavering belief that she could protect him stirred something profound within him. For a moment, the looming anxiety of his journey ebbed. He knelt beside her, brushing a stray strand of hair behind her ear, his fingers lingering on her soft cheek.

"I'll be back before you know it, I promise. But I have something for you too."

Daniel reached into his bag and drew out a small, framed photograph—one of their cherished moments. It captured the three of them at his ham radio, smiling as if the world had paused just for them.

"Keep this by your bed, so you'll always have me with you," Daniel said, handing the photograph to Ava.

She cradled it carefully, her eyes wide with wonder.

Just then, Mei Lin stepped into the room, catching the tail end of their tender exchange. Her gaze shifted from the photograph to Daniel's packed bag. She pressed her lips together—a quiet gesture of support, tinged with concern. Their eyes met, and in that glance, a thousand unspoken reassurances passed between them.

"Everything ready?" she asked softly.

"Yes, I reckon so. Ava helped me pack, so I should be sorted," he said, grinning down at her.

Ava giggled, proud of her role in the morning's preparations.

Daniel rose to his feet, pausing to soak in the quiet comfort of his family. A growing sense of conflict churned within him. Ambition tugged at his sleeve—the opportunity in Korea could transform their lives—but the thought of leaving Mei Lin and Ava, even briefly, weighed like a stone in his chest.

"I'm all set," Daniel said, infusing confidence into his voice as he turned to Ava. "Can you be a good girl and look after your mummy while I'm gone?"

"I will!" she chirped, her voice brimming with earnest promise. Yet Daniel caught the flicker of uncertainty in her eyes, that delicate trace of worry children can't quite name.

He knelt again and drew her into a hug, holding her close, her tiny heart beating against his chest.

"Remember," he murmured, his voice low and steady, "no matter how far I go, I'll always be thinking of you."

As he lingered in the embrace, Mei Lin stepped forward and enveloped them both, sealing them in a cocoon of warmth and love.

"And we'll always be here waiting for you," Mei Lin whispered, her voice laced with quiet affection as she pressed a tender kiss to his cheek. Their embrace held more than warmth—it was a silent vow of love, hope, and the fragile uncertainty of change. In that moment, wrapped in each other's arms, they dwelt in a bubble of shared trust, blissfully unaware of what lay ahead.

As they reluctantly parted, Daniel's heart grew heavier. Adrenaline thrummed beneath his skin as the weight of the journey ahead loomed larger. He gathered his belongings, each item a reminder of the purpose—and the sacrifice—this trip demanded. Glancing back at his family, framed in the soft light of the doorway, he offered a final smile.

"I'll be back soon," Daniel called over his shoulder, the words meant to reassure them—but mostly himself.

With every step away from the comfort of home, something within him tugged. A quiet instinct murmured that this wasn't merely a business trip. It was the first time since Ava's birth that they would be apart for more than a few days, and the unfamiliar distance already weighed on their hearts.

The horizon ahead was lined with uncertainty—a truth that clung to Daniel as he ventured into the unknown. The air brimmed with possibility, yet shadows lingered at the edges of his thoughts. Doubt tried to creep in, but he clung to the belief that this was his moment. His chance.

As the taxi wove through the bustling rhythm of city streets towards the airport, Daniel sat quietly, his thoughts a tangle of hope and hesitation. The opportunity ahead gleamed like a promise, yet it pressed uncomfortably against the ache of all he was leaving behind. Each passing landmark—a park bench, a corner café, a mural Ava loved—felt like a farewell.

The drive stretched longer than Daniel expected, each traffic light a reminder that the world kept turning while his own seemed momentarily paused. Outside, the city pulsed with life. Within, Daniel clung to memories of home: Ava's radiant smile, the weight of her small hand in his, Mei Lin's soft voice echoing from the kitchen. Those memories, delicate yet grounding, enveloped him like a protective shield.

Upon arriving at Paya Lebar Airport, Daniel stepped out of the taxi into the cool humid embrace of the evening air. It offered a welcome contrast to the lingering warmth inside the car, and for a moment, he simply stood—taking it all in. The terminal thrummed with activity: the shuffle of luggage wheels, the soft murmur of announcements, the occasional ripple of laughter or tearful farewell. Around him, people moved with purpose—travellers immersed in routine, families reuniting, friends sharing final hugs before parting.

He made his way through the terminal towards the British Overseas Airways Corporation (BOAC) desk, his suitcase rolling steadily behind him. His flight included a stopover in Hong Kong for the night before continuing to Gimpo

International Airport, just outside Seoul, the following evening. The weight of the journey ahead settled on his shoulders, equal parts hope and hesitation.

The check-in process was smooth, almost disarmingly so. With practised efficiency, the staff handled his documents. Daniel presented his passport and, moments later, received his handwritten paper boarding pass—its fragile creases a tangible emblem of this new chapter. He held it a moment longer than needed, then tucked it away.

As he passed through security, the hum of the terminal faded, giving way to the quiet pulse of reflection. He glanced at the sea of travellers, wondering about the stories they carried, the farewells they'd exchanged. The journey ahead was real now, no longer merely an idea sketched on blueprints or discussed in late-night conversations. He was truly departing.

Though excitement stirred in his chest, a dull ache lingered too. Each step forward was a step away from Ava's small arms and Mei Lin's steady calm. Yet Daniel knew— sometimes the path to something greater began with a single, difficult farewell.

After navigating the queue, Daniel made his way to the departure lounge, his footsteps echoing softly on the polished tile floor. He purchased a cup of coffee from a nearby kiosk and settled into a seat by a large window. Outside, planes taxied slowly across the tarmac, their sleek silhouettes glinting in the afternoon light. Beyond the airport grounds, the city stretched towards the horizon, its mid-rise buildings standing as quiet sentinels of Singapore's growing ambition.

The rhythmic hum of the airport enveloped him—low conversations, the occasional rustle of newspapers, and the steady announcements over the PA system. Daniel unfolded his newspaper, scanning it more out of habit than genuine interest. His thoughts lingered on home—on Ava's small hand pressing the flower into his palm, on Mei Lin's brave smile.

Suddenly, a fresh announcement crackled over the intercom, stirring a ripple of attention among the waiting passengers. Daniel looked up, listening as a weather update was delivered in clipped, formal tones. The alert concerned South Korea—specifically, the Taebaek District, a mountainous region he knew he would need to traverse en route to Donghae, where the transistor factory awaited.

Daniel's pulse quickened. Severe weather warnings had been issued: torrential rain, landslides, flash flooding. The words struck him with force, turning the abstract thrill of travel into something far more uncertain. He sat up straighter, his coffee cooling in his hand, as anxiety seeped in like a tide. Donghae had always seemed distant, but now it felt almost unattainable.

His fingers tightened around the newspaper as he scanned the details again, searching for specifics—anything to gauge the true severity of the situation. It was no longer just his invention or career at stake. It was the very real risk of navigating treacherous terrain alone, far from the comfort of home and those he loved.

"Authorities are advising caution for travellers," the announcer's voice rang out across the lounge, steady and grave. "Evacuations are underway in some areas, and residents are urged to stay informed and safe. If travel is not essential, please cancel."

Daniel's stomach tightened. The words echoed in his mind, anchoring a knot of unease deep in his chest. Cancelling was not an option—not now. This meeting in Donghae was more than a presentation; it was the breakthrough he had worked towards for years. The future of his invention—and perhaps his family's financial security—depended on it.

Still, Daniel reminded himself, he had one night in Hong Kong. The weather might shift. It could pass. He clung to that hope like a raft in rising waters.

His gaze drifted back to the window. The landscape he would soon face—the Taebaek region—was renowned for its breathtaking beauty, a hidden gem nestled among dramatic mountains. Yet beauty could deceive. That same terrain was also notorious for treacherous roads and unpredictable conditions, especially during heavy rainfall. Mudslides. Washed-out roads. Delays—or worse.

For a fleeting moment, the spark of excitement that had carried him this far dimmed under the weight of the broadcast. Doubt seeped in, persistent and unsettling.

He reached for his coffee, now cold, and stared at the swirling clouds gathering on the distant horizon. This journey was no longer merely a step forward—it was a gamble.

Daniel felt a lump rise in his throat as the implications settled over him. The meetings he'd arranged—potential partnerships that could elevate his invention and transform everything—now seemed fragile, uncertain. Questions crowded his mind: Could he travel safely through the region? Would he even reach his destination?

Daniel swallowed hard, pushing the doubts aside, drawing strength from Mei Lin's steadfast belief in the opportunity. Just a business trip, he told himself firmly, slipping his phone back into his pocket. He resolved to remain optimistic, to keep his focus fixed on what lay ahead, despite the shadow cast by the severe weather warnings.

Minutes later, the boarding announcement rang clearly through the terminal: "Flight BOAC375 to Kai Tak Airport, Hong Kong, now boarding at Gate 12." The call jolted him from his thoughts, and Daniel gathered his belongings with renewed resolve, steeling himself for the journey ahead.

As he walked towards the gate, a swirl of emotions stirred within him—excitement, anxiety, and an urgent longing to return home soon. He cast one final glance over his shoulder at the bustling airport, the familiar comfort of home fading behind him. Ahead lay the unknown—a path that would shape not only his future but that of his family in ways he could scarcely have imagined.

Settling into his seat aboard the Douglas DC-6, the steady hum of the engines enveloped Daniel—a comforting drone hinting at the adventure ahead. He gazed out of the window as the ground slipped away, the sprawling cityscape of Singapore shrinking into a mosaic of buildings and greenery.

The journey brimmed with anticipation; he aimed to expand his company's reach across Asia, seizing the promise of a burgeoning market that beckoned with opportunity.

A friendly flight attendant approached, interrupting his reverie.

"Good evening! Would you care for a drink?" she asked with a warm smile.

Daniel nodded and requested soda water. The bubbles fizzed pleasantly as he took a sip, easing him into the gentle rhythm of the flight. Soon after, the meal arrived—a fragrant chicken curry paired with aromatic rice, a comforting nod to the culinary delights of his homeland. He savoured each bite, letting the familiar flavours wash over him as the plane soared through the clouds.

As the first hour of the flight passed in relative calm, Daniel let his thoughts drift homeward. He could still picture Mei Lin and Ava standing at the front door, waving him off—Ava's small fingers fluttering like leaves in the breeze, Mei Lin's eyes reflecting a complex blend of pride and quiet concern. That image clung to him like a cherished photograph in his mind. It was the last time they would see him—though he didn't know it then—and the weight of that realisation threatened to settle in his chest. He pushed it aside.

Kai Tak Airport stood defiantly at the edge of Kowloon Bay, nestled amid the sprawl of tenement rooftops and narrow streets that formed the vibrant heart of 1960s Hong Kong. Even in 1963, its approach was already legendary—a harrowing descent that tested every pilot's nerve and offered window-seat passengers a view like no other.

Daniel was fortunate. He had the seat.

As the aircraft banked sharply on final approach, it swept low over the city's patchwork of laundry-lined balconies, neon shopfronts, and rooftop kitchens. From his vantage point, Daniel could discern families dining, children darting through corridors, a woman brushing her hair before a mirror. Life below unfolded in fleeting vignettes, intimate and ordinary. The roar of the engines seemed unnoticed by the city.

Oddly, the sight calmed him. It drew his mind from the earlier flight announcements and the unease still lingering at the edges of his thoughts. By the time the wheels screeched onto the tarmac, Daniel felt strangely centred.

He moved briskly through the modest but efficient terminal and checked into the nearby airport hotel. He needed a few hours' rest before the next leg of his journey: a late-afternoon flight to Korea—and the start of something new.

Daniel woke early the next morning, invigorated by the prospect of what lay ahead. He reviewed his notes over a pot of tea in the hotel lounge, rehearsing the key points of the presentation he'd deliver later that week—an idea he believed could revolutionise communications.

With time to spare, he ventured into the streets, captivated by the colours and sounds of early-morning Hong Kong. The city thrummed with energy—rickshaws wove between market stalls, vendors called out over sizzling woks, and the scent of roasted chestnuts mingled with the salty tang of the harbour air.

He didn't need to look long. A rich blue satin cheongsam adorned with hand-stitched plum blossoms caught his eye— a perfect gift for Ava. For Mei Lin, he chose a delicate jade pendant, cool and smooth to the touch, its pale green glow almost translucent in the sunlight. Small tokens, yet brimming with meaning.

By late afternoon, Daniel found himself back at the terminal. The sky had deepened into a soft violet, with strokes of amber and rose painting the horizon as the last light of day lingered. The airport, though bustling, moved with a rhythm that now felt comfortingly familiar. His flight included a brief stopover in Taipei for refueling.

He boarded quickly and settled into his seat. As the engines began to hum, Daniel leaned back and exhaled deeply. Ahead lay Korea — a land of opportunity, purpose, and a life that, though still elusive, was on the verge of change.

The first leg of the journey to Taipei passed uneventfully. After a swift refueling stop, they were back in the air. Exhaustion overtook Daniel quickly, and he drifted into a soothing sleep. When he finally stirred, the cabin lights were dimmed, and the plane had begun its descent.

At first, everything seemed calm, but the serenity didn't last. A sudden jolt snapped him fully awake. The seatbelt sign lit up urgently above as the plane dipped again, swaying through turbulence that rattled his nerves. Daniel gripped the armrests instinctively, a flicker of unease rising in his chest as he braced for the unpredictable skies ahead.

"Just a spot of bumpy air," he muttered under his breath, trying to steady himself. He recalled past flights—some smooth, some nerve-racking—but all ultimately safe. Air travel, he reminded himself, was an unpredictable dance with gravity.

Yet, as the turbulence intensified, the aircraft lurched violently, drawing startled gasps from around the cabin. Daniel felt a knot tighten deep in his stomach. The once-steady hum of flight now sounded uneven, erratic.

Flight attendants moved with brisk efficiency, securing carts and fastening compartments, their practised calm a stark contrast to the unease rippling among the passengers.

Then came the captain's voice, crackling over the intercom. His tone was steady, yet an edge—subtle but unmistakable—betrayed his composure.

"We're encountering weather-related turbulence as we approach. Please remain seated and keep your seatbelts fastened."

Daniel complied instinctively, tightening his belt, the fabric digging slightly into his lap. He closed his eyes and tried to steady his breathing, willing his thoughts towards what lay ahead.

Focus.. He needed to stay focused. This journey was the turning point—his chance to break new ground, to make a lasting impact in Korea. The future of his business, everything he had worked for, could hinge on the meetings arranged for the next few days.

Just a few more hours.

But the turbulence didn't ease. It persisted, a relentless battering that shook the aircraft like a toy in a storm. With each jarring lurch, Daniel felt his composure fraying. Then the plane dipped—sharply and suddenly—drawing a collective gasp from the cabin.

He gripped the armrests until his knuckles ached, a cold sweat prickling along his back. His heartbeat pounded in his ears.

And then came the images—Mei Lin's serene eyes, Ava's playful giggle, the way her tiny fingers had reached for the flower now nestled in his jacket pocket.

He squeezed his eyes shut, willing the storm outside to abate. Their faces—soft, bright, brimming with life—served as his anchor, his silent prayer.

His beacon of hope.

At last, the plane began to stabilise, and the Captain came over the intercom to confirm they are now approaching the airport. The descent into Gimpo Airport brought a tentative sense of relief. As the wheels touched down, the aircraft trembled slightly before settling into a smooth roll along the runway. A gentle ripple of polite applause spread through the cabin—an unspoken nod to shared tension and collective gratitude.

Daniel loosened his grip on the armrests, belatedly aware of how fiercely he'd been clutching them. His pulse still raced—not from fear precisely, but from the surge of adrenaline yet to subside. He inhaled deeply, steadying himself with the reassuring truth: they had landed safely. The solid ground beneath him, though unfamiliar, felt like an anchor after the uncertainty of the flight.

As soon as the seatbelt sign clicked off, the cabin sprang to life with movement—passengers stretching, retrieving bags, murmuring to one another in a blend of languages. Daniel rose and fetched his carry-on from the overhead compartment, its familiar weight anchoring him further. His thoughts turned swiftly to what lay ahead: the critical meetings, the prospects for growth, the expectations he bore from home.

Stepping off the plane into the crisp Korean air, a wave of cold clarity washed over him. It was bracing—invigorating in its sharpness, a reminder that this was real. This was the next chapter. Yet, with that clarity came a flicker of unease. The terrain beyond Seoul, towards the Taebaek Mountains and Donghae, promised not only opportunity but also isolation and risk. The uncertainty clung to him like the chill in the air.

This was no longer merely a trip. It was a trial.

As Daniel made his way into the airport and to the baggage claim, the weight of his briefcase dug into his palm, tethering him to the moment. The airport, modest in scale, exuded an undeniable charm—quaint decorations lined the halls, reflecting the local culture with quiet pride. Paintings of the surrounding mountain landscapes adorned the walls, capturing both the region's rugged beauty and its subtle warmth.

He paused, letting the unfamiliar atmosphere envelop him. The terminal hummed with life: a chorus of conversations in myriad languages, the steady beep of baggage carts reversing, and the occasional muffled announcement resonating overhead. It all felt alien, distinctly foreign, yet imbued with the same promise that had spurred his decision to come.

After what seemed an eternity, his suitcase finally emerged on the conveyor belt. He stepped forward, retrieving it in one smooth motion, and headed towards the exit. Outside, he would hail a taxi to Donghae, the coastal city where his meetings would commence.

As he navigated the terminal, his mind buzzed with anticipation—visions of business discussions, potential partnerships, and opportunities ripe for the seizing. The earlier turbulence was already receding into the background, overtaken by the familiar cadence of determination. Doubt still lingered in the corners of his mind, but for now, purpose forged ahead.

As Daniel stepped outside, a rush of cold, damp air, laden with the scent of rain-soaked earth, enveloped him. The storm had intensified, sheets of rain pouring from the sky and pattering against the pavement. The valley air was thick and rich—moisture mingling with the fragrance of pine and distant mountains.

Scanning the dimly lit kerb for a taxi, Daniel spotted a driver approaching through the downpour, umbrella in hand. The man offered a brisk nod and gestured towards his car.

"Hotel?" the driver asked, his voice warm, his smile bridging the language barrier with ease. Daniel had studied Korean language at school, so could get by with his high school skills

"Yes, please," Daniel replied, retrieving a slip of paper from his coat pocket and handing it over. The address was neatly inscribed, just in case.

The driver's expression shifted slightly as he read it. "Ah… heavy rain on that road. Can be treacherous."

Daniel's pulse quickened. He couldn't afford to be stranded, not now. Sensing the hesitation, he leaned forward slightly.

"I understand," he said earnestly. "But it's vital I reach there tonight—I've an early meeting tomorrow. I'd be immensely grateful."

The driver regarded him for a moment, then nodded once, decisively. He assisted Daniel in loading the suitcase into the boot and gestured for him to take the back seat. Moments later, they pulled away from the terminal, merging onto the slick roads winding through the valley.

The headlights sliced through sheets of rain as they climbed steadily, the outside world reduced to streaks of water and blurred silhouettes. Each bend in the road felt like a step deeper into the unknown.

Yet, as they wove through the picturesque landscape—lush greenery unfurling beneath a misty sky, with the distant peaks of the Taebaek Mountains rising like silent sentinels—

Daniel felt a growing unease settle in the pit of his stomach. The earlier weather warning resurfaced in his mind, its urgency now undeniable. A creeping sense of foreboding took hold.

Perhaps he should have heeded the warning more seriously. But then, surely the local authorities would have assessed the safety of travel conditions before permitting flights to land. Wouldn't they?

The taxi pressed on, navigating cautiously along the narrow roads that hugged the mountainsides. The scenery, once idyllic, now appeared more rugged—wild and almost indifferent to the human lives within it. This was a place untouched by the haste of modern development—raw, majestic, and unpredictable.

Daniel gazed out the window as they passed glimpses of rural life. Farmers stood ankle-deep in muddy rice paddies, bending in rhythm with the earth. Women balanced baskets atop their heads, moving with quiet grace along the roadside as the rain came down. Children played with sticks and stones, their laughter brightening the air, untroubled by the storm. Each scene wove a rich tapestry of a culture Daniel deeply admired—and yearned to understand more deeply.

Yet the beauty of the moment was overshadowed by a gnawing tension within him, a quiet whisper that things might not unfold as planned.

Just as he began to ease, a sudden jolt startled him as the taxi swerved to avoid a pothole. Daniel's heart raced as he gripped the door handle tightly, feeling the wheels skid momentarily before the driver deftly regained control. Laughter erupted from a group of locals nearby—a reminder that, in this unfamiliar land, life carried on with its usual cadence, untouched by his sense of unease.

As the unsettling moment passed, they approached an isolated stretch of road high in the mountains. The driver muttered something under his breath, then glanced at Daniel through the rearview mirror.

"Very remote. The roads are poor up here. This storm is fierce. I'll take a different route to avoid danger," he said, his tone grave enough to stir a fresh wave of caution within Daniel.

The vehicle pressed on along the uneven path towards the village, unease seeping back into every fibre of his being.

As they veered off the main road onto a narrower track, Daniel spotted a weathered sign with a faded arrow reading

Donghae. A surge of excitement coursed through him—they were heading in the right direction.

Yet, even as the unfamiliar landscape unfolded around him, shadows of doubt crept into his thoughts. Something felt amiss. An ominous feeling whispered that this journey was unfolding differently than he had envisaged.

"Are we nearly there?" he asked, attempting to lighten the mood.

But the driver's frown, visible in the rearview mirror, spoke volumes. Something heavier hung in the air.

"We're about halfway, but the road is dreadful, so we must go slowly," the driver replied curtly as they continued jolting along the winding track.

Daniel peered through the mud-streaked windows, straining to glimpse signs of life in this remote region. The few houses they passed were sparse, built from local materials—simple, yet imbued with a rustic charm. But as the taxi ventured deeper into the mountains, the road grew worse, and the weather deteriorated. The sky darkened as clouds gathered overhead, swallowing the light.

Soon, the houses vanished entirely. Only mountains and vast stretches of wild countryside remained.

A tightness gripped Daniel's chest as shadows deepened around them. The vibrant openness of earlier yielded to an encroaching sense of isolation. Trees loomed over the road, their branches curling like skeletal fingers reaching through the mist. The air grew heavy, damp, laced with the scent of impending rain.

He glanced upward. The sky had turned a bruised grey, clouds swirling ominously.

"Will this storm ease?" he asked, striving to keep his voice steady despite the dread coiling in his stomach. He knew the driver likely had no answer—but he needed to hear something, anything, to anchor him.

"No. This is dreadful—we must turn back. The heavy rain is making it too perilous," the driver said, glancing over his shoulder, his eyes shadowed with concern. "Road's treacherous… not safe."

The words hung in the air, heavy and unwelcome. Tension coiled in Daniel's stomach like a taut spring. This wasn't what he had envisaged when he boarded the plane. He had pictured opportunity, new beginnings, meaningful partnerships—not slick roads and mountain storms threatening to unravel everything before it even began.

He clenched his jaw, shoving the fear aside. He had to remain resolute—for his family, for the business they had poured everything into. This journey could transform their lives. He couldn't turn back now.

As the taxi rounded a sharp bend, the wind surged, howling through the trees, bending them low like bowstrings drawn taut. Thick drops began to patter against the car's roof—at first erratic, then faster, louder, as if fate itself were drumming an urgent warning.

Was it merely a downpour… or something more?

Suddenly, the driver slammed on the brakes.

Daniel lurched forward, striking his head against the back of the driver's seat. Pain flared, and he felt warm blood trickling down his forehead. Outside, the tyres screeched and skidded, kicking up mud as the taxi teetered perilously close to the road's edge. For a heartbeat, everything tilted.

Through the passenger window, Daniel glimpsed the river far below—swollen from the rains, a violent torrent raging through the gorge. One misstep, one wrong move, and they could be swept away without a trace.

"Is everything all right?" he asked, pressing a handkerchief to his bleeding forehead, his voice taut with alarm.

The driver didn't respond at once. He squinted through the deluge, hands gripping the wheel tightly as thunder rumbled in the distance.

"Road's damaged!" he barked, eyes darting across the broken path ahead. "Too perilous. We must turn back—I'm turning back!"

His urgency was unmistakable, his composure fraying at the edges as he reached for the gearstick. Outside, the rain intensified, hammering the windscreen and blurring the world into a storm-drenched haze.

But before they could react, a deep rumble tore through the valley—low and thunderous, shaking the very air around them. Daniel's heart seized. This wasn't thunder.

It was the earth shifting.

The driver gripped the wheel tightly, his knuckles white as he fought to maintain control.

Then, in a horrifying instant, the ground gave way—a gaping, muddy chasm yawned open before them. He swerved instinctively, trying to avoid it, but the vehicle spun out of control, veering off the road as Daniel braced for impact.

"Hold on—I can't hold it!" the driver shouted.

But it was already too late.

The car flipped violently, the world spinning in a chaotic blur of sound and motion as it plunged down the valley. Daniel was hurled against the interior, his body battered by each jolt—the chaos felt surreal, like a nightmare unfolding in slow motion. Glass shattered around him, the frame crumpling under the force of the crash. He barely registered the driver's panicked scream before everything plunged into darkness—and then, his body was flung from the wreck, tumbling over rocks before coming to rest. Moments later, the car erupted into flames.

Time blurred into nothingness.

When Daniel finally stirred, it was like emerging from a dream steeped in pain. He floated in a haze of confusion, the sharp ache in his legs and head tethering him to reality. Cold rain lashed his skin, and he gasped for air, disoriented. The fire's glow flickered at the edge of his vision as he blinked against the glare, struggling to make sense of it all. Panic crept in—he couldn't recall what had happened, and the throbbing agony enveloping him offered no answers.

Raising his head, Daniel glanced around. Panic surged—he was sprawled on the cold, wet ground, dirt and debris scattered about him like the wreckage of a nightmare. Then everything faded to black again.

The burning taxi lay nearby, twisted metal engulfed in flames, fire clawing at the sky. Smoke billowed, thick and acrid, mingling with the damp, earthy scent of the forest floor—a grim reminder of the crash's violence.

He drifted back to consciousness, groaning. When he tried to move, pain erupted through his limbs, sharp and searing.

Anxiety gripped his chest. His mind reeled.

Where am I? The question echoed in his head, desperate and wild.

Am I alive?

The silence offered no answer. Only the crackle of fire, the sting of rain, and the pounding in his skull persisted.

In his fog of confusion, thoughts of Mei Lin and Ava flickered across his mind like fireflies—brief, fleeting lights in the encroaching darkness. A wave of longing surged over him. He clung to one desperate hope:

Please, let me return to them.

His lips barely moved, but the words slipped out, soft and raw.

"Please… let me return to them," he whispered into the chaos, each syllable laden with yearning.

But just as that hope settled deep in his chest, darkness returned—cold and merciless. And then, just like that… they were gone. He could no longer recall them. Not their faces. Not their names. Only silence remained.

From a distance, the sharp crackling of flames and the acrid smell of burning reached Jung-Sook, a local woman gathering firewood. Alarmed, she shoved her cart aside and hurried towards the smoke. As she slid down the muddy bank towards the wreckage, her foot caught on something. She stumbled—then gasped. It wasn't debris. It was a man.

Daniel cried out in pain as she accidentally brushed his side. Without hesitation, she knelt and wrapped her arms around him, heaving with all her strength.

"Hold on," she muttered, her voice trembling as she dragged him uphill, feet slipping on the rain-slicked earth.

She called for help, though she knew no one would hear. The mountains stood silent, remote.

Breathless, she laid him in the wooden cart, shielding him as best she could from the biting cold. Then she began the slow trek back to her cabin, nestled high among the trees—her sole thought now to save this stranger from the jaws of death.

When Daniel awoke, the world was hushed and strange, shaped by shadows and dim lights that flickered at the edges of his awareness. The air carried a sharp blend of smoke and disinfectant—jarring and unfamiliar. He tried to move, but his limbs felt sluggish, alien, as though they no longer belonged to him.

Panic flared in his chest as the fog in his mind began to clear. Above him stretched a rough-hewn wooden ceiling, wholly unfamiliar. The room around him was dimly lit, its details swimming in and out of focus.

Where am I?

The thought echoed in his head, spiralling as confusion tightened its grip. He blinked, straining to make sense of the shapes around him, but nothing resolved. The walls, the sounds, even his own body felt foreign.

And deeper still—something worse. Not merely the strangeness of the room or the dull ache in his body, but a vast emptiness within.

He didn't know who he was.

Faces and names hovered just beyond reach, like dreams dissolving in daylight. He sensed there had been people—vital people—but they were gone now. Forgotten.

Frustration surged within him, sharp as fire. The harder he tried to recall, the more it slipped away. All that remained was a hollow ache in his chest.

Then, piercing the silence, a gentle voice spoke in Korean. Soft. Strangely familiar.

"Sir? Can you hear me?"

The voice, calm and steady, cut through the fog. Daniel turned his head slightly, a stab of pain flaring in his neck. He winced, the movement slow and stiff.

A woman leaned over him—her features sharp yet kind, illuminated by the flicker of lamplight in the dim room. Her eyes held quiet concern, grounded and resolute.

"You're in my home," she said gently, her Korean clear in his ears. "You were in an accident. Do you know your name?"

Daniel blinked. The word accident echoed in his skull, stirring something faint—an image, a sound—but nothing solid enough to grasp.

"I… I can't recall," he rasped. Speaking felt like lifting a mountain. His throat burned. Even forming words seemed to sap his strength.

"You've been asleep for five days," the woman said. "You had severe injuries. I had to set your leg—it was badly broken. There's no hospital here, no way to call for help. But it's mending now. Don't fret."

"Do you speak English?" Daniel asked her.

Yes, I speak English," she said with a smile.

She dipped a cloth in cool water and laid it gently across his forehead. Her touch was practised, careful.

Daniel closed his eyes briefly, the weight of her words settling into his bones. Five days. A broken leg. No memory. No name.

Yet something in her voice—the steady cadence, the quiet care—tethered him, if only faintly.

A wave of dread surged over him as he searched the void within his mind. Fragments of his life flickered—faces, voices, moments—but they slipped away like grains of sand through trembling fingers. He strove to grasp something—anything—that might anchor him to who he was. But nothing endured.

Panic surged, tightening his chest like a vice.

"I need to know… Where—what is this? What am I doing here?" he gasped, desperation fracturing his voice.

Jung-Sook reached out, her hand resting gently on his arm.

"Your car veered off the mountain road during the storm," she said softly. "The ground gave way. You were fortunate—you were flung from the vehicle before it plunged into the valley below and caught fire. If that hadn't happened… no one would have found you."

She dipped a sponge into a bowl and pressed it gently against his forehead. The coolness tethered him, if only faintly.

"I'll do everything I can to help you," she continued. "But for now, you must rest. You've lost a lot of blood. Your body needs time to mend."

Her words were calm, but beneath them Daniel detected an undercurrent of worry, quiet and sincere.

He closed his eyes, striving to breathe through the fear. The question still echoed in his heart, unanswered: Who am I without my memories?

A chill washed over him, flooding his mind with anxious thoughts and hollow voids. The weight of his situation settled like a mantle of fog—thick, oppressive, and impossible to dispel. How had he ended up here? Where was the warmth he'd felt moments ago—the flicker of connection, the sense of belonging that now slipped away like a dream at dawn?

As if sensing the turmoil within him, Jung-Sook spoke again, her voice low and steady.

"When you're feeling stronger and the weather clears, we'll contact the village authorities. They may be able to help identify you. But snow is coming, and once it arrives, it'll be some time before we can reach anyone. For now, focus on mending. I'll handle the rest."

Her words were pragmatic, yet carried a quiet comfort—like a fragile thread tethering him to something tangible.

Still, a cold detachment gripped him, sharp and unsettling. He was trapped within a life he couldn't recall, surrounded by fragments that didn't yet fit. The memories he yearned for were locked deep within, and the name Daniel—if it was his—felt remote, a fading echo just beyond reach.

He sank back against the thin pillow; eyes fixed on the rough-hewn wooden ceiling as his thoughts spiralled into shadows. What had his life been? Whom had he loved? Whom had he lost?

Outside, the wind brushed against the windows, while inside, only the faint, rhythmic ticking of the wall clock broke the silence. He drifted in and out of sleep, cold uncertainty seeping into his bones, silence filling the empty corners of his mind. He drifted in and out of consciousness, sensing Jung-Sook beside him as time blurred—more ghost than presence, a flicker of warmth amidst the relentless cold. Yet he was powerless, trapped in a void where memories were a luxury he could no longer grasp. Whenever he reached for clarity, he found only fog—merciless, unyielding, absolute.

In the days that followed, snow fell—thick, silent, unending. As winter closed in, Daniel embarked on the slow, painful journey of rehabilitation. Each movement demanded effort, each breath a trial. His battered body responded with stubborn resilience. Yet, as his strength returned, so did the crushing weight of all he couldn't recall.

Jung-Sook remained a steadfast presence, tending to him with quiet care. Her voice, her footsteps, even the way she stirred soup on the stove brought a measure of calm. Yet it couldn't fill the vast emptiness within him. The absence of identity and memory gnawed at him ceaselessly. Beneath the surface of his healing, fear festered—quiet yet ever-present. Not only fear of the unknown, but also fear of who he might have been—and what awaited when memories returned.

4

The Static Sound of Silence-Winter 1963

Sunlight filtered through the gauzy curtains of their Singapore shophouse, casting faint golden lines across the floorboards. Yet it brought no warmth to Mei Lin—not to the cold weight pressing on her chest, nor to the stillness clinging to the air like dust.

Daniel had departed for his business trip days earlier. Since his brief call from Hong Kong before flying to Korea, there had been nothing. No messages. No voice. Only silence—sharp, endless, unforgiving.

She paced the narrow living room, arms folded tightly across her chest, as if sheer tension could hold her together. The phone lay untouched on the side table. Whenever it buzzed, she flinched, only to be disappointed.

95

Khian-Seng had visited, offering comfort—gentle words, awkward reassurances—but none reached the part of her unravelling. Even Ava, typically a whirlwind of laughter and chatter, had grown quiet. Her toys lay scattered, untouched, her voice's melody replaced by long silences and hesitant glances.

'Khian-Seng, people don't just vanish. Why can't anyone discover where he is?' Mei Lin sobbed.

Khian-Seng draped a comforting arm around her, offering words of solace he knew would likely not ease her pain.

Mei Lin closed her eyes, leaning her head against the wall, willing the emptiness to fade. Yet all she heard was the clock's ticking—and the void where Daniel's voice should have been.

Daniel had flown to Hong Kong, then to Korea. Mei Lin clung to that timeline like a lifeline, something to grasp amid the growing silence. After that—nothing. No message. No call. Not even one of his cheerful postcards, with their rushed sketches and notes scrawled in blue ink. He always sent one, even for a two-day trip.

'This isn't like Daniel. Something terrible must have happened,' she continued.

'There's no point speculating, Mei Lin, until we know more. I know this is grim—he's my brother too,' he replied.

'I know, I'm sorry. It's this endless waiting that's unbearable,' she said.

'Mummy, can we make another drawing for Daddy?' Ava asked.

Ava's voice was soft, hopeful. She sat cross-legged on the floor, encircled by a chaos of crayons—sunbursts of yellow, violet scribbles, and smiling stick figures with arms outstretched.

Mei Lin swallowed hard, fighting the lump in her throat. She knelt beside her daughter, smoothing a hand over her silky hair. 'Of course, sweetheart,' she murmured.

The soft shuffle of footsteps drew her gaze to the doorway. Nur entered, calm and steady. 'Let me take Ava, Ma'am,' she said softly, already reaching for the little girl's hand. 'You need rest. I'm certain we'll hear something soon.'

Mei Lin nodded, yet remained still. Her gaze lingered on the bright drawings scattered across the floorboards. They seemed like little prayers, etched in crayon.

Mei Lin nodded, though the dread in her chest deepened further. Daniel should have been home by now. She should have heard something—anything.

Then the phone rang. Its sound sliced through the stillness. She flinched, her breath catching in her chest. For a moment, her feet wouldn't move. Then she lunged for it, her heart pounding.

'Hello? Chris?' she gasped.

A brief silence lingered on the other end. Then his voice came—strained, weary, brittle at the edges.

'Mei Lin…'

Her heart sank.

'I'm sorry, Mei Lin. I've no updates yet.' He paused, his words' weight pressing through the line.

'People don't just vanish, Chris,' Mei Lin said, panic clawing up her spine.

'He did,' Chris confirmed, his voice taut. 'The airline logged his arrival. But he never checked into the hotel. No taxi booking. Nothing.'

Mei Lin felt the room tilt.

'I've spoken to the police,' Chris continued. 'No reported incidents. No accidents. As far as the system's concerned, Daniel just… vanished. I'm filing a formal missing person's report today. I've contacted Soong, the firm Daniel was meeting, and they've got people searching too—we're doing everything and will keep digging.'

'Please,' she whispered, her fingers gripping the receiver until her knuckles whitened.

Khian-Seng stepped forward, gently prising the phone from her and speaking with Chris, his voice low and measured as they discussed next steps.

'We'll find him,' Chris promised, then hesitated. 'I'm sorry I've no better news.'

The line went dead.

Mei Lin stood frozen, pressing her hands to her face as tears came—soft at first, then steady. Around her, the world felt eerily still, as if holding its breath, awaiting something she couldn't name.

'We'll find him, Mei Lin,' Khian-Seng said gently, wrapping his arms around her.

She gazed at him through tear-blurred eyes, then nodded faintly. Silently, she turned and climbed the stairs, step by step, to Ava's room.

'Ava,' she said softly, as her daughter glanced up, crayon in hand. 'Don't worry, darling. Daddy's just taking a bit longer than we thought, and Mummy's missing him—that's why I'm crying. He's… delayed because of work, but he'll be back soon, sending all his love to you.'

She drew Ava close, resting her cheek against her soft hair, listening to the clock's faint tick—and the silent static of a world gone mute.

'Will he come home soon? Don't cry, Mummy. I miss Daddy, but he's busy at work,' Ava said, her soft voice laced with a comforting tone.

'Of course, sweetheart,' Mei Lin replied, forcing the words past the lump in her throat as doubt twisted in her heart. 'Daddy loves us and wants to be with us.'

She kissed Ava's forehead and held her a touch closer.

Yet as the hours dragged on, Mei Lin couldn't quell the gnawing fear. She kept glancing at her phone, waiting—hoping—for any sign from Daniel. Each minute that passed without news seemed to thicken the air around her heart, pressing with an unseen weight.

Far away, in a remote mountain cabin, Daniel drifted in and out of consciousness, trapped in a fog of pain and confusion. He remained unaware of the chaos unfolding at home—oblivious to the worry and heartache weaving into Mei Lin's life.

Within his mind, he wandered a labyrinth of shadows, grasping for fragments of his former self. Familiar feelings stirred—an ache for connection, a flicker of love—but faces and names stayed just beyond reach.

Around him, the world carried on, indifferent. Yet, deep within, a flicker endured—a pull towards something real. Towards someone.

Every effort to mend his body reminded him he was still trapped in the void of forgotten connections. Somewhere, the world outside searched for him—but his identity slipped further away with each passing hour.

As days stretched into weeks, Daniel's body slowly mended, but the emptiness in his mind remained a raw, unyielding void. Each morning, he awoke in the mountain cabin to the silent hush of falling snow. The scents, the sights—

everything around him remained unfamiliar. The warmth of home lingered at the edge of memory, tantalising yet unreachable.

He could now sit up in bed unaided, often gazing through the frost-laced window. Beyond the glass, the Korean mountains stretched, vast and solemn beneath a heavy quilt of snow. Towering pines stood like silent sentinels along the ridge, their branches laden with snow, their quiet almost sacred.

The beauty was undeniable—yet it deepened his loneliness. The landscape was nearly monochrome—whites, greys, muted greens—broken only by the dark slopes of distant peaks and the thin curl of smoke rising from a chimney far below.

The village, a short distance away, clung to the mountainside like a secret, its wooden houses bowed under winter's weight—a truly remote place. Stillness hung in the air—not emptiness, but a sacred quiet—echoing the blank slate of his memory.

He watched an older woman, bundled in a thick coat, trudge along a snow-laced path, a woven basket in her hands. Her pace was slow and deliberate. Somewhere out of sight, a dog barked once, then fell silent.

Daniel blinked, trying to weave meaning from the scene. It felt both familiar and alien, like a half-remembered dream. The mountains loomed around him—vast and indifferent—like silent keepers of stories beyond his reach. As if they had witnessed his fall and now guarded the shattered fragments of his former self, buried beneath the snow.

Within the cabin, the wood stove crackled with life. A faint scent of herbs and something earthy lingered in the air—comforting, yet unfamiliar. Daniel shifted in bed, wincing at his limbs' soreness, yet grateful for the sensation—for anything real.

The woman tending him moved softly in the next room. Her name still eluded him. She was kind yet cautious, her words sparse, her presence steadfast. He sensed a guardedness in her—a solitude mirroring his own.

Unbeknown to him, her name was Jung-Soo. That she had lived alone for years, nursing her own wounds, trusting no one. That she had found him near death on the mountain and, for reasons she couldn't fathom, chose to save him.

Yet what he knew—what had taken root in the hollow of his chest—was a question: where had he come from, and was a family waiting for him somewhere?

A child's laughter wove through his dreams. A woman's hand, warm and familiar, clasped his own. The faint scent of jasmine—or perhaps lemongrass—in a sunlit room. A voice—soft, insistent—called through the static. Were they mere dreams? Or was his mind playing tricks again?

Daniel exhaled slowly, watching his breath mist the window before it faded into the cold morning air. He still didn't know who he was—not fully. Yet something deep within had begun to stir. Somewhere beyond these snow-draped mountains, he felt certain someone held the pieces he lacked. And perhaps—just perhaps—he could find his way back to them.

Yet each day, the faces in his dreams faded further. The visions, once vivid, now slipped further from his grasp, like smoke curling through his fingers.

His body was mending—slowly, steadily—under the gentle care of the woman who had pulled him from the wreckage. Her name was Jung-Soo. It suited her—graceful, resilient, quietly fierce. Like the strength she offered him, without ever seeking anything in return.

She was diligent and attentive, her hands steady, her presence grounding. Each day, she worked tirelessly to help him regain movement and strength. Unbeknown to Daniel at first, but now clear, was that she had served as a nurse during the Korean War. Those hard-earned skills, forged in crisis, now saved his life.

'One step at a time,' she would say in halting English, learned from American soldiers she had cared for in a hospital during the war. She gently encouraged him, guiding him through rehabilitation exercises.

'You're doing well,' she often said, her voice soft and steady—a balm against the frustration threatening to weigh him down. 'You are strong, and we'll get you back on your feet. I have something for you'. With that, Jung sook walked over to the desk and presented a book to Daniel. Pressed within the pages of the book was a flower.

"When I was cleaning your jacket, I found this flower in your top pocket. I thought it must be important, so I kept it. Do you know why you had it in your pocket?"

Daniel looked back at Jung Sook and shook his head. "No, I have no idea why I had that flower. Thank you for keeping it, hopefully it will come back to me"

As she aided him with daily recovery tasks, Daniel drew comfort from her presence. Something deeply nurturing imbued her movements through the cabin—warm,

unhurried, always attentive. Her laughter—rare yet bright—
was infectious. Despite the fog still clouding his past, their
quiet moments offered a fragile peace.

At times, Jung-Sook brought him local treats during his
breaks—sweet rice cakes wrapped in leaves or steaming
dumplings filled with minced vegetables. She explained
their cultural significance, sharing family stories, and Daniel
listened intently, drawn into a world that, though not his
own, felt oddly anchoring.

'Thank you for everything,' he said one afternoon, his voice
soft as he watched her refill his cup with warm water.

She turned to him, her expression earnest.

'You are a good man. It's my duty to help,' she replied softly,
brushing stray strands of hair behind her ear. Then she
smiled, the lines around her eyes deepening with quiet
resolve. 'Truly… you're healing faster than I expected. Have
you recalled anything—anything at all—about who you
are?'

Her question hung heavily between them. Daniel longed to
say yes—to offer some fragment of truth. Yet all he could do
was shake his head.

'Not yet,' he admitted, the words bitter on his tongue. The emptiness within him pulsed like a bruise, dimming even the brightest moments. Each small step forward was a victory—yet the shadow of not knowing never fully lifted.

'At first, I had cloudy images, too vague to decipher. But as time passed, they faded entirely. I wish I could recall something—anything,' he confessed one day, his voice laced with longing.

'Memories will return,' Jung-Sook said softly, her gaze holding his. 'Sometimes they return when least expected. You must be patient.'

Yet patience remained just beyond his grasp.

Day after day, Daniel gazed out the cabin window, his eyes tracing the snow-capped peaks encircling them like ancient sentinels. The mountains were beautiful—yet alien and unfamiliar. He stared as if they might hold answers. Yet no matter how long he looked, his past remained hidden, like the valley beneath the snow. Who was he? Where had he come from? The questions swirled endlessly, unanswered.

As days blurred into nights, his bond with Jung-Sook quietly deepened. She was no longer merely his caregiver but a quiet companion in his solitude. She began sharing stories of her life: the hardships she had endured, her family, the strength of her community, and the traditions of her people. She asked him to call her Jung. 'No need for the Sook—it's far too complicated,' she said. Her voice brought colour to his grey world, painting a tapestry of resilience and quiet beauty.

Though he still couldn't recall his family—or whether he had one—Daniel found solace in her warmth. Her stories wove threads into the fabric of his new reality, and though his mind remained a blank canvas, he felt the stirrings of belonging.

Yet, as Daniel felt a fragile thread of solace weaving between them, the absence of his memories haunted him—an ever-present void where his identity should have been.

He often caught himself watching Jung—the way her hands danced when she spoke, the quiet resolve in her eyes, the calm assurance of her presence. Grace imbued her every motion, a quiet resilience that comforted and captivated him. In those hushed moments, something stirred within him—something warm, familiar, yet elusive—like a song he almost recalled.

One evening, after a particularly gruelling physiotherapy session, Daniel stepped outside to breathe the crisp mountain air. A homemade crutch supported him, his limp evident. The sun hung low in the winter sky, painting the horizon in hues of rose and gold. The snow beneath the trees shimmered like powdered glass, the silence around him profound and still.

Jung joined him softly, two steaming cups in her hands. 'Thought you might like this,' she said, offering him one with a faint smile.

He accepted it gratefully, the warmth seeping into his hands.

'Thank you,' he said, taking a slow sip. The tea was fragrant and soothing, its heat easing the cold and the frustration clinging to him like a shadow.

'It's beautiful here,' he murmured, his eyes tracing the valley's curves below.

'How long will I limp, Jung?' he asked, hoping for reassurance.

'It's hard to say—you may always have one. Yet we must take one step at a time, one day at a time, and hope for the best,' Jung replied softly.

Daniel smiled at her and nodded.

'It's beautiful here,' Daniel murmured. Jung smiled in agreement, leaning against the stone wall. Her gaze softened at his words.

'That's why I returned here after the war. I've had no interest in the outside world since.'

'Do you ever think about it—the war, I mean? What happened?' Daniel asked, a faint smile tugging at his lips.

'Of course,' she said softly. 'Yet I came here to leave those memories behind. This place… it lets me breathe.' She paused, her expression brightening. 'Anyway, you're my favourite patient ever. No more talk of war—I have all I need here.'

Daniel gazed towards the mountains as he stood. 'When will the snow clear?' he asked gently. The question hung in the air, gentle yet weighty. He felt a thread of vulnerability weave between them, fragile yet real.

Then, without warning, his foot slipped on a patch of ice near the edge of the steps. He twisted, lost his balance, and fell hard, his cup flying from his hands and shattering on the frozen ground.

"Damn it!" he snapped, scrambling to his knees. "I'm sorry, Jung. I'm so bloody clumsy." His breath hitched, frustration sharpening his voice. "I just… I wish I knew who I was. Where I came from!"

Jung knelt beside the broken pieces of the cup, her hands moving with quiet grace. She looked up at him, her expression calm and steady.

"Then we shall find out," she said gently. "One step at a time."

"I hope you'll remember where you came from, who you are," Jung said softly. "But if you don't… we'll sort it out together."

A smile crept across Daniel's face, the warmth of her words easing the ache within him. In the cold wilderness of his forgotten life, her presence was a steady flame. Their bond, forged through shared silence and slow healing, had become a fragile thread—one he now clung to with growing hope.

"Every day, I feel a bit stronger," he said, meeting her gaze. "Thanks to you. I just… I wish I could remember. Find my way back."

She reached out, taking his hand with quiet strength.

"When the snow clears, we'll head to the town," she said. "See if anyone knows you. But for that, you'll need to keep walking, build your strength." A playful firmness edged her voice. "Now, sit on the porch. I'll fetch you more tea."

She disappeared into the cabin and returned moments later with a fresh cup, placing it gently in his hands.

They sat side by side, gazing across the vast valley below. The sun dipped behind the mountains, casting a golden glow that faded into the shadows of nightfall. In that moment, with the quiet hum of the stove behind them and the cold air brushing their cheeks, Daniel made a silent vow:

He would fight for his memories.

For the truth.

And for those waiting beyond the snow.

Days passed, and as Daniel continued his rehabilitation, he felt his strength slowly returning. Each session with Jung marked quiet progress—he stood for longer stretches, took steadier steps, and the old hospital gown that once hung loosely from his gaunt frame now fitted more snugly about his shoulders. They celebrated the small victories together, her encouragement never overstated but always sincere, her praise laced with a warmth that bolstered his courage.

One morning, after completing a round of exercises, Daniel paused to catch his breath. A strange discomfort flickered at the edge of his awareness—elusive and maddening. Something stirred in the depths of his mind: images, sounds, broken fragments surging forward with sudden intensity… then slipping away just as swiftly.

He clenched his jaw, exhaling sharply as he leaned against the wall. The taste of hope soured into frustration. The memories were there—he could sense them—but they refused to take form.

"Are you alright?" Jung asked, her brow furrowing with concern as she stepped closer.

"Just… I think I might've had a memory," he admitted, his voice low, eyes clouded with a mix of hope and anguish. "But it vanished—just like that. It's like trying to grasp smoke with my hands."

She rested a gentle hand on his arm, her touch steadying, grounding him in the present. "Don't be disheartened," she said softly. "Even fragments matter. They show you're beginning to heal—not just your body, but your mind as well

5

Footprints of Hope – Spring 1964
(Korea)

The April air was crisp, no longer biting, and the last traces of snow had thinned into scattered patches beneath the trees and in the mountain's shadowed corners. Morning light streamed through the wide cabin windows, casting long streaks of gold across the worn wooden floor.

Inside, the scent of jasmine tea wafted through the room—earthy and calming.

Daniel sat, legs stretched out by the small table, his gaze following Jung as she moved quietly about the kitchen area, pouring hot water over loose leaves in a clay pot. The ritual was slow, deliberate—something Daniel had come to cherish in these still, unfamiliar mornings. He cradled his tea in both hands, grateful for its simple warmth and comfort.

"You're walking stronger each day," Jung said, setting down a second cup beside him. "But I'm afraid that limp may linger, though it's far less pronounced than before."

"I feel it too," Daniel replied, carefully stretching his legs back and forth.

"My body aches less now. I think I'm ready to venture further."

Jung nodded, thoughtful. "After lunch, you can try walking a bit further—down past the second ridge."

After their midday meal, Daniel set out from the cabin, following a narrow path that wound down the slope through a thicket of early-blooming shrubs and fresh undergrowth.

The forest was stirring from winter's grip—buds breaking open, birds calling through the canopy above, weaving song into the afternoon air.

Daniel took slow, measured steps, the walking stick Jung had carved for him tapping softly against the ground. He breathed deeply, letting the cool air fill his lungs. It carried the scent of damp earth and pine, with a faint trace of wildflowers beginning to bloom. Here and there, the forest floor was soft and dark where the snow had finally melted away.

He walked in silence for some time, his footsteps the only sound aside from birdsong and the occasional creak of trees swaying gently in the breeze.

Daniel welcomed the quiet. Out here, in the open air and living woods, something within him began to stir—a flicker of identity, a faint pull towards something once known.

After nearly half a mile, he paused. A clearing lay ahead, and he sat to rest.

A few minutes later, his breath steadied and legs strengthened, he pressed on a bit further—until something caught his eye. Among the trees, blackened trunks stood out like scars.

Curiosity overcoming fatigue, Daniel pushed through the brambles and reached the ridge's edge.

Deep in the valley below, a shape emerged: a burnt-out car, twisted and skeletal, half-swallowed by the forest. Its metal frame was blackened and rusted, the glass shattered and strewn like ice across the ground. There was no smoke now, but the air held a strange stillness, as if the earth hadn't yet released its memory of what had happened there. He crouched slightly, scanning the wreckage below. No footprints. No signs of recent life—just silence. The kind of silence that thrummed with questions.

Then—a sudden noise. A loud rustle.

Daniel turned sharply.

A wild boar, large and bristling, emerged from behind a cluster of trees, its eyes fixed on him with wary intensity. For a moment, they stared at each other, frozen.

Then, with a sharp grunt, the animal turned and bolted into the woods, crashing through the undergrowth as swiftly as it had appeared.

Daniel stood still, heart pounding.

The forest closed in around him once more, its quiet returning like a held breath released.

He cast one last glance at the car before turning back towards the cabin.

The walk back felt heavier. His steps were slower.

Something about the wreck—its presence so deep in the woods, unspoken, untouched—had stirred an unease in him. Not fear exactly, but something harder to name.

As the cabin came into view, Daniel realised the forest wasn't merely a place of recovery. It was a keeper of secrets.

And somewhere among those secrets, a part of himself lay waiting.

He reached the small cabin soon after, his breath heavy from the walk, eyes wide with urgency.

Inside, Jung was waiting. Her face remained calm, but her hands paused mid-fold in the fabric she was mending. She studied him closely as he crossed the threshold.

"Jung," Daniel said slowly, rubbing his cold fingers together. "I saw the car today. Nothing's left—just twisted metal, broken glass. No body… no sign of anyone. It's as if whoever was there simply vanished. Wiped away, as though they were never there."

His voice trembled. The image still clung to him—the eerie stillness around the wreckage, the silence pressing on his thoughts.

Jung nodded, her gaze steady, though a flicker of sadness passed behind it.

"I went back… after I found you," she said softly. "There was someone, but the fire's heat had been so intense that little remained—nothing to identify them. So I buried the body."

She paused, letting the weight of her words settle.

"I didn't want you to see that—not while you were healing. It was difficult, but... it felt right. Though we don't know who they were, they were human, and it was the proper thing to do. I've seen enough inhumanity to last ten lifetimes."

Daniel stared at her, struck by her quiet strength and by what she had borne in silence. His chest tightened with a mix of sorrow and gratitude.

The silence that followed held more than words: understanding, pain, and the beginnings of trust.

He turned to the window, watching the fading light stretch across the horizon. Shadows danced along the treetops, and the soft hush of the forest reminded him how isolated they were... yet not alone.

"That poor person, who were they, how was I connected to them? Were they my relative? They also could have had a family and never returned home."

"If they had, I'm sure we would have heard from them now. It is clear they were not connected to family. Maybe they were like me, alone. We did our best for them to have peace". Jung said touching his shoulder.

The burnt car.

The wild boar.

Jung's admission.

They were pieces of a puzzle he didn't yet understand.

But something inside him shifted—a fear eased, just a little, by the truth now laid bare.

The question hung in the air, a tether connecting him to a past he couldn't quite reach.

"I… I don't know, Jung," he said, his voice barely above a whisper, a tear glistening in his eye. "I think about who I am, where I came from… but then, nothing. It's as though everything is shrouded in fog."

Seeing the sorrow clouding his face, Jung nudged him gently, a playful smile softening the moment.

"I'm certain it will come. In the meantime, we'll forge new memories! With time, the fog will lift, and you'll remember. And whatever your family is like, I know they love you. You're strong. They'll be waiting for you."

Her encouragement lifted his spirits. That evening, for the first time in days, he felt a glimmer of hope amidst the uncertainty.

Jung's light became a quiet source of strength, urging him to embrace the healing process—both physical and emotional.

A few days later, as he ventured further into his rehabilitation with longer walks, Daniel surprised himself with how far he could go. He now relied less on his stick, though it remained with him, as did the limp. He was gradually regaining confidence in his movements.

Each extra step was a small triumph, every exercise an affirmation of his will to reclaim his life.

But in quiet moments of reflection, the shadows of missing memories crept in. Despite the healing, the space where his past should have been remained a vast, silent expanse.

Then one morning—while Daniel was practising standing without his cane—a spark ignited.

A memory flickered like a flame.

In his dreams, faces had begun to emerge. One in particular: a woman with dark hair and warm eyes. It felt as though she were right beside him, whispering words he couldn't quite catch.

The image blurred in and out of focus, like a dream barely held at dawn.

Panic surged through him. The fear of losing that flicker of recognition—of watching it slip away—was overwhelming.

"Jung," he called, urgency sharp in his voice as he stumbled backward, nearly losing his balance in his effort to hold the image.

She rushed to his side, concern etched into every line of her face. "What is it?"

"I saw someone…" he stammered, hands trembling as he gripped the edge of the bed. The memory danced just beyond his reach.

"A woman. I can't recall her name, but she feels familiar. Deeply familiar. I think… she might be important."

"Then we'll try to capture it together," Jung said gently, her eyes shining with quiet resolve. "What else do you recall?"

"I don't know," he replied breathlessly, frustration tightening his chest. He clutched the bed harder. "It's like a puzzle— slipping away the moment I draw near. I just… I need to know who she is. Or if she even exists. What if it's all my mind playing tricks after the accident?"

"We'll find that piece," she said firmly, squeezing his arm. Her touch was steady, grounding.

"Close your eyes. Think of her. What do you feel? Is she someone you love?"

As he closed his eyes, Daniel focused intently, letting himself sink into the dim recesses of his mind. If there was a connection to be found, he had to delve deep.

He concentrated on the feeling—the warmth, the laughter. Then, a jolt stirred in his chest, a flicker of resonance.

He glimpsed fragments of home. A life filled with love, echoing through him like a melody.

"I… I feel warmth when I think of her," he murmured, holding back tears of frustration and longing. "It feels right, as though I should know her… but it's not real. It's a dream."

"Hold on to that feeling," Jung said gently. "Memories sometimes live in emotions. This could be the start."

He nodded, clinging to her words.

Yet the uncertainty lingered.

It haunted him—this ache of not knowing. Healing was on the horizon, but parts of him remained out of reach. A puzzle half-built, its missing pieces scattered across time. Then, suddenly, it all vanished, leaving only empty darkness in his mind.

Despite the struggle, something within him sparked—a renewed sense of hope.

In the days that followed, Daniel continued his walks with quiet resolve, treating each step as a chance to reclaim a part of himself. With Jung's steadfast support, even the smallest triumphs felt monumental, urging him to persevere through the mounting frustration of his amnesia.

One afternoon, they sat outside on the bench overlooking the mountains. Clouds drifted lazily across the sky, and Daniel felt a wave of peace wash over him—a gentle reminder of the beauty still present in life, even amidst uncertainty.

"Tell me more about your life here," he said, turning to Jung. "What are your dreams?"

She paused, thoughtful, her gaze following a cloud as it stretched into the distance. Then, slowly, she began to share her aspirations.

"As you know, I was a nurse during the Korean War," Jung began, her voice soft yet steady. "That is where I learnt to speak English, working with the American soldiers, and hospital staff. Afterwards, I returned to the family home—to escape the chaos, but also to hold on to the memories I had left. This place… it's my last tie to my family."

She paused, her eyes distant.

"Before the war, my parents moved north to be closer to my mother's sister. I never saw or heard from them again. I can only assume they perished in the conflict. My aunt's village was heavily bombed."

Daniel listened intently, moved by her quiet resilience, by the way she had chosen to rebuild a life from the ashes of war.

"You've rebuilt your life beautifully," he said. "But… why did you never marry?"

Jung gave him a small, wistful smile. "Some paths choose us, Daniel," she said softly. "After the war, I needed to find peace, not just for myself but for others. This cabin, this life—it's where I could do that. Perhaps love will find me yet, but I've found meaning here."

"I was married once," she said. "Very young. He was a soldier, incredibly handsome, too," she added with a smile. "Sadly, he was killed in the war, not long after we wed. We were only married a few months."

She looked away, her voice barely above a whisper. "I don't talk about it much. He was the love of my life, and now he's gone."

Hearing this, Daniel felt a strange shift within him—a sense of connection deeper than the friendship they had built. It was as if their separate stories were slowly weaving into a shared tapestry, threaded with understanding, vulnerability, and the quiet hope of healing.

"So, we've both lost important things in our lives," Daniel said, gently placing an arm around Jung's shoulders.

"At least I know what I've lost," she replied with a soft smile.

Then, with a slight shake of her head, she added, "Enough of this talk. You need your rest. We can walk further tomorrow."

With that, they stood and walked back towards the cabin. The evening light spilled across the porch as they stepped inside and quietly parted for the night, each retreating to their own room—carrying a shared warmth neither had expected but both had begun to welcome.

6

A Family's Grief - Spring 1964 (Singapore)

The loss felt unbearable. From the moment the news reached her, Mei Lin's world spiralled into a vortex of despair and confusion. December 1963—she would never forget that date. It was the moment when laughter, love, and dreams collided with the harsh, unrelenting reality of Daniel's disappearance.

Weeks turned into months, and the absence of her husband grew heavier with each passing day. He had left for Korea with ambitious plans to expand his business, his voice brimming with excitement as he spoke of new opportunities. Now, his silence tore through the rhythm of their family life, leaving only echoes—his laughter fading in the corners of their home, the warmth of his embrace reduced to memory.

"Please come back," she whispered into the stillness of their shophouse, clutching Ava's tiny hand as if it might somehow bridge the widening chasm between presence and loss.

The family gathered as best they could, offering kind words and quiet support. It wasn't what Mei Lin truly wanted, but she was grateful, nonetheless. Their presence meant something. Still, in the quiet corners of her heart, it was Daniel she longed for most.

Desperate for answers, Mei Lin refused to give up. She made phone calls, contacted his business partners, and reached out to friends and colleagues in Korea—she tried every angle. But every lead dissolved into uncertainty. No one had seen him. No one knew anything. It was as if the universe itself had swallowed Daniel whole, and with every passing day, the weight of not knowing burrowed deeper into her soul.

Mei Lin had just endured the worst Christmas of her life. Trying to comfort Ava through her heartbreak had been almost unbearable—especially with her daughter still clinging to the hope that Daddy would return. But Daniel hadn't come back. He had missed one of the most cherished times for their family. His father had been British and Christian, so they always celebrated Christmas with warmth and tradition, alongside other religious festivals. This year, though, their home was silent, hollowed out by his absence.

One day, there was a knock at the door. "Mei Lin, I want to help," her brother-in-law, Khian-Seng, said gently. He had been watching her struggle; the weight of grief etched into every movement. "I can go to Korea now that the snow has cleared. Perhaps I can find out what happened to him—it'll be easier being on the ground than at the end of a phone."

Despite the knot of fear and uncertainty in her chest, Mei Lin nodded. She knew that any action—any hope—was better than the helpless limbo they were trapped in.

"Shall I come with you?" Mei Lin asked quickly, her voice taut with urgency. "Surely two people are better than one."

Khian-Seng shook his head gently. "No… I think it's best you stay here—with Ava. The last thing she needs right now is to lose both her mum and her daddy, even if only for a little while."

Mei Lin looked away, nodding reluctantly. Her throat tightened. "You're right," she said softly. Then, after a pause, her voice fell to a whisper. "But please… just find some answers."

Khian-Seng departed soon after, carrying with him a fragile piece of Mei Lin's hope. His resolve was unwavering: he would search the mountain villages of Korea, no matter how remote or rugged. The terrain was unforgiving, but he pressed on, driven by determination and a brotherly love that refused to falter.

He travelled tirelessly across the stark landscape, moving from village to village, speaking with locals who greeted him with polite curiosity but offered no real answers. Each enquiry seemed to dissolve into silence.

"Have you heard of a foreigner… an engineer?" he would ask again and again, showing the same photograph, repeating the same words.

Faces would tighten with confusion. "No one has seen him. I'm sorry."

The days slipped by faster than he expected. He had only a week to search, and the hours were vanishing. No leads. No breakthroughs. Just cold winds and colder roads.

On the final morning, as the sun rose over the frostbitten mountains, Khian-Seng paused for a moment. The air was sharp with the scent of pine and damp earth. Fatigue weighed heavily on his shoulders. He had climbed, walked, questioned—and yet, Daniel remained a ghost in the snow, a name without a trace.

Still, he had one more village to try along this stretch of road. And hope, though frayed, had not yet broken.

Today, Khian-Seng found himself walking along a narrow dirt path winding through dense woods, the trees arching overhead like clasped hands against the pale morning sky. The trail felt endless, silent save for the crunch of his boots and the occasional whisper of wind through the branches.

Up ahead, an old barn emerged from the tangle of foliage— its slanted roof sagging under years of snow and storms, its weathered wood silvered with age. It stood like a forgotten sentinel from another time; its silence steeped in memory. His breath caught as he approached, heart pounding with a mix of exhaustion and final hope. This might be his last chance—the last stretch of land before he'd be forced to return empty-handed. He couldn't bear to face Mei Lin or little Ava with nothing but silence.

Circling the barn slowly, he scanned the area with sharp, cautious eyes. Every creak of old timber, every rustle in the undergrowth, tugged at his attention. The air felt heavier here, a stillness that made one feel watched.

"Daniel…" he called softly, his voice nearly lost to the breeze. It trembled, not with fear, but with desperation. He didn't dare shout—didn't want to startle a man who might be injured, confused, or afraid. Yet he couldn't shake the gnawing urgency rising in his chest.

He took another step forward, listening, hoping, searching.

As Khian-Seng crested the brow of a hill, his breath caught. The forest opened before him, revealing a sweeping expanse of emerald green bathed in the glistening glow of morning light. He paused, momentarily transfixed by the beauty—the gentle shimmer of dew on leaves, the golden beams filtering through the branches. Yet the stillness only deepened the urgency pounding in his chest.

Then, at the edge of his vision, something stirred.

A flash—quick and subtle, almost imperceptible—cut through the dense line of trees. His heart slammed against his ribs as he squinted into the shadows. There, slipping between two trunks, was a figure. Just a glimpse, but enough to ignite hope.

"Daniel!" he called, louder this time, his voice cutting through the morning's hush. It echoed off the trees, laced with breathless anticipation. Could it truly be him?

He surged forward, driven by instinct. The ground sloped downward, the underbrush crunching beneath his boots like brittle bones. Every sound felt loud and intrusive against the forest's quiet, but he couldn't slow down now. His pulse roared in his ears.

As he reached the next rise, he paused just long enough to listen—then caught sight of movement again. A figure, taller than most locals he'd seen, weaving through the trees with deliberate steps. It wasn't an animal. It wasn't his imagination.

Someone was out there. Someone who didn't want to be found.

Khian-Seng's breath came quickly now, his limbs aching with fatigue but driven by something stronger—hope. He pressed forward, deeper into the thicket, determined not to lose the trail.

In that fleeting moment, Daniel glanced over his shoulder, a flicker of awareness rippling through him. He sensed a presence—not threatening, but unfamiliar—moving just beyond the edge of clarity. Partially obscured by the trees, Khian-Seng hadn't crested the hill high enough to be seen clearly. Yet something in Daniel recoiled instinctively.

Uncertainty gripped him, and without pausing, he turned and moved deeper into the woods.

Khian-Seng's frustration surged. He had come too far, sacrificed too much, to let Daniel slip away now.

"Wait!" he shouted, his breath catching. "I'm here to help you."

His voice shattered the stillness, echoing through the trees, desperate and raw. "Daniel! Please, it's me—Khian-Seng! Where are you?"

Branches clawed at his sleeves as he pressed forward, the dense underbrush resisting every step. His heart pounded like a war drum, the mingled weight of fear and hope urging him onward. The woods were quieter now, the wind whispering through the trees like a secret he couldn't quite catch. Why wouldn't Daniel respond?

"Daniel!" he cried again, his voice cracking with urgency. "You're not alone! Your family is searching for you!"

The silence that followed was almost cruel. Yet Khian-Seng didn't stop. He couldn't. Something told him Daniel was close—lost, yes, but listening. And perhaps, just perhaps, something in that voice might reach whatever remained of the memories buried in the man's fractured mind.

Moments passed, the silence thick and suffocating. Khian-Seng's voice lingered in the air, a fragile thread pulled taut through emptiness. Still, he pressed on.

"I won't leave without you!"

Deeper in the woods, Daniel halted, his breath catching. That voice—it tugged at something buried deep within him. A flicker of recognition sparked, faint but undeniable. His heart pounded. There was something in the way it called to him— urgent, familiar, achingly real.

He clenched his fists, the instinct to flee warring with a sudden pull of memory. Fear gripped him. What if it was a trap? What if he was mistaken? He remained hidden, crouched behind a cluster of pines, his breath misting in the cold air. Yet the urge to respond, to reach out, gnawed at him.

"Where are you going?" Khian-Seng shouted again, his voice raw, cracking with desperation. He pressed through the undergrowth, thorns and branches tearing at his sleeves and arms, heedless of the scratches blooming across his skin. "I'm here! It's me!"

Still, only the rustle of wind answered, brushing through the trees with a whisper that mocked his hope. The forest offered no sign—no confirmation, no rejection—only stillness.

Yet Khian-Seng could sense it. He was close. Something in the air had shifted. His pulse thudded with urgency, a deep, primal insistence not to give up. Was it truly Daniel? Could their long search finally be nearing its end?

He quickened his pace, eyes darting through the foliage, refusing to let the moment slip away. Every step felt like a heartbeat, every breath a plea.

He whispered once more, softer this time, almost to himself: "Daniel… please."

As he pressed through the dense underbrush, Khian-Seng's mind churned with memories—of Mei Lin's weary eyes, Ava's innocent questions, the weight of the promise he had made. I'll find him. I'll bring him home. That vow rang louder than the crunch of leaves beneath his feet, louder than the fatigue tugging at his limbs.

Was he so desperate to find his lost brother that he was now imagining figures, hearing noises?

If the fleeting figure he had seen was Daniel, he had vanished deeper into the wilderness—slipped through his fingers like mist. Khian-Seng stood at the edge of the trees, breathless and aching, the stillness pressing in on him.

His heart sank. The forest offered no sign of life, no voice answering his desperate call.

"Daniel!" he shouted again, the name torn from him like a final plea. But only the wind answered, brushing the leaves with indifferent quiet.

For a long moment, he stood motionless, battling the weight of defeat. The sense of failure coiled tightly around him, squeezing the air from his lungs. So close. Just moments too late. The thought was unbearable.

Yet he refused to let it consume him.

Khian-Seng thought to himself that maybe his mind was playing tricks. Was he so desperate to find Daniel that he imagined it.

After a brief pause, Khian-Seng clenched his jaw and forced himself to move. Every step away from the clearing ached, each one a silent struggle between hope and despair. But even as doubt gnawed at his resolve, he made a vow.

I'll return. I'll keep searching. I won't let Daniel stay lost.

With the wind at his back and a fire reignited in his chest, Khian-Seng vanished into the forest once more—not in retreat, but in pursuit.

As he emerged from the dense woods, the last trees giving way to a narrow, winding path, Khian-Seng paused. His breath came quickly, his chest heaving with exhaustion. The forest behind him stood silent and indifferent, branches swaying gently as though oblivious to the urgency that had driven him. He turned back one final time, his eyes scanning the treeline, willing a sign—any sign—to appear.

But there was only stillness.

No voice answered his calls. No movement stirred the silence.

The journey to the airport was cloaked in a silence so profound it seemed to press against his skin. No radio. No idle conversation. Just the dull hum of the engine and the endless stretch of road winding through the mountains like fading hope. Khian-Seng sat rigid, his hands still, his mind replaying every turn he'd taken, every person he'd questioned, every glimpse of possibility that had slipped through his fingers.

There had been a moment—brief, fragile—when he thought he'd seen Daniel. A figure in the trees. A head turning. A shadow slipping away. But it had been too fleeting, too distant. Now, it felt like a mirage, a memory conjured by desperation.

His forehead rested gently against the cool glass of the car window. Outside, the forest blurred into shifting streaks of green and shadow. He watched it pass, his reflection faint in the glass—eyes weary, jaw clenched.

He had come seeking answers, hoping for truth, needing closure.

But the mountains had offered only silence.

Yet he made a vow—quiet but fierce—to himself, to Mei Lin, to Daniel.

This isn't over. I'll return. Every year, if I must, and search every inch of the mountains leading to the factory. Until I know the truth.

Back in Singapore, the city's heat and noise struck him like a shock after the stillness of the mountains. He found Mei Lin waiting in the kitchen, her eyes a fragile blend of hope and dread.

He sat her down gently, taking her hand in his, grounding them both in that moment of uncertainty.

"There's… no sign of him," he said, his voice low and heavy. "No one's heard of a foreigner passing through. No one has seen him. Mei Lin, I've done all I can—for now."

She stared at him, her fingers tightening around his as though clinging to hope itself.

"I'll go back," he said quickly, earnestly. "Every year, if I must. But I think—" he hesitated, the words catching in his throat, "—we may have to face the possibility that Daniel is… gone."

Mei Lin wrenched her hand from his, stumbling back with a broken cry, the sound sharp and raw in the quiet room.

"No. No, I won't accept that!" she cried, her voice breaking as tears brimmed in her eyes. She turned abruptly and fled down the hallway, the bedroom door slamming shut with a final, echoing thud.

Khian-Seng stood frozen in the silence that followed, the air heavy with grief. Guilt settled deep in his chest, pressing like a stone. He had returned with nothing but unanswered questions and a heartbreak he couldn't mend. He knew Mei Lin was clinging to hope—fragile, flickering hope—even as some part of her had already begun to mourn.

Behind the closed door, Mei Lin wept into the pillow that still held the faint scent of Daniel. Deep down, she knew. He was gone.

And somehow, she and Ava would have to learn to live in the emptiness he left behind.

7

A Quiet Bloom – Spring 1965
(Singapore)

Back in Singapore, as weeks bled into months, Mei Lin's grief slowly hardened into quiet, melancholic acceptance. Friends and family offered comfort in measured doses, but none could fill the void Daniel had left behind. His absence clung to the walls of their home, a presence in the silence, a ghost in every routine.

Ava, now old enough to sense the shift in their world, began to ask questions.

"Mummy, where's Daddy?" she would ask softly, her voice carrying the gentle, innocent lilt that twisted Mei Lin's heart.

Mei Lin hated lying to her, but the truth felt too heavy to share. So she crafted a version to fit a child's world—something gentle enough to carry them both through.

"Daddy's on a long journey, sweetheart," she'd say, brushing the hair from Ava's forehead. "He loves you dearly, and he'll come back."

But even as the words left her lips, they felt like echoes—faint, hollow, and uncertain. She longed for the day she could tell Ava the whole truth. But for now, this would have to be enough.

As time pressed forward like a relentless tide, Mei Lin began to build a life for herself and Ava—laying the fragile foundation of a new reality amid the persistent ache of grief. She returned to work, channelling her energy into her career, and in doing so, started to rediscover herself—not only as a mother but as a woman shaped by loss, resilience, and quiet strength. Yet Daniel's absence lingered, ever-present, like a shadow stretching across each day.

After years of searching and exhausting every possibility, Khian-Seng returned—his shoulders heavy, his spirit worn.

"It's over," he said softly one afternoon, seated across from her at the kitchen table. His voice was gentle, threaded with sorrow and care. "He's… officially declared dead. The Koreans have confirmed it. I have the paperwork here."

Mei Lin felt her world crack again, grief flooding in like a wave she'd tried to hold at bay. Even after all this time, even after bracing herself for this possibility, the finality stole her breath. She didn't weep—not at first—but sat in silence, numbness cocooning her heart.

"This is the second hardest day of my life," she whispered. "Now I must tell Ava that her daddy is never coming back."

"Do you want me to do it with you?" Khian-Seng asked softly.

"No, this is something I must do, and I've avoided it for far too long. I'll speak with Ava now," Mei Lin replied.

With that, Mei Lin walked slowly upstairs and into Ava's room, closing the door behind her.

"Ava, Mummy has something to tell you," were the only words Khian-Seng heard before the door shut.

Months passed in muted mourning, though Daniel had been gone for years. The confirmation of his death extinguished the last embers of hope Mei Lin had kept alive. In the quiet that followed, she withdrew from the world, tending to Ava with fierce devotion but leaving little room for herself.

It was Bo—her lifelong friend—who gently broached the subject one evening over tea.

"Mei Lin," she said carefully, watching her friend's expression, "you've been alone for a long time now. Perhaps it's time to consider… starting again. Not to forget him, but to let yourself live."

"Don't be silly, Bo," Mei Lin replied with a faint smile, though her voice quivered slightly. "I've only ever loved Daniel. What would I know about seeing other people? He was the love of my life—my soulmate—and now… he's gone."

Bo sighed softly, refusing to let her friend slip back into grief.

"Oh, come on, Mei Lin. You're far too young to talk like that. And think of Ava—it might do her good to have a father figure."

Mei Lin glanced away, her expression tightening.

"I'm not certain. It just feels… wrong. I'd be terribly uncomfortable. Besides, I must be cautious—for Ava's sake. She still hasn't fully accepted that her father isn't returning."

Bo reached across the table, gently touching her hand. "Look, I'm hosting a dinner party next Saturday. Why not come? No pressure, just good food and pleasant company. You never know—you might actually enjoy yourself."

Mei Lin narrowed her eyes. "This sounds suspiciously like a setup. What are you scheming?"

"Nothing mad, I swear!" Bo chuckled. "But yes, I do have a friend attending—Gerry. He's a widower, though I loathe that term. His wife passed away from cancer three years ago. He's still navigating his loss, too. And—full disclosure— he's remarkably handsome."

Mei Lin let out a reluctant chuckle, her first in ages. "Alright, I'll come. But this is just dinner, Bo. No matchmaking. Understood?"

"Understood," Bo replied with a cheeky grin. "Just dinner. Besides, you haven't seen the house since I had it thoroughly remodelled."

The front door opened to warm light, the gentle clink of glasses, and soft music drifting from within. Mei Lin stepped tentatively into Bo's elegant home, where the scent of jasmine mingled with something rich and savoury wafting from the kitchen. She had dressed with quiet care—nothing flashy, just enough to feel presentable—but beneath her composed exterior, nerves fluttered.

Bo appeared at once, her smile radiant as she enveloped Mei Lin in a warm hug. "You made it! I'm so chuffed."

"Thank you for inviting me," Mei Lin said, slipping off her shoes. Her gaze swept the room. "It's a stunning home; I love what you've done to transform it."

Bo beamed. "Isn't it gorgeous, I'm so glad you like it. Come in, come in—you're right on time."

Bo guided Mei Lin into the living room, which glowed with soft ambient light. Laughter and hushed conversation flowed through the space like a warm current, gently easing Mei Lin's tension. The air carried a quiet elegance—subdued tones, flickering candles, and the occasional chime of a fork against a plate.

Bo leaned in with a conspiratorial grin. "Let me introduce you to everyone."

Their first stop was by the wine table, where a couple stood chatting, glasses in hand.

"This is Anya and her husband, Vikram," Bo said, gesturing between them. "They've just returned from London."

Next came two younger guests, chuckling over a photo one held as they leaned close together.

"That's Joshua and Claire," Bo said with a playful wink. "They work with me at the agency. They keep us old folk from turning into fossils."

Mei Lin offered a polite nod as Bo steered her through the remaining introductions, keeping the mood light and effortless. With each warm exchange, the evening's conviviality grew, and gradually, the tightness in Mei Lin's chest began to loosen.

They reached the dining table, where several seats were already taken. Glasses gleamed in the ambient light, and soft instrumental music played faintly in the background. Bo gestured towards a man who had just risen from his chair.

"And here," she said with a cheeky grin, "is Gerry."

He stood and extended his hand with an easy smile. "So, you're Mei Lin. I've heard nothing but good things."

Mei Lin returned the handshake, his grip firm yet gentle. There was something unassuming about him—no forced charm, no overstated warmth. Just quiet sincerity.

Bo lightly placed a hand on her shoulder. "You're here, Mei Lin—right beside Gerry. He doesn't bite, I swear."

Mei Lin gave a soft chuckle as she slipped into the seat. "Well, that's a comfort."

As the other guests settled into their places and the table buzzed with conversation, Mei Lin stole a glance at Gerry. He wasn't flashy or overly chatty, but there was a calm steadiness about him—someone at ease in his own skin. Someone who listened more than he spoke.

Mei Lin relaxed a touch more. Perhaps Bo had been right. Perhaps it was merely dinner… and perhaps that was enough for now.

The meal began with light banter, flowing wine, and laughter that gradually warmed the table like a slow-burning hearth. Conversation drifted effortlessly among the guests, punctuated by the clink of cutlery and bursts of mirth. During the first course, Gerry leaned towards her and made a quiet quip about the "small army of cutlery" lined beside their plates. Mei Lin chuckled—more than she'd anticipated—and for a moment, the tension she hadn't even realised she was carrying melted from her shoulders.

By the time the main course arrived, they were chatting with the ease of old friends. They swapped favourite books, quirky travel tales, and childhood dishes that still brought comfort in adulthood. At one point, Gerry shared a tale of losing a bet and having to run a charity race dressed as a pineapple. Mei Lin laughed aloud, a full, unguarded sound that surprised her—warm and genuine, like sunlight breaking through a long-clouded sky.

Across the table, Bo noticed. She glanced between them, a gentle smile tugging at her lips. She gave a small, contented nod to herself.

When dessert was cleared and the evening began to ebb into soft farewells and lingering chats, Gerry turned to her again. His voice was softer now, more reflective.

"Thanks for the company tonight," he said. "It's been… truly lovely."

Mei Lin met his gaze, surprised by how genuine her own response felt. "It has. Thank you—for making me laugh. It's been ages."

He paused, as though weighing his words carefully. "Would you perhaps like to have dinner again sometime? Just the two of us. No pressure, just as two friends who enjoy each others company ”

Mei Lin hesitated, not from unease, but from the unfamiliar stirring of something new beginning to blossom where only silence had lingered for so long. She smiled, softly and a touch shyly.

“I think I’d like that.”

She paused, feeling a flicker of something unfamiliar—yet not unwelcome. Then she nodded.

“I’d like that.”

A week later, as Singapore’s city lights flickered to life beneath a gentle dusk sky, Gerry pulled up outside Mei Lin’s home in a modest silver sedan. The hum of evening traffic drifted through the air, faint and subdued.

Mei Lin stepped out of her shophouse in a flowing navy dress, simple yet elegant. Her hair was swept back with a pearl clip that glimmered faintly in the warm glow of the porch light. For a moment, Gerry simply gazed at her, his expression open and genuine.

"You look lovely, Mei Lin," he said, stepping out of the car and rounding it to greet her. He offered his arm with a gentle smile.

"Thank you," she replied, tucking a strand of hair behind her ear. "I've not been to Raffles in ages."

"Well, tonight we'll remedy that," he said with a chuckle. "They still serve that absurd cocktail tourists can't resist."

"The Singapore Sling?" she asked, laughing. "I've never actually tried one."

He feigned shock. "A born-and-bred Singaporean who's never had a Singapore Sling? That's practically a crime."

She laughed again, feeling lighter than she had in ages. "Perhaps tonight's the night for breaking old habits."

As they drove through the tree-lined avenues, the city outside shimmered—alive with motion and light. For once, Mei Lin allowed herself to savour it, leaning gently into the warmth of the moment. No expectations. No comparisons. Just a quiet, budding sense of companionship that asked nothing of her but presence.

And for the first time in what felt like ages, that was something she could offer.

"Then we'll make a night of firsts," Gerry said with a grin.

The grand colonial façade of Raffles Hotel stood tall, bathed in soft golden and white lights, raffles palms in the pristine gardens. Inside, the restaurant hummed with subdued conversation and the delicate clink of glasses. They were ushered to a table by the window, where the city's glow filtered gently through sheer curtains. For a moment, they both simply soaked in the ambience—the smooth jazz drifting faintly in the background, the crisp linen on the table, the quiet charm that seemed to slow time just a touch.

As they placed their orders, the conversation flowed effortlessly—books, travel tales, and the absurdities of bureaucracy across different countries. Gerry's dry wit caught Mei Lin off guard more than once, eliciting genuine laughter from her, light and liberating.

"So," he said eventually, resting his chin lightly on one hand, his eyes earnest. "What about your family? You mentioned you were married before…"

Mei Lin paused, a shadow fleeting across her face before she smiled softly. "Yes, I was. He… vanished some years ago. It's complicated."

Gerry nodded slowly, offering her space to choose how much to share.

"It was ages ago now," she continued softly. "But it left its mark, as you'd expect."

He reached across the table, his gesture gentle and reassuring. "I'm glad you came tonight. No pressure, just companionship."

Mei Lin met his gaze, sensing something fragile yet genuine blossoming in the quiet between them.

Her smile softened, her eyes distant for a moment. "Yes. Daniel. He was… one of those people who made everything feel possible. We met at school—childhood sweethearts, really. He was a radio engineer. Loved signals, frequencies—as if he were always reaching for something just beyond grasp."

She paused, her voice steady yet tinged with fragility. "He went on a business trip to Korea in 1963… and never returned. We searched for him, of course. Frantically. But nothing. He simply vanished. Never seen or heard from again."

Gerry didn't interrupt. He simply listened, his expression open and respectful.

"We had a daughter together, Ava. She's ten now. Bright, cheeky, fiercely protective of me." Mei Lin gave a soft chuckle, swirling her glass. "Sometimes she says things that sound far wiser than her years."

"I'm truly sorry about Daniel," Gerry said softly. "Losing my wife hit me hard, but at least I had closure. I knew what happened. I can't fathom that kind of uncertainty. My heart goes out to you, Mei Lin."

They sat in a gentle silence, letting the weight of their words settle without pressing further.

Gerry exhaled and added, "Ava sounds wonderful. What a remarkable girl."

Mei Lin smiled warmly. "She is. She's kept me anchored."

Gerry nodded, glancing down briefly before speaking again. "I was never so fortunate. My wife, Lillian, and I… we tried for years. It just wasn't meant to be. She passed away three years ago. Cancer."

"I'm so sorry, Gerry," Mei Lin said gently, reaching across the table to mirror his earlier gesture. "That's its own kind of sorrow."

"It is," he said, meeting her gaze. "But… nights like this remind me that something good can still rise from the ruins."

"Thank you," Gerry replied, his voice soft yet steady. "It's odd, isn't it? People talk of grief as if it eventually fades away. But it's more like a tide—sometimes calm, sometimes it sweeps you off your feet."

Mei Lin nodded, her eyes shimmering. "Yes. I still expect to hear his voice at times. In the mornings… or when Ava does something clever, I want to turn to him and say, 'Did you see that?'"

They fell into a gentle silence—one that didn't demand words, only the shared comfort of being understood without explanation.

"But Ava… she must be the light in your days," Gerry said after a moment, offering a warm smile.

Mei Lin's face brightened. "She is. She's the reason I rise each morning, the reason I press on. Sometimes she'll do or say something so like Daniel it catches my breath. And other times… she's entirely her own. Fierce, funny, and brimming with life."

"She sounds like the sort of girl who transforms a room just by stepping into it."

"She truly does," Mei Lin said, her smile laced with pride. "She asks the toughest questions, too. The kind that make you pause and rethink everything."

Gerry chuckled softly. "Perhaps one day I'll meet her. I reckon she'd terrify me—and I mean that in the best possible way."

"She might interrogate you," Mei Lin said with a laugh. "She doesn't trust easily. But once she takes to you… she'll never let you go."

"I'd consider that an honour," he said, meeting her gaze.

This time, the silence that followed felt different—softer, brimming with possibility.

"Well," Gerry said, raising his glass with a gentle smile, "to Ava, then. And to unexpected dinners."

Mei Lin lifted her glass too, her eyes warm. "To Ava. And… to new beginnings."

Their glasses met with a delicate clink, the quiet chime lingering between them like a whispered promise.

In the weeks that followed, dinner at Raffles marked only the first of many quiet, shared moments. Gerry and Mei Lin began meeting more often—sometimes for coffee after work, other times for strolls along East Coast Park, where the sea breeze softened the lingering warmth of the day.

One evening, they watched the sunset from the Botanic Gardens, seated on a bench beneath a sprawling banyan tree. Mei Lin pointed out a turtle gliding through a shallow pond nearby. Gerry smiled, sharing a tale of trying to adopt a turtle as a boy in Wales—only for it to vanish on the very first day.

"I spent hours searching for it," he said, shaking his head. "Named it Trevor, of all things."

Mei Lin laughed softly. "You don't strike me as a Trevor sort of person."

"And yet, I was gutted when he disappeared."

They settled into an easy rhythm. No pressure. No grand declarations. Just warmth and comfort—the quiet assurance of someone simply being there.

On a humid Saturday morning, they met at a bustling market near Tiong Bahru. Mei Lin strolled beside Gerry, sipping sugarcane juice and pointing out spices and fruits, weaving tales of recipes her grandmother used to make. Gerry listened intently, his eyes brightening with each new detail, asking questions that showed he was genuinely invested— not just in the stories, but in her.

"Do you always gesture so much when you're passionate about something?" Gerry asked, smiling as she mimed kneading dough in the air.

Mei Lin rolled her eyes playfully. "Only when I'm trying to make a point."

"Noted. I'll start bringing hand signals to our chats."

Later that week, he presented her with a small tin of Welsh cakes he'd tried baking himself. They were slightly charred at the edges, but Mei Lin accepted them as if they were treasure, placing them gently on the kitchen counter and smiling as she brewed tea.

Increasingly, she found herself eagerly anticipating his presence—the quiet comfort, the ease of his company. The way he allowed her space to grieve, to breathe, to hope again.

One evening, they sat on the balcony of Gerry's flat, the city humming softly below. The sky was dark, the stars veiled by Singapore's vibrant glow.

Gerry turned to her, gently brushing a lock of hair from her face. "I've truly enjoyed getting to know you, Mei Lin. These moments with you… they've meant more than you might realise."

Mei Lin looked down briefly, then met his gaze with a soft smile. Her heart beat steadily—not the crushing ache of grief she once bore, but something gentler now. Something akin to healing.

"I feel the same," she said softly. "And I think… it's time."

He tilted his head slightly. "Time?"

Mei Lin nodded, her voice barely above a whisper. "I think it's time you met Ava."

Gerry's expression softened—a blend of surprise and quiet honour. He didn't speak at first, but the glimmer in his eyes conveyed everything.

"I'd like that," he said at last.

Mei Lin smiled, a weight lifting that she hadn't even realised she still carried.

8

A Step Towards Us, Autum 1968
(Singapore)

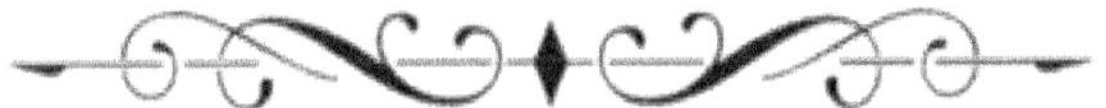

The sun gleamed off the waters around Sentosa as soft music and laughter drifted through the warm air. A travelling fair had sprung up near the shoreline—stalls aglow with flashing lights, the scent of popcorn and fried treats carried on the breeze, and the gleeful shrieks of children on spinning rides echoing across the island.

Mei Lin stood near the entrance, her hair dancing in the wind, one hand resting gently on Ava's shoulder. Ava wore a cotton sundress adorned with yellow daisies, a small canvas bag slung over her shoulder.

Nur stood beside them, scanning the crowd with curious eyes—until they settled on Gerry approaching.

"There he is," Mei Lin whispered, nudging Ava gently. "That's my friend Gerry."

Ava studied him with cautious curiosity as Gerry reached them. He wore light khakis and a pale blue shirt, a warm smile softening the moment he saw the young girl standing shyly beside her mother.

"You must be Ava," Gerry said, offering his hand. "I've heard quite a bit about you."

Ava didn't respond at first, glancing at Mei Lin, who gave her a reassuring nod. Then she offered a quiet, "Hello," gripping Mei Lin's hand a little tighter.

"She's a touch shy," Mei Lin said softly.

"That's quite alright," Gerry replied with a wink. "So am I."

"And this is Nur, my lifeline and dearest friend," Mei Lin added, gesturing towards Nur.

"Nur, I've heard so much about you. I'm delighted to meet you," Gerry said warmly.

"Thank you, sir," Nur replied politely.

"Oh, please," Gerry chuckled. "I'd need a knighthood from the Queen for 'sir.' Just Gerry will do."

They all shared a laugh.

It didn't take long for the group to settle into a comfortable rhythm. They strolled through the fairground together, Nur snapping photos with her small camera while Ava gradually warmed to Gerry—especially after he won her a small stuffed rabbit at the ring-toss stall.

"His name's Pepper," Ava declared, cradling the toy in her arms. "Because of his ears."

"Splendid name," Gerry said with mock gravity. "He looks like a chap who'd choose adventure over salad."

The four of them queued for the Ferris wheel, and Ava insisted Gerry join her in the pod. High above, the city skyline glimmered in the distance. Gerry pointed out Fort Siloso and the tiny figures strolling below.

"Do you think they can see us?" Gerry asked Ava, nodding towards the distant figures below.

She leaned against the pod's window. "Maybe… if they've got sharp eyes."

Later, they paused at a food stall shaded by a red-and-white umbrella. The fair's take on local favourites was humble but delicious—sweetcorn in buttered cups, wok-fried rice served in paper bowls, and chilled lime juice that cut through the afternoon's heat.

They settled on benches beneath a canopy of fairy lights. Nur chatted with a vendor in Malay, her laughter mingling with the hum of the crowd, while Ava sat beside Gerry, stirring her rice and occasionally slipping bits to Pepper the Rabbit as if he were a proper guest.

Mei Lin watched quietly for a moment, taking in the gentle ease of it all. The way Gerry chuckled at Ava's wild tale of a "moon rabbit" and teased whether Pepper might need his own passport. The way Ava, in turn, leaned slightly towards him, her guard softening almost imperceptibly.

By sunset, they were all a touch sun-kissed and weary. Gerry treated each of them to a small scoop of coconut ice cream, and they ambled slowly back towards the entrance.

"Thank you," Mei Lin murmured softly as she strolled beside him. "For today. You were… splendid with her." "She's a remarkable child," Gerry replied, glancing at Ava, now perched on Nur's back, Pepper dangling from her bag. "You've done a splendid job, Mei Lin." She smiled, her heart brimming. This day—ordinary, joyful, a mere afternoon at a fair—felt like a subtle turning point. Not only in her bond with Gerry, but in her life. A gentle new chapter, unfolding. The promise of many days out.

 "Is Gerry my new daddy now?" Ava asked one evening, her innocent curiosity prompting the question as they sat round the dinner table. Mei Lin paused, the words tugging at her heart as she set down her fork. She had seen how Gerry treated her daughter—his patience, his laughter, the way he encouraged Ava to explore and play without ever overstepping.

 "Gerry is a very kind man," Mei Lin said gently, choosing her words with care. "He cares for you deeply, and we cherish our time with him. But your daddy will always be your daddy. No one could ever take his place."

Ava nodded slowly, her young mind grappling with the intricacies of love and loss. "But it's nice to have someone to play with," she said simply, a faint smile tugging at her lips.

"It is," Mei Lin replied, her own smile softening as she gazed at her daughter. "And it's quite alright to love your Daddy and still cherish your friendship with Gerry."

 As time passed, Gerry's steadfast presence brought vibrant moments seeping back into their lives. He became a devoted partner—caring not only for Mei Lin but for Ava too—gradually weaving himself into their daily rhythm. He offered thoughtful gifts, sparked their laughter, and always seemed to know how to brighten their spirits after a weary day.

Yet in the hushed corners of the night, as Ava drifted into dreams of adventure, Mei Lin often wrestled with memories of Daniel. In those quiet moments, she could almost hear his laughter, see his warm smile lighting up the spaces of their former life. At times, she caught herself glancing at the door, half-expecting him to step through—an ache blossoming gently beneath her ribs.

Gerry, attuned to her silences, never pressed. During their tranquil evenings together, he would often reach for her hand and say softly, "You needn't forget him, any more than I can forget my wife. They were part of our lives. That doesn't fade with time."

She cherished his understanding—his patience, his quiet strength. With him, there was no urge to let go, only room to breathe. The bond they shared was comforting, even as it bore traces of sorrow. In her heart, she knew Daniel would always endure—a memory tenderly preserved for Ava's sake, a steady light woven into the tapestry of their lives. Not a shadow, but a presence. Everlasting.

As Ava blossomed into her own vibrant personality, balancing her role as both daughter and friend to Gerry became second nature. She called him "Daddy Gerry," and though it felt odd at first, Mei Lin saw how seamlessly they fit together—like two pieces of a grander puzzle finding their place. Ava flourished in their new family rhythm, laughing and playing, forging fresh memories while still honouring the love that had gone before.

Yet as the years drifted by, Mei Lin often found herself wondering—could Daniel ever be found? Could miracles still unfold, like a hand emerging softly from the shadows? But whenever that thought weighed too heavily on her heart, she gently guided her thoughts back to Ava and the love enveloping them now. Life was still evolving, still enduring. Despite the persistent ache of loss, it was also undeniably beautiful.

On an ordinary afternoon, seated in a garden ablaze with colour as they celebrated Ava's birthday, Mei Lin glimpsed something precious—happiness, cradled in her daughter's laughter. She watched as Gerry chatted beside her, his face radiant with joy, wholly present in the moment. In that simple scene, Mei Lin permitted herself to dream—not of what was lost, but of what might yet be. A future brushed with love, even if it differed from what she once envisioned.

In that moment, Mei Lin found a measure of peace—holding both memory and possibility within her heart. The past and present intertwined gently, and though a part of her would always long for Daniel, she embraced the love surrounding her now. Life, with all its intricacies, had woven the unlikeliest threads into something whole—rich, vibrant, and uniquely its own. A tapestry of family, stitched together by both loss and love.

As they celebrated Ava's birthday amidst blooming flowers and the laughter of friends, Mei Lin felt a deep, quiet gratitude for all the moments life had bestowed upon her— the joy, the resilience, the beauty of watching her daughter thrive in a world brimming with possibility.

"Make a wish, Ava!" Mei Lin called out, her eyes gleaming as everyone gathered round the small cake adorned with vibrant icing and glowing candles. Ava squeezed her eyes shut, a slight pout forming as she clasped her hands together, capturing every hope in that pure, unguarded moment. "I wish for... a grand adventure!"

Ava exclaimed, her face radiant as she opened her eyes. The candle flames danced brightly, as if stirred by the very energy of her words.

Mei Lin felt a surge of emotion well within her—a tender blend of pride and nostalgia. In Ava's radiant face, she glimpsed echoes of Daniel: the same glint of mischief, the insatiable curiosity. That spirit of wonder, so vibrant in their daughter, felt like a subtle thread weaving past and present, binding them all in a shared, unspoken legacy.

Gerry leaned forward, his voice warm and teasing. "What sort of adventure do you have in mind?"

"Perhaps we could visit the beach, or the zoo—or even a forest in a far-off land!" Ava's excitement spilled forth, her words tumbling like bright marbles, each one brimming with possibility.

Gerry chuckled, his eyes twinkling. "That sounds like a wonderful idea. Shall we plan a family outing next weekend? We'll find somewhere thrilling to explore—just the three of us."

"Yes, yes!" Ava clapped her hands, laughter bubbling from her chest. The joy radiating from her sent ripples through the garden, as though her happiness had taken root and blossomed amidst the flowers.

Mei Lin watched the pair—her daughter and her partner—and, despite the threads of nostalgia that sometimes wove through her joy, she granted herself a moment of stillness, of clarity. This was life, unfolding in ways she hadn't foreseen. In that moment, acceptance settled gently in her heart. Though Daniel's memory would always be tenderly cherished, there was room now—for new love, for new joy.

Later, as the celebration eased into a quieter evening, laughter softened into a murmur of gentle conversation. In the living room, Gerry—with his natural warmth and ease—had Ava giggling over a fanciful debate: if they could become any animal, would they choose the majestic elephant or the graceful gazelle? Their playful voices wove through the space, echoing off the walls like a soft, familiar melody.

Yet amidst the joy, a thought drifted unbidden into Mei Lin's mind, briefly drawing her inward. Would Daniel have enjoyed the cake? Would he have joined the games, laughed with them thus? The questions, tender and unanswerable, stirred a fleeting ache—one she knew well. A quiet pang for all the moments that might have been.

And yet, as she gazed at the scene before her—Ava's face radiant with joy, Gerry's eyes brimming with affection—Mei Lin felt a subtle shift within. This was their reality now. One not defined by absence, but shaped by presence. Not merely by loss, but by the courage to love anew.

She smiled, letting the warmth of the moment seep into her bones.

It wasn't the life she had envisioned. But it was full. It was real.

And it was hers. "Let's plan more adventures—beginning with our trip to Malaysia!" Mei Lin chimed in, gently drawing herself back to the present. "I want to see you both become true explorers."

"Yes! We'll be bold adventurers!" Ava declared, her eyes gleaming as she beamed up at her mother and Gerry.

Laughter flowed freely between them as they schemed over slices of cake and glasses of lime soda. Mei Lin felt something stir deep within—a quiet, blossoming hope taking root. Life had transformed, reshaped in ways she could never have foreseen. Yet here they were, together. In that moment, she glimpsed the beauty of the uncharted path ahead and embraced it. With Ava's joy, Gerry's steadfast presence, and

Daniel's memory tenderly nestled in her heart, she could move forward—not despite the past, but alongside it.

The days melted into weeks, and the gentle rhythm of their new life unfurled like a melody, simple and true. Though echoes of yesterday still murmured at the edges of her thoughts, Mei Lin clung to what mattered most: the present. The laughter filling her home. The quiet strength of love, not lost but transformed. The family they had woven—real, resilient, and brimming with promise.

More adventures lay ahead. She could sense it.

And this time, she would greet them with open arms.

9

Blossoming Connections – Summer 1964
(Korea)

As the months slipped into a rhythm of healing and quiet routine, Daniel gradually began to settle into his surroundings in the Korean countryside. With his memories still shrouded in fog, Jung gently suggested one day that he should have a name—one chosen for him by her.

"Hey," she said with a playful smile, "it's time you had a proper name. I can't keep shouting 'hey' whenever I need you."

Daniel chuckled. "Fair enough. What do you propose?"

She paused, thoughtful, then said, "I think you should be called Bark Eun-soo. It means kind and graceful."

"Wow, Jung," he said, raising an eyebrow, "you reckon I'm kind and graceful?"

"Yes," she replied simply. "That's precisely what you are, and that's what we'll call you." "Very well," he smiled. "Eun-soo it is."

Their laughter mingled with the rustle of the trees and the soft hum of the wind, filling the air with warmth.

In the weeks that followed, life in the small village grew less foreign. Each day offered its own quiet comfort, the unfamiliar gently becoming familiar. Mornings began with the soft trill of birdsong and the faint creak of wood as the cabin stirred with the first light. Jung would already be outside, a woven basket poised on her hip, barefoot and ready to greet the land with hands steady and sure.

One morning, a delicate fog clung to the hills, draping the valley in a soft, silvery haze. The sun had yet to pierce the clouds, and the fields glistened with dew like scattered glass. Jung handed Daniel a warm, cloth-wrapped bun and nodded towards the winding path leading to the rice paddies.

"Today, we plant together," she said, her voice gentle yet certain.

Daniel followed her into the ankle-deep water, hesitating only briefly before stepping in. The mud embraced his feet with a soft suction, tugging gently as he adjusted to the unfamiliar terrain. He sought to mirror her movements—stooping low, spacing the seedlings, pressing each one tenderly into the earth.

Jung moved with the fluid grace of one who had worked the land her entire life. Her tasks held a quiet, meditative rhythm, her hands gliding with poise and certainty. Daniel, by contrast, was awkward yet resolute. His fingers fumbled, splashing more than planting, but he pressed on.

She glanced at him from the corner of her eye and offered a gentle smile.

"You're learning," she said. "Not bad for a city fellow."

Daniel laughed, wiping sweat from his brow with the back of his hand. "I used to dream of rice, not mud squelching between my toes."

"Perhaps the mud suits you better than your dreams," she teased, her eyes sparkling with mischief.

They settled into a companionable silence, the only sounds the whisper of wind through the trees, the faint murmur of voices from the village, and the rhythmic splash of water as they waded through the field. Jung taught him how to gauge the soil's health, how to spot the subtle signs of pests, and when the earth murmured it was time to harvest. Each lesson was accompanied by a patient smile, a light touch on his shoulder, and a quiet word of encouragement.

Over time, Daniel grew to relish the physicality of the work. It anchored him. There was a quiet pride in the labour—in watching life emerge where once there had been nothing. It echoed, in some subtle, unspoken way, the growth stirring within him.

They often shared lunch beneath a sprawling willow tree at the edge of the fields. Jung would bring steamed rice and pickled vegetables wrapped in cloth, sometimes a thermos of warm barley tea. On one such afternoon, as they sat side by side gazing across the patchwork of fields, Daniel asked, "Do you ever dream of leaving? Of living elsewhere?"

Jung paused, pensive. "Sometimes," she murmured. "Not to flee, but… to see the world. To tread a street where no one knows your name."

Daniel nodded. "I understand that longing."

She glanced at him then, her eyes probing. "Are you remembering more now?"

He paused. "Fragments and glimpses. Feelings more than facts. I know I've lost something precious. Yet sometimes I wonder if… perhaps it's alright not to rush back to who I was."

They sat in silence after that, not uneasy—just rich with unspoken understanding. The breeze tugged gently at the hem of Jung's sleeve, and Daniel found himself watching the way her hair lifted at the nape of her neck. Something unspoken was taking shape between them—tender, cautious, yet inevitable.

Evenings were when their guards softened, when words flowed more freely. They'd sit by the fire, sipping broth or tea, sharing fragments of themselves. Jung spoke of her parents, lost to the war, and the grief that had settled into quiet resolve. Daniel offered what little he could—hazy recollections, flickers of a little girl's laughter, a woman's scent, a name called through a fogged memory.

One evening, the moon cast its silver light across the wooden floor of the cabin. Jung sat beside him on the low bench by the window, hands cradling a warm mug. Daniel had been particularly quiet, gazing at her from the corner of his eye, something stirring within him—tentative, yet real.

"I don't know who I was before," he said at last, "but I know I've never felt this… at peace."

Jung turned to him, her expression gentle. "Sometimes the person we become after the storm is who we were always meant to be."

Silence followed—not hollow, but rich. It hummed with something unspoken, something alive.

Daniel reached out, slowly, letting his fingers graze hers.

She didn't draw back.

When their eyes met again, it was with the quiet certainty of two souls who had come to mean something profound to each other—woven through the gentle folds of ordinary days, through shared silences and soil-stained mornings.

He leaned in, tentative at first, then with quiet resolve, and kissed her.

It wasn't urgent. It wasn't dramatic. It was warm. Real. Like planting roots in soil that had patiently awaited something true to take hold.

When they parted, Jung said nothing. She simply rested her head on his shoulder, and together they listened to the wind beyond the cabin—the soft murmur of the world settling a little more into place.

The next morning dawned with a rare brilliance—not only in the sky but within Daniel's chest. He rose earlier than usual, drawn by the familiar lilt of Jung's soft humming outside.

She was already at the field's edge, sleeves rolled high, hair tied loosely in a bun, placing baskets near the water with the serene efficiency of one who knew her rhythm.

As Daniel approached, she looked up, meeting his gaze with a grin that lingered a touch longer than before.

"You're late," she teased.

"I was dreaming," he replied, stepping into the water beside her. "Perhaps of this place. Or perhaps of you."

Jung shook her head, laughing, but the subtle blush that warmed her cheeks betrayed her. They worked side by side for a time—kneeling in the warm shallows, hands moving in quiet harmony as they planted the final rows of seedlings. Birds trilled overhead, and somewhere in the distance, the village dog barked, its voice carrying across the fields.

Then, as Daniel reached into the water for another seedling, Jung flicked a splash of muddy water at him with the back of her hand.

He blinked in mock disbelief. "Oh, you didn't just do that."

Her smile grew mischievous, her eyes sparkling. "I rather think I did."

With exaggerated indignation, Daniel scooped up a handful of water and flung it at her, catching the hem of her tunic. She squealed, half-laughing, half-dodging, but lost her footing and tumbled into the shallows with a splash.

For a moment, she sat there, drenched and blinking up at him—then erupted into laughter, full and radiant, the kind that welled from the chest and danced on the breeze.

Daniel stepped forward, offering his hand. "Truce?"

She grasped his hand—but instead of rising, she tugged him down with her, sending a wave of water over them both. They collapsed into laughter, breathless and sodden, their faces streaked with droplets and earth. No words were needed—only the joy of the moment, the quiet intimacy of shared laughter carrying across the fields.

When they finally stood, drenched and caked in mud, they resembled two mischievous children caught in something unexpectedly beautiful.

"You look utterly ridiculous," Jung said, brushing water from her brow.

"So do you," Daniel replied, grinning. "But I rather like it."

They trudged back to the cabin, their baskets largely forgotten, clothes clinging to their skin, leaving a trail of wet footprints in the waning light.

That evening, after drying off and donning clean clothes, they sat on the porch steps, gazing at the moon's ascent— full and golden, as though bestowing a quiet blessing on whatever was blossoming between them.

Jung rested her head against Daniel's shoulder. He remained still, gently pressing his cheek against her hair.

For a moment, they sat in silence. The air was thick with warmth and the hum of cicadas—a soft rhythm enveloping them, as if the world itself had paused to breathe.

Finally, Jung whispered, "I never thought I'd feel like this again."

Daniel closed his eyes. "Nor I."

They had no need to name what was growing between them. It was tender yet certain—like green shoots steadily rising in the fields they now called home.

That evening, after the laughter in the fields and the serene calm of dinner, Daniel and Jung stood on the modest porch of the cabin, gazing as stars flickered to life across the deepening sky. Crickets chirruped, and a gentle breeze whispered through the trees, carrying the scent of earth and woodsmoke.

Jung leant against the wooden post, her eyes agleam in the moonlight. Daniel edged closer, his heart steady yet brimming. "Let's not sleep in separate rooms tonight," he murmured, his voice barely above a whisper. He met her gaze, seeking something—assurance, trust, a sense of belonging.

Jung's eyes held his, tender and steadfast. A flush warmed her cheeks, and a soft smile curved her lips" I'd like that," she replied, her voice hushed, slightly tremulous, but certain.

She reached for his hand, and together they stepped inside, closing the door softly behind them—ushering in not merely a night of closeness, but a quiet crossing into something profound.

That night, as they lay entwined in each other's arms, no words were needed. The steady cadence of their breathing, the warmth of skin against skin, and the stillness that enveloped them like a protective veil spoke more than words ever could. In that humble cabin, beneath the gentle hush of the hills, they found sanctuary in one another—a safe haven after years of solitude and sorrow. Daniel began to grasp how deeply Jung's life was bound to the land, and, in turn, he felt himself becoming part of it too.

As days blended into weeks, and weeks into months, life settled into a gentle, steady rhythm—quietly fulfilling. Mornings dawned with shared meals and the simple joy of tending the garden side by side. Jung patiently taught Daniel the craft of cultivating rice—the meticulous care of fragile seedlings, the cadence of the seasons, and the quiet satisfaction of harvesting food with their own hands. Together, they sowed rows of chillies, beans, radishes, lettuce, and fragrant herbs for soups and teas. They made the long trek to the main town, their cart laden with surplus rice and vegetables, and held a stall in the local market once a month—produce that not only sustained them but yielded a modest income, the fruits of a life they had built from the soil up.

Afternoons were spent wandering trails that wound through the hills, foraging wild berries, or visiting neighbours' homes for tea and conversation. Evenings often saw them cooking together—chuckling as they chopped vegetables or knelt by the hearth. At times, they danced to the crackle of the fire, their movements slow and unhurried, hearts perfectly in tune.

With each passing season, the ache of Daniel's past began to fade. He no longer woke with a start, nor bore the heavy weight in his chest. Instead, he carried baskets of vegetables, books Jung lent him, or firewood from the grove behind their home. And through it all, he carried love—for the life they were crafting, and for the woman who had helped him rediscover himself.

Then, on a warm evening in late spring, as golden light bathed the valley, they hiked to a hillside dotted with wildflowers. There, enveloped by the scent of blossoms and the murmur of distant birdsong, Daniel turned to her. "My life has changed so much since I came here," he said, his voice steady yet laden with emotion. "I didn't know what I expected to find... but I found you. And with you, I feel whole again."

Jung's eyes glistened as she listened, her hand resting gently in his.Daniel reached into his pocket and drew out a small wooden box. Nestled inside was a simple silver ring—modest yet elegant, adorned with a single jade stone. He opened it slowly and met her gaze."Jung," he said, his voice steady despite the emotion welling within, "I want to spend the rest of my life with you. Will you marry me?"

For a moment, her breath hitched. Then her eyes brimmed with tears, and a radiant laugh escaped her—a bright, joyous sound that reverberated across the hillside. "Yes," she whispered, nodding as the words came to her. "Yes, of course I will."

He slipped the ring onto her finger, and they fell into each other's arms, holding one another tightly as the sun dipped below the horizon, bathing the world in a golden, hopeful glow.

In the weeks that followed, the village buzzed with delight over the news. Neighbours arrived bearing gifts—baskets of freshly harvested rice, jars of preserved fruit, and embroidered cloths stitched with care. Elders bestowed blessings with weathered hands and warm smiles, while children roamed the hills, gathering wildflowers to strew along the path from the village to the cabin.

Jung planned a wedding that honoured both tradition and the quiet, steadfast love they had forged. They chose to wear hanbok, meticulously hand-sewn by the village tailor. The colours were deliberate—deep forest green for Daniel, symbolising growth; soft coral for Jung, evoking love and renewal.

On the morning of their wedding, the air thrummed with anticipation and birdsong. Beneath a trellis adorned with white blossoms, the ceremony unfolded. Friends and neighbours encircled them, some beaming, others dabbing at their eyes, each bearing witness to something rare and true.

Daniel stood beneath the floral canopy, his breath catching as Jung approached. She was radiant—her hanbok embroidered with birds in flight and delicate plum blossoms, her dark hair swept up and adorned with silver pins. When her eyes met his, the world seemed to pause—just for them.

They exchanged vows amid laughter and music, sealing their love with a promise as enduring as the hills cradling their home. And when they kissed, a hush fell over the gathering—a quiet reverence for something rare and beautiful.

Together, they stepped into a new chapter, hand in hand. In the months that followed, Daniel and Jung settled into married life, their days interwoven with growing intimacy and ease. Their home, once a refuge, became a haven of warmth—brimming with shared meals, soft laughter, and dreams murmured beneath the covers as the stars wheeled overhead.

As the seasons turned and blossoms returned to their garden, their conversations shifted toward the future. They often spoke of family—not merely the one they had forged together, but the one they hoped to nurture.

One golden afternoon, as they harvested vegetables from the soil they had tilled together, Jung paused, sunlight glinting on her hair. A thoughtful expression crossed her face, tender yet resolute.

"I want to give you a family," she said, her voice steady, brimming with warmth and quiet conviction. Daniel turned to her, his hands still clutching a bundle of lettuce. His heart swelled at her words.

"I want that too," he murmured softly. "More than anything."

In that moment, he could envision it—children scampering through the garden, laughter echoing across the hills, the two of them growing old in the life they had crafted, rooted in love and sustained by all they had overcome.

"Let's take our time," Jung said, her smile softening. "We have each other, and that's what matters most for now. But I believe we'll have a family someday."

A warmth enveloped them as they resumed their work, the simplicity of their shared life anchoring them in the present. Each day, the love story that had begun in uncertainty blossomed into something quietly extraordinary—a life woven with laughter, trust, and shared dreams.

As the months passed and spring returned with its vibrant hues and new life, something shifted once more. Jung discovered she was pregnant. The news arrived like sunlight through an open window—startling, radiant, and brimming with wonder. It transformed everything, yet deepened the bond already forged between them.

Their connection grew even more rooted as they prepared to welcome new life. Evenings became sacred—filled with murmured dreams and quiet planning, the future glowing softly around them.

"What if it's a girl?" Jung mused one night, her hand resting gently on her swelling belly, her eyes agleam with hope. "I want her to be just like you—strong, kind, and curious."

Daniel smiled, his fingers brushing lightly across her cheek. "No matter," he said, his voice low with affection. "Whether a boy or a girl, I'm certain they'll have your spirit."

The months passed in a whirlwind of excitement and anticipation. With the aid of village men, they extended the cabin, transforming the old storeroom beside their bedroom into a nursery. It became a labour of love—walls painted in warm, soothing tones that echoed the joy blossoming between them. Together, they attended prenatal classes, chuckling through awkward demonstrations and marvelling at the miracle unfolding within Jung.

As they decorated the nursery, they shared stories, imagined their future family, and dreamt aloud about what lay ahead. Each brushstroke and every shared plan deepened their bond—quiet and steadfast, like the steady turning of the seasons beyond their window.

One golden afternoon, while tending their garden, they found a moment of serene calm beneath the sun's gentle rays. Jung knelt among the sprouting herbs, her hands deftly pulling weeds, when she glanced at Daniel and asked, "Do you ever think about your own family?"

Daniel paused, his fingers grazing the leaves of a young chilli plant. The question stirred something within him—a breeze rustling through forgotten pages. "Sometimes... I do," he said slowly. "I want to remember, but it's hard. Like grasping a dream after waking. As time passes, it fades further and further away."

Jung gazed at him, her expression tender, her eyes brimming with unwavering love. "You've forged a new family with me," she said softly. "Whatever lies behind you, I'll always ensure there's a place for you here—with me, with us."

Emotion welled in Daniel's chest. "Thank you," he murmured, his voice thick with gratitude. In her words, he felt something settle into place—the sense that his past and present were threads in the same tapestry, guiding him here. Home.

As the seasons turned, anticipation swelled, and excitement hung in the air like a gentle promise. Then, one evening, Jung felt it—the unmistakable waves of labour beginning. Brimming with exhilaration and nervous energy, Daniel remained by her side, gently rubbing her back and murmuring steady words of encouragement through each rising tide of pain.

Hours passed, long and arduous, until, with the first light of dawn piercing the darkness, their daughter arrived. Soon Hee's cry filled the room, her small hands wiggling in the doctor's tender grasp. In that moment, everything shifted— the world around them bursting into vibrant hues, a sense of completeness blossoming where uncertainty had once lingered.

Jung cradled Soon Hee close, her heart swelling beyond measure, tears of joy streaming freely down her cheeks. "She's perfect," Jung whispered, her eyes locking with her daughters for the first time.

"Yes, she is," Daniel breathed, his own tears glistening with overwhelming love. In that instant, he felt not only a father but a vital part of a greater whole—redefined, fulfilled, and utterly at home.

As they sat, enveloped in love, laughter, and the fragile new life they had created, Daniel realised he had finally found his way—a different path home. The memories of his past, though still shrouded in shadows, began to intertwine with the joy of his present, forming a new horizon lit by hope, promise, and the quiet certainty of belonging. With Jung and Soon Hee beside him, Daniel felt the warmth of family take root in his heart, guiding him toward whatever lay ahead. For the first time in years, he felt whole.

Later that week, sunlight streamed through the kitchen windows, casting soft golden glows across the wooden floors. Their home had settled into a gentle rhythm— feedings, lullabies, and warm meals shared amid weary smiles. At the kitchen table, Jung sat sifting through a modest stack of documents and official forms, her brow furrowed in quiet concentration.

"We need to visit Gangseo-gu next week," she said, glancing up at Daniel, who stood nearby, gently bouncing Soon Hee in his arms.

"Oh?" he replied, his thumb brushing across his daughter's soft cheek, marvelling at the tiny miracle cradled in his arms.

"To register her birth," Jung replied, setting the papers aside with a calm, resolute expression. "It's important. She needs to be officially recognised. She deserves to have her name recorded, her presence affirmed beyond just us."

Daniel nodded slowly, his gaze lingering on Soon Hee's serene face. He understood Jung's meaning—this was more than mere paperwork. It was the act of anchoring their daughter in the world, proclaiming to the universe: she is here, she matters.

"Quite right," he murmured. "She does. Of course. She deserves everything."

Jung paused, her voice softening. "And while we're there… I think it's time we register you too."

Daniel looked up, bemused. "Me?"

"Yes," she said, reaching for his hand. "We'll register you under your Korean name—Bark Eun Soo. We'll say the paperwork was lost during the war. It's not uncommon. Countless records were destroyed or never properly filed in those years. No one will question it."

He blinked, struck by the simplicity of her plan—and the profound weight of what it offered. A name. A past. A place. An official identity.

"Is that… even possible?"

Jung offered a small, reassuring smile."It's more common than you think. You've been here, living a full life. You're a husband, a father. You belong. We'll do it properly. Together."

Daniel sat in silence, the weight of her offer anchoring him more deeply than he had anticipated. He had wandered through the fog of lost memories for so long that the prospect of being seen—truly seen—as someone whole, someone real, felt almost surreal.

"Are you certain?" he asked softly.

"I've never been more certain," she replied. "This is your home now. Let's make it official."

He took her hand and squeezed it gently, his heart brimming. "Very well. Let's do it."

The decision—so rooted in love and quiet practicality—felt monumental. Not only would their daughter have her place in the world from the outset, but Daniel—Bark Eun Soo—would finally step into the light, no longer adrift in the shadows of uncertainty.

As the days drew closer to their appointment in Gangseo-gu, the paperwork gradually took shape. A few old letters, community testimonials, and a scheduled visit to the district office were all that was required. Jung managed every detail with steadfast determination, shielding Daniel from the burden of bureaucracy with the same quiet grace she had shown throughout her pregnancy and motherhood.

When the day arrived, they dressed simply yet with care. Soon Hee was snugly bundled and secured to Jung's back in the traditional manner. Together, they walked to the bus stop in the pale light of early morning. After a brief wait, the bus arrived. They boarded and found their seats, Jung now cradling Soon Hee in her arms. As the countryside slipped past the window, giving way to the city, Daniel felt something stir within him—a quiet strength, a sense of beginning. He was no longer merely passing through. He was becoming.

The district office in Gangseo-gu nestled among a quiet row of government buildings, its concrete facade softened by spring vines beginning to climb its walls. Inside, the air carried the familiar scent of ink and paper—efficiency, bureaucracy, lives being officially recorded.

Jung stepped forward confidently, presenting the documents to the clerk behind the glass window. Soon Hee slept serenely in a sling across her chest, unaware that her name was being inscribed in the world's records.

The clerk, a middle-aged woman with silver-rimmed spectacles and a patient expression, offered a polite smile as she accepted the forms.

"A beautiful name," the clerk remarked as she entered it into the government records. "Soon Hee—it means 'goodness and joy.' Most fitting."

Jung smiled. "That's precisely what she's brought us."

Daniel stood beside them, observing quietly, his hand resting gently on Jung's back. When the time came for the second part, she turned and gave him a subtle, encouraging nod.

"And this," Jung said, presenting a second set of documents, "is for my husband."

The clerk glanced at the papers. "Bark Eun Soo?"

"Yes," Jung replied, calm and composed. "His records were lost during the war. He's been here since, contributing to the community. He had no need to register before, but with Soon Hee now, he wishes to ensure everything is in order. Thus, he needs formal registration."

The woman studied Daniel briefly, then returned to the documents. There was a momentary pause—Daniel's heart thudded once, heavily—before the clerk gave a small nod.

"That's not uncommon, though you certainly took your time," she said simply, stamping the form. "We've seen many such cases. The family record will be issued in a few weeks. In the meantime, here's the temporary certificate."

Daniel gazed at the slip of paper bearing the name Bark Eun Soo. For years, he had drifted—stateless, rootless, undefined. But in this moment, something settled into place. He was no longer a mere shadow.

He existed.

"Thank you, and I'm sorry for not addressing this sooner," he said, his voice low and thick with emotion.

The clerk nodded kindly. "Welcome home, at last." She offered a warm smile.

Afterwards, the city seemed brighter, more vibrant. They strolled hand in hand down the main street, Soon Hee nestled against Jung's chest, the gentle rhythm of her breathing a comforting constant.

The bustle of Gangseo-gu unfolded around them: vendors hawking sweet roasted chestnuts, children tugging at their mothers' sleeves, bicycles weaving through dawdling traffic.

They paused at a small, family-run eatery with low wooden tables, where the aroma of sesame oil and grilled fish wafted from the kitchen. Settling near the window, Daniel ordered hot noodle soup with dumplings, while Jung chose bibimbap, vibrant and steaming in its stone bowl.

They ate in companionable silence, pausing only to exchange smiles or tend to Soon Hee when she stirred.

"This feels real now," Daniel murmured between bites, his voice barely above a whisper. "Like the life I was always destined to live."

Jung reached for his hand across the table. "That's because it is."

After lunch, the city blurred into a tapestry of honking taxis, street vendors, and the ceaseless murmur of voices in motion. Daniel and Jung strolled side by side along the narrow pavement, weaving through the bustling crowd.

As they rounded a corner near the government offices, Daniel halted—something had caught his eye in the window of a cluttered antique bookshop nestled between a noodle stall and a tailor.

Its smudged glass and sun-faded awning lent it an almost forgotten air. In the display rested a framed, yellowing map of Southeast Asia, its inked coastlines curling slightly at the edges. Below it, a stack of weathered books leaned precariously, one bearing gold-embossed letters barely legible: Memoirs of the East: Tales from the Straits Settlements. Daniel stood transfixed.

"What is it?" Jung asked, pausing beside him.

He didn't answer immediately. His gaze remained fixed on the book, a faint sensation stirring within—like hearing the echo of a half-forgotten melody.

"That…" he murmured. "That looks familiar." His eyes lingered on the cover, which bore a large photograph of Singapore from the early 1900s.

Jung peered into the window. "The book?"

"Perhaps. I'm not certain. The cover… or maybe the map." He furrowed his brow, his voice low and uncertain. "It feels as though I've seen it before. Somewhere."

Jung tilted her head, her expression curious. "Are you certain?"

He gazed a moment longer. Then, with a soft chuckle and a shake of his head, he said, "No… it can't be. Just resembles something else, I suppose."

With a quiet exhale, he turned from the window. Jung gave his hand a gentle squeeze, and together they strolled down the street toward the bus stop.

Behind them, the bookshop melted back into the city's rhythm, fading into the hum of noise and movement as they made their way to the bus—and home.

10

Little Light
(Korea)

As the sun rose over their cosy village home, Daniel and Jung tumbled out of bed, morning light streaming into their bedroom and bathing it in warmth. The walls rang with laughter, sleepy footsteps, and the rustle of quilts pushed aside.

From the moment Soon Hee could walk, her zest for exploring the world had captivated Daniel. Now a bright, curious six-year-old, she brimmed with questions and giggles. Daniel cherished nothing more than their time together—playing, learning, and wondering. They had made a conscious choice to ensure Soon Hee could speak both Korean and English fluently.

"Daddy, come look!" Soon Hee would shout, tugging his hand towards the garden or the tree line beyond their house, her little legs propelling her forward with boundless enthusiasm, pigtails bouncing as she ran.

The garden was their kingdom—a realm where sticks transformed into swords, flowers became crowns, and the clouds above held secret tales waiting to be discovered.

One afternoon, as they lay on a blanket spread across the grass, Daniel pointed to a cloud drifting lazily across the sky.

"Do you see that one, Soon Hee?" he asked, his voice brimming with playful curiosity.

"Is it a dinosaur?" she squealed, her eyes wide with wonder.

"Almost! A big, fluffy one," he chuckled. "But did you know that clouds—and the stars above—can tell stories?"

"Stories?" she echoed, tilting her head, her brow furrowed with curiosity.

Daniel smiled, closing his eyes for dramatic effect, and began, "When I was a lad, I'd lie in the grass like this and gaze at the stars. I fancied they were part of a grand tale— constellations dancing across the night sky. There's the Plough, which is part of Ursa Major, the Great Bear. Each star has a name and a story waiting to be shared." Daniel had no true memory of his childhood, of course; he wove this tale to keep Soon Hee enchanted.

Soon Hee's face glowed with excitement, her imagination soaring. "Like superheroes?" she asked, eyes sparkling with wonder.

"Exactly! Just like superheroes. The stars guide travellers by night, reminding them they're never alone. If you look closely, they form patterns—just waiting for you to discover them."

These small moments wove their days together with golden thread. Whether chasing dragonflies, gathering smooth stones from the riverbank, or helping Jung knead dough in the kitchen, Soon Hee's world brimmed with warmth, exploration, and boundless love.

By the time she turned seven, she was reading storybooks with growing confidence—favourites about explorers, scientists, and inventors. She often pestered Jung for bedtime tales of "when she was little," delighting in stories of her mother's mischief and courage.

One rainy afternoon, she surprised Daniel with a carefully drawn picture of their family standing beneath a star-filled sky.

"This is us," she declared proudly. "That's you, Mama, and me. And those stars are ours."

Daniel fought back tears, his heart swelling with an emotion too deep for words. The drawing stirred something within him—memories that weren't quite memories, mere glimpses: another child, another sky.

That night, as he lay beside Jung in bed, the quiet stillness pressed around him. The afternoon replayed in his mind—Soon Hee's laughter, the way her imagination soared, the way she gazed at him as if he held the universe's secrets.

And then came the dream. He stood in a grassy field, surrounded by children. One small girl stood out, her dark hair falling over searching eyes, her face alight with the same wonder Soon Hee had shown earlier that day.

"Each star is special," he heard himself say. "They shine not just for us, but to connect us to everything we love—our hopes, our dreams, our memories."

The next morning, Daniel stirred earlier than usual. The warmth of the dream lingered, as did the ache it left behind. He gazed across the bed at Jung, her breathing slow and peaceful, then towards the hallway beyond their room—

towards Soon Hee's bedroom, brimming with drawings, model rockets, and fairy-tale books.

Life had granted him a second chance. Though he still didn't fully grasp the past he had lost, he knew this: he was exactly where he belonged.

11

New Horizons - Summer 1977
(Singapore)

As the summer of 1977 dawned, the world hummed with anticipation. Humanity stood poised on the cusp of history with the imminent launch of the two Voyager spacecraft. For Ava—now a bright, ambitious twenty-year-old—the season brimmed with even greater promise.

She had excelled at school, particularly in her science classes, and her curiosity about the stars, the universe, and all that lay beyond had only deepened. When the chance to attend a summer internship at NASA arose through Billy's connections, she was elated. It was a dream realised—a chance to immerse herself in the realm of space exploration and connect with others who shared her passion.

As she packed her bags, her heart swelled with excitement. Visions of the future danced in her mind.

"This is just the beginning," Ava told her mother, Mei Lin, who watched proudly as her daughter meticulously arranged her belongings, newspapers about the forthcoming Voyager launches strewn across the bed.

"Remember to return with tales and experiences to share," Mei Lin replied with a warm smile, her heart aglow with pride. "You can do anything you set your mind to, Ava."

The weeks leading up to the internship passed in a whirlwind of anticipation, study, and preparation. When the day of her departure finally arrived, Ava embraced her mother tightly at the airport. She kissed Gerry's cheek, a blend of excitement and nervousness fluttering in her chest like wings poised for flight.

"I can't wait to share everything with you both!" Ava exclaimed, her eyes aglow with enthusiasm.

After arriving in the U.S. and settling into her temporary lodgings, the days blurred into a flurry of learning—meetings, experiments, and even a chance to meet astronauts. Ava thrived in this world, absorbing every scrap of knowledge as if it were gold dust.

The month raced by, and soon she was back in Singapore. One rainy afternoon, curiosity beckoned, and she ventured to explore the attic—a space long since relegated to storage, brimming with mementos of her childhood and relics of her father's past.

As she climbed the creaky stairs and pushed open the door, a musky scent of old books and wood enveloped her, rich with nostalgia. Dust motes danced in the slanting light as she stepped inside. Sifting through boxes—decorations from past birthdays, long-forgotten school projects—something in the far corner caught her eye: a small, dusty box, half-hidden beneath an old blanket.

Her curiosity ignited, Ava knelt and gently lifted the lid. Inside lay a collection of photographs and yellowing letters, their edges curled with age. As her fingers traced the faded prints, a wave of emotion swept over her—these were cherished fragments of a life she'd only ever heard about, never fully known.

Her gaze fell upon a photograph that sent memories flooding back—a picture of her younger self nestled between her mother and father at the ham radio. All three were beaming, Daniel's face alight with the enthusiasm that transformed every moment into an adventure. His hands were mid-gesture, showing them how to communicate across the airwaves, his eyes aglow with life.

A surge of warmth coursed through Ava, stirring memories she had only ever grazed. She could hear the static's hum, feel the thrill of tuning into distant frequencies, and recall the wonder of hearing voices from far-off lands. Her father had spoken of the stars as if they were old friends, each one bearing a story.

That photo—a single frame—held a world of laughter, curiosity, and love. It reminded her how deeply Daniel had shaped her path, even through the silence of his absence.

Yet alongside the joy of the memory came a quiet ache—a poignant sense of loss that settled deep in her chest. "Daddy," she whispered, the word heavy with a weight she didn't fully grasp. She didn't recall everything about him— some memories were vivid, others mere flashes, stories, or secondhand echoes—but this photograph stirred something deeper: a longing not just to remember, but to truly know him.

Sitting cross-legged on the attic floor, she clutched the picture to her chest, her thoughts spiralling with questions about the man behind the smile. Daniel had been an engineer, a dreamer, a lover of stars—just as she was now. She couldn't help but wonder: would he be proud of her? Of the path she'd chosen, the curiosity that burned in her like starlight?

As sunlight streamed through the small attic window, casting golden beams through drifting dust motes, Ava made a silent vow to herself. She would learn all she could about space, the moon, and the vast universe beyond—and perhaps, along the way, uncover more about her father and the legacy he'd left behind.

With renewed resolve, she gently closed the box, feeling a newfound connection to her past. She carried the photograph downstairs and placed it beside her bed. It radiated warmth and love, like the embrace of a cherished blanket—a constant reminder that she was never truly alone.

After lingering among memories, Ava descended from the attic, her heart lighter and her vision for the future sharper. The experience at NASA, woven with newly stirred memories of her father, had kindled a deeper passion within her.

She felt an exhilarating sense of purpose. Ava knew, without a doubt, that she wanted to forge a path blending her love for science, her yearning to explore the universe, and the enduring threads of her father's legacy.

12

Nurturing Dreams – Winter 1977
(Korea)

More than two decades had elapsed since the war, and though its scars lingered in Korea's soul, life had quietly woven itself back together—like a quilt stitched from resilience.

For Daniel and Jung, the tranquil village they now called home offered a gentler rhythm—one shaped by routine, relationships, and the steady pulse of family.

Now, a new milestone loomed: their daughter, Soon Hee, was poised to start school.

Each morning, Daniel rose early, a quiet thrill stirring in his chest. He took care in preparing Soon Hee's breakfast—her favourite always—warm rice porridge adorned with a dusting of sugar and a fresh slice of fruit. Her bright eyes would sparkle with each bite, and the kitchen would brim with giggles as they dreamt up what she might learn that day.

"Daddy, do you think I'll meet someone who loves the stars as much as we do?" Soon Hee asked one morning, her hair bouncing as she perched eagerly on her chair.

"I'm certain you will," Daniel replied, gently tucking a stray lock behind her ear. "There are heaps of children who adore learning about the cosmos. And remember, you can be whomever you wish to be."

"Like an astronaut!" she declared, her smile illuminating the breakfast table.

"Precisely," he said, his heart swelling with pride. "Just like an astronaut."

After breakfast, Daniel would escort her to school each morning—a ritual they both treasured. The path was framed by cherry trees swaying in the breeze and modest market stalls just stirring for the day.

Soon Hee skipped alongside him, her small hand nestled in his, bombarding him with questions about planets, clouds, and what made the moon's glow.

Every step wove a thread into the tapestry of their shared memories, quiet moments destined to glimmer in hindsight—glimpses of a childhood cherished and a father's steadfast love.

The sights along the way—flowers blooming beside the path, children's laughter floating through the air, and warm waves of friendly greetings from neighbours—infused each step with gentle joy. Daniel felt profound contentment in sharing this new chapter of Soon Hee's life.

As late summer gave way to autumn, the leaves turned to fiery hues of crimson and gold, heralding the school year's approaching end. One crisp morning, as they strolled together, Daniel paused to absorb the changing world around them.

"Look at how splendid the trees are, Soon Hee," he said, gesturing to the vibrant colours overhead. "They're like stars in the sky—ever-changing, yet thriving."

"They're ever so lovely, Daddy!" Soon Hee exclaimed, her eyes wide with wonder as she watched the leaves drift down like tiny flames.

Her delight warmed Daniel's heart, a tender reminder of the bond they shared—a connection forged between a father and daughter who sought inspiration in the world's beauty.

Yet preparations loomed on the horizon. A journey to Seoul was required to formally register Soon Hee at the local school and ensure Daniel had all the necessary paperwork in order. Daniel and Jung also needed to renew several of their own documents, promising a day both full and brisk.

One early morning, they set off for the capital. Jung packed their essentials with care, including a simple lunch to keep their spirits buoyant. As they neared Seoul's outskirts, the city's vibrant energy began to envelop them. Storefronts lined the streets, a harmonious blend of sleek glass facades and traditional wooden signage. The air buzzed with life— the hum of traffic, chatter from the pavements, and the tantalising aroma of sizzling street food wafting on the breeze. After completing the registration process with the authorities—no need this time for explanations about misplaced paperwork from the war, merely a straightforward renewal of essential documents—they stepped back into the city's vibrant bustle.

As they ambled along the lively street, Daniel's gaze wandered, settling on a quaint second-hand shop nestled between a teahouse and a tailor's. He halted abruptly, his eyes fixed on something beyond the smudged glass window.

"Wait, Jung—look at that!"

She paused beside him, tracing his line of sight.

There, resting haphazardly on a dusty shelf, stood an old ham radio. Its metal casing was tarnished with age, yet the knobs and dials retained a certain allure, like an artefact from a bygone era. A familiar wave of nostalgia surged through him, stirring long-buried memories.

"This look familiar, I don't know why, but it could be fun," he murmured, almost to himself. "And splendid for Soon Hee—to connect with people far away, to hear distant voices and places."

Jung smiled gently, her gaze shifting from the radio to Daniel's face. "Are you certain? It looks ancient, and likely won't work."

He nodded, already picturing the wonder in Soon Hee's eyes the first time she heard a voice crackle from across the globe "Even if it needs a bit of work to get it back to working, I'll enjoy that. I could likely mend it. Yes, it definitely feels oddly familiar, though I can't quite place why," Daniel mused.

"Perhaps you should pop in and check if it works," Jung suggested, her voice brimming with gentle encouragement. "It could be a smashing project for you and Soon Hee to tackle together."

Brimming with enthusiasm, Daniel stepped into the shop, drawn by the tug of memory and possibility. He approached the shelf and began examining the radio's components, his fingers instinctively turning knobs and pressing buttons, as though guided by a long-forgotten familiarity.

"Good day," the shopkeeper greeted cheerily, emerging from behind a curtain. "What can I do for you two fine people today?"

Daniel pointed to the radio. "I see you've an old ham radio here. Is it still functional?"

"Indeed, sir," the shopkeeper replied with a nod. "Likely just needs a spot of cleaning, and maybe a touch of care, but she's still works. After several minutes of scrutinising the machine—checking the dials, noting the wear, envisaging it sputtering back to life—Daniel was certain he had to have it. The price was reasonable, especially for something so meaningful.

Once they had paid and stepped back onto the bustling street, the weight of the radio in Daniel's hands felt curiously familiar—though he couldn't quite pinpoint why.

Over the following weeks, he dedicated his evenings to reviving the old ham radio, its once-dormant dials and wires gradually stirring under his meticulous care. Soon Hee perched beside him, her curiosity boundless, her hands eager to assist however she could.

"Daddy, will we be able to speak to people from other countries?" she asked one evening, propping her cheek on her palm, eyes aglow with wonder.

"I hope so," Daniel replied, smiling as he tightened a screw. "Isn't that thrilling? But first, we've a few more tasks before we can test it."

He gathered tools and spare parts, diving into the project— more trial and error than precision, yet guided by an instinct he couldn't quite grasp. As he painstakingly cleaned components, deftly soldered wires, and tuned the aged dials, faint memories flickered, like echoes just beyond reach, steering his hands.

After a week of steadfast effort, the radio sprang to life. The moment he connected it to power and heard the familiar crackle of static, Daniel's heart soared. It was as though the machine had roused from a deep slumber—ready once more to murmur tales and tunes from far-off lands across the airwaves.

One evening, as the sun sank low, bathing the room in amber light, Daniel called softly, "Soon Hee, come here! It's ready, you've got to see this. I've fixed it!"

Daniel announced, beaming as he turned the knobs, demonstrating how the components worked in harmony. "Now we can tune into different frequencies and chat with people far away!"

With a spring in her step, Soon Hee bounded into the room, curiosity illuminating her face.

"What is it?" she asked, eyes wide with anticipation as she approached the table where the radio now sat, humming softly.

Her mouth fell open in awe. "Really? Can we talk to people now, even astronauts?"

"Maybe one day!" he chuckled, drawing her into the moment. "For now, we can listen to all sorts of fascinating conversations, but the astronauts will have to wait. Fancy helping me tune it?"

With excitement bubbling between them, Soon Hee eagerly accepted the challenge, and together they began exploring the radio's frequencies. Daniel felt a surge of joy wash over him as he watched her face light up, eyes aglow as voices crackled through the speaker.

"Listen!" he said, tweaking the dial. They leaned in, their heads nearly touching, as distant chatter filled the room—conversations in English, Chinese, Russian, and Korean weaving together like threads across the airwaves.

As days turned to weeks, Soon Hee's fascination grew ever deeper. Her curiosity knew no bounds, and Daniel found himself utterly charmed by her zeal to learn. He began teaching her about wave frequencies, transmissions, and how sound journeyed invisibly through the ether.

Late into the evenings, they would huddle by the radio, tuning into distant voices and playfully imagining replies—weaving tales about who might be on the other end. Sometimes it was an astronaut in orbit, at others a scientist in a snowy outpost, or a child in a far-off land, much like her. Their imaginations soared, transforming static and signals into pure magic.

"I want to study science! This is ever so thrilling!" Soon Hee proclaimed one evening, her eyes aglow with fervent aspiration. "I want to master everything about space—and how the radio reaches folk so far away!"

Daniel's heart swelled with pride, sensing the torch of curiosity passing from him to his daughter in a profoundly fulfilling moment. "You absolutely can, Soon Hee. You've a brilliant mind, and I'm certain you can achieve anything you set your heart on. The radio became more than a mere device; it blossomed into a focal point for their shared passion—a symbol of their unbreakable bond. For Daniel, who had felt adrift for so long, parenting was a transformative odyssey. Through these moments with Soon Hee, the fragments of himself he thought lost were gradually weaving back together, stitched anew by love and hope.

As summer faded into autumn, each garden harvest marked more than a shift in seasons—it mirrored the quiet growth within their family. Daniel and Jung marvelled as their daughter flourished, her mind blooming alongside the chrysanthemums. Daniel, in particular, revelled in her discoveries, ever eager to forge deeper connections through science and creativity. He urged her to gaze at the stars twinkling in the night sky and ponder the unseen threads binding people across distance and time.

One evening, as sleep gently tugged at his thoughts, Daniel slipped into a dream. The stars above gleamed brightly, casting light across a vast, boundless sky. He stood barefoot in the garden of a tranquil home, the air still and heavy with promise. Beside him stood a small girl—a mere silhouette— her hand nestled in his. He leaned down and whispered softly, his voice melding with the silence, intertwining with the glow of the stars overhead.

"They shine for you," he said, "every single one. They carry our stories, our dreams, and they never forget."

The little girl tilted her head upward, listening raptly, her presence warm and familiar—yet just beyond grasp.

"Stars are like tiny lanterns," he continued, gesturing to the sky. "They illuminate the darkness, and even though we can't see everything, we know they're there, shining for us. Sometimes, if you peer closely, you can spot patterns—like tales etched across the night sky. That's why we call them constellations. They weave stories. And just like the stars, each of us has a tale to tell."

The mysterious girl tilted her head, her silhouette bathed in starlight as she tightened her grip on his hand.

"And can we talk to the stars? Like with your radio?"

He smiled, the corners of his eyes crinkling with warmth. "Yes," he murmured. "In a way, we already are."

But then, the dream began to fade—the edges softening like ink in water—as though the universe itself were gently drawing him away. The stars gleamed more faintly, and the air grew still. His voice, now softer and more heartfelt, lingered in the waning moment.

"Just keep listening," he murmured. "Even when it's silent. Sometimes, the stars whisper back."

And with that, the dream melted into stillness, leaving only the hush of night and the distant echo of connection.

The faint echo of his own words lingered in his mind: "Remember, no matter where I am or what I forget, I'm always gazing at the stars, just like you."

As the dream faded into the serene hush of dawn, Daniel awoke with a lingering warmth glowing in his chest. That sense of connection—of hope, of purpose—still pulsed quietly within him. He sat up slowly, sunlight streaming through the window in soft golden ribbons. The world felt still, suspended in that early morning calm. Jung lay beside him, her breathing steady and serene, untouched by the dream that had stirred him so profoundly.

Across the room, the old ham radio rested where he had placed it the previous evening—silent yet brimming with potential. Daniel reached out and gently touched its edge, the metal cool beneath his fingertips. He fancied he could sense a faint hum of possibility, as though the radio still held whispers waiting to be heard and tales yet to be told.

He knew fragments of his former life were resurfacing, seeping through in slivers. Yet nothing was clear—it was all shrouded in a fog of dreams. Oddly, there was comfort in that haze, even though not remembering troubled him less than recalling just enough.

The dreams had grown more frequent, their echoes lingering longer each morning. Yet with them came a renewed sense of purpose. Each day, Daniel embraced the simple joys of village life—tending the fields, sowing vegetables, and watching Soon Hee flourish. Now a teenager, she carried herself with burgeoning confidence, shouldering more responsibilities on the farm when not at school. One radiant morning, with the scent of dew still fresh in the air, they resolved to spend the day working together on the farm—a tranquil expanse of land beyond their home, rich with freshly turned soil, thriving crops, and the gentle chorus of birds and breeze. The hum of nature enveloped them like a soft lullaby, anchoring them in the present, even as the past murmured from the shadows.

Soon Hee walked beside Daniel, balancing a brimming bucket of water in each hand. They lingered at the well, filling containers, watering the plants, and chuckling as stray splashes soaked their shirts and trousers. At one point, Soon Hee squealed with glee and flung a handful of water at Daniel, droplets glinting in the sunlight like tiny crystals.

Nearby, Jung watched the scene unfold with an amused smile, shaking her head.

"Hey, you two," she called, laughing. "We've work to do, not playtime!"

Daniel chuckled and bent to adjust a watering can—but then, something shifted. A sudden wave of dizziness surged through him, disorienting and fierce. The ground seemed to tilt beneath his feet. His vision blurred into a haze of light and colour.

Without a word, he crumpled, his knees buckling as he collapsed silently into the field. The soft earth cushioned his fall, but it did nothing to ease Soon Hee's shock. Her eyes widened in alarm "Daddy?" Soon Hee cried, rushing to his side. "Daddy!"

She dropped to her knees beside him, her voice rising in pitch. He lay motionless, unresponsive, as though the laughter from moments before had been eclipsed by something far graver.

Jung, who had been tending the chickens nearby, heard Soon Hee's cries and raced over in a panic. Kneeling beside Daniel, she gently shook him, her voice quivering as she called his name—but his eyes remained shut, his body limp.

With trembling hands and urgent care, Soon Hee helped her mother lift and steady him. Together, they guided Daniel back to the house, their hearts pounding with fear, the afternoon's light dimmed by mounting dread.

Inside, they gently laid him on the bed. Jung acted swiftly, phoning the village doctor, her voice taut with worry. The doctor arrived promptly, his face etched with concern as he examined Daniel with the limited tools at his disposal.

After a prolonged pause, the doctor looked up, his tone measured yet grave.

"He needs more thorough tests than we can provide here," he said. "You should take him to the city—a larger hospital a few hours away. They'll have the equipment to properly assess what's happening."

Jung nodded, swallowing her fear. Soon Hee clung to her hand, their worry etched in every breath.

"I'm fine, everyone. I just felt a bit dizzy, that's all," Daniel insisted, attempting to ease their concern. "Truly, I'm fine."

"Let the doctor decide that," Jung said firmly, her gaze steady. "You're going to do as we say."

Daniel sighed but yielded. "Alright, alright. If it'll set your minds at ease, we'll go to the city—but it's likely just a waste of time."

The next morning, Daniel and Jung embarked on the long, bumpy journey to town. They left Soon Hee in the trusted care of one of the village "aunties"—a gentle, silver-haired woman who had nurtured generations of children and offered a reassuring smile as she placed an arm around Soon Hee's shoulder. Jung lingered for a moment, her fingers brushing Soon Hee's cheek, loath to let go.

They boarded an ageing bus that creaked and groaned as it wound through the rugged mountain terrain. The narrow roads twisted like ribbons, hugging the hillsides, while dense forests and mist-shrouded valleys glided past the window in soft, watercolour hues. Daniel sat quietly, his hand resting in Jung's. She clasped it tightly, her thumb tracing slow circles over his knuckles. Neither spoke, their silence brimming with unspoken worry and quiet fortitude.

When they reached the town hospital, the air felt chillier, the sterile corridors unfamiliar. The head doctor—a kind-eyed man with a warm, steady demeanour—greeted them and guided Daniel through a thorough examination. He spoke gently, clearly attuned to the tension beneath their courteous smiles. Blood tests followed, then scans, each step methodical and essential.

"If you can return later this afternoon," the doctor said, jotting notes with care, "I should have the results ready for you."

Jung nodded, her expression composed yet her hand never releasing Daniel's. They stepped back into the corridor, clinging to each other a touch more tightly than before.

"We could pop out for a bite to eat," Jung suggested with a hopeful smile. "There's that lovely noodle stall just down the road."

"Excellent," the doctor nodded. "Return in a few hours after your food, and we'll review everything."

When they returned to the hospital, they were ushered into the doctor's office. He greeted them with the same gentle smile.

"Did you enjoy your lunch?"

"Yes, it was lovely, thank you," Jung replied courteously, then glanced at Daniel, her expression tightening. "But we're rather anxious to hear the results."

The doctor's smile faded slightly. He paused, his demeanour growing graver as he regarded them both.

"Right, I'll be straight with you," the doctor began softly. "Some of your test results suggest a concerning issue."

Daniel leaned forward. "What sort of issue?"

The doctor glanced at the papers before him, choosing his words with care. "Have you ever experienced significant trauma—such as a serious accident?"

Before Daniel could respond, Jung interjected. "Eun Soo was in a car accident... years ago."

The doctor nodded. "That fits. It appears you sustained a blunt cardiac injury at the time—what we'd call a cardiac contusion or bruising. While your body healed, it left scar tissue. Over time, that scar tissue has weakened the heart muscle."

Daniel's expression tightened. He glanced at Jung, then back to the doctor. "So… am I going to die? Can this be treated?"

"Well," the doctor said with a reassuring smile, "we're all going to die someday. But in your case, Daniel, I want to keep that day far off. We'll need to conduct a few more tests over the coming months. For now, rest is paramount."

He fixed Daniel with a firm look. "You'll need to make significant lifestyle changes. No more dashing about the fields or heavy labour. That sort of exertion could be dangerous now."

Jung stepped in at once. "Don't worry, Doctor. I'll ensure he takes it easy. No more hard work for him."

The doctor nodded. "Good. I'll prescribe some tablets to help if you feel dizzy again. And I'd like you back here in a month for a follow-up."

"Thank you, Doctor," Daniel said, rising slowly from his chair. He reached for Jung's hand, giving it a gentle squeeze. Together, they stepped out of the office and began their journey home—hearts heavy with the weight of change, yet grateful for the time still ahead.

13

Paths of Discovery – Summer 1977
(Singapore)

After sifting through memories a while longer, Ava descended from the attic with a heart somewhat lighter and a vision for the future clearer than ever. Reflecting on her past, her time as an intern at NASA, and the spark of passion kindled by memories of her father, she felt an exhilarating sense of purpose surging within her. Ava knew she wanted to forge a path that wove together her love for science, her yearning to explore the cosmos, and the threads of her father's legacy.

Her university application followed swiftly. Ava set her sights on a prestigious institution in the United States, determined to pursue a dual degree in physics and medicine. She believed fervently in the potential to blend these fields one day. The prospect of contributing to the medical aspects of space exploration thrilled her—a fusion of dreams inherited from Daniel and reborn in her heart.

As she prepared for this new chapter, Ava felt a blend of excitement and trepidation, her father's memory a quiet constant she carried within. She had made the journey from Singapore to America in the autumn, crossing the vast ocean that separated her from the only home she had known. Now, standing on the bustling university campus, with its historic buildings towering around her, Ava felt both insignificant and invincible—a mere speck in an expansive universe, yet a budding scientist on the cusp of discovery.

Navigating university life brought its challenges. The cultural shift was tangible, and Ava often felt the strain of adapting to a new environment while keeping pace with her rigorous coursework. Yet, even amidst frustration, she found herself flourishing. Late-night study groups, inspiring lectures, and bonds forged with fellow aspiring scientists fuelled her passion. She joined the university's astronomy club, where she discovered kindred spirits who shared her dreams. Together, they organised stargazing evenings that transformed the night sky into a shared sanctuary—a haven where Ava felt belonging, purpose, and wonder.

One crisp winter evening, as the astronomy club gathered on a rooftop to observe the Leonid meteor shower, Ava gazed at the cosmos, captivated by the brilliance of shooting stars streaking across the heavens. The icy air nipped at her cheeks, but she scarcely noticed. The moment was electric—alive with awe—and it stirred something profound within her.

Memories of her father surfaced unbidden: the two of them lying on their backs in a tranquil field, his voice tracing constellations, weaving tales of science and magic. In the stillness of the evening, with stars cascading overhead, Ava could almost hear his voice again, carried on the breeze and entwined with the whispers of the universe.

"Look, there it goes!" her friend shouted, pointing at the sky as a brilliant streak of light arced across the darkness.

Ava laughed and cheered with the others, her breath misting in the chilly air, her heart brimming and eyes sparkling. In that moment, the thrill of the meteor shower blended with the lingering warmth of memory, kindling a deeper spark within her—a steadfast belief that she was precisely where she belonged.

"Each of those stars has its own tale," Ava mused, her gaze locked on the shimmering sky. Her thoughts drifted to the adventures and discoveries she yearned to embrace—the myriad stories waiting to be woven, somewhere beyond the horizon. "Out there, tales are waiting to be told."

As she progressed in her studies, Ava pursued her dual path with fierce resolve. She immersed herself in astrophysics lectures, delving into the intricacies of space travel—exploring not only the vast unknowns of the cosmos but also the emotional and psychological trials it entailed. Concurrently, her medical courses demanded equal rigour, anchoring her in anatomy, physiology, and the core tenets of health sciences. With each lesson, she honed a deeper understanding of the unique medical challenges faced by space explorers, intertwining her passion for science and care.

The years sped by, each shaped by Ava's unyielding resolve. By her junior year, she had forged a reputation as a fiercely dedicated student, her passion illuminating all she pursued. She immersed herself in research that blended her dual interests, exploring the effects of microgravity on human health and developing innovative safety solutions for astronauts.

Despite the demands of her academic life, Ava found camaraderie and connection in unexpected corners. She gravitated towards a diverse group of students—scientists, engineers, and even artists—each offering a unique perspective on life, growth, and creativity. One friendship, in particular, began to flourish: a fellow physics major named Tommy, whose playful banter and boundless enthusiasm transformed even the most gruelling study sessions into moments to cherish.

As they settled into a steady rhythm of classes and late-night conversations, a warm camaraderie blossomed between them. They spurred each other through exams, celebrated small triumphs, and occasionally slipped away from their demanding schedules to explore local art exhibitions or music festivals. These moments allowed Ava to embrace facets of herself beyond her academic ambitions, savouring the rich tapestry of university life.

Yet, beneath the excitement and achievements, the memory of her father lingered in her heart. On quiet evenings under star-filled skies or during solitary study sessions, she often found herself reflecting on the dream she held: to honour him. With every calculation she solved, every word she spoke in class, and every stand she took for her beliefs, she sensed his presence quietly guiding her—an unseen but steadfast light in her journey.

Then, one summer, a pivotal moment unfolded. NASA and her university launched a Cooperative Education Programme, seeking bright young minds to contribute to their ambitious projects in space exploration, including cutting-edge medical research for long-duration missions. With her heart racing, Ava meticulously crafted her application, weaving in her prior experience as a NASA intern, her aspirations, and the deep love she bore for her father's legacy.

The moment she submitted her application, Ava's heart raced with a heady blend of hope and nervous anticipation. Staring at the screen, she felt the weight of the path ahead— a path that was not merely an opportunity, but a chance to weave her dreams with the honouring of her father's memory in the very realm that had sparked her passion.

In the days that followed, Ava immersed herself in her studies, fuelling her curiosity and deepening her zeal for both physics and medicine. Every lecture, every late-night reading, and each hands-on experiment drew her closer to the future she envisaged. The prospect of working with NASA—contributing to the frontier of space medicine— shone brightly within her, a guiding star in her academic journey.

While awaiting a response, Ava found solace in the familiar ritual of stargazing. Using the telescope her parents had given her years ago, she spent evenings wrapped in a blanket beneath the open sky, her gaze tracing the constellations. The stars evoked memories of childhood nights beside her father, listening to tales of the cosmos.

"I'm going to make you proud, Daddy," she whispered to the stars, the night air cool against her skin. In that stillness, she felt the universe enfold her like an embrace—vast, silent, and brimming with promise.

During a term break from university, back in Singapore after weeks of anticipation, the long-awaited letter from NASA arrived in the post. Ava's hands trembled as she tore it open, her heartbeat thundering in her ears. Her gaze swept the page—then froze. She gasped.

"Congratulations..."

"Yes! Yes! Yes!" she cried, leaping into the air. Her room rang with joy as she bounded up and down, barely containing the surge of elation in her chest.

Without pause, she raced downstairs to share the news. Mei Lin and Gerry were seated in the living room, chatting idly about dinner plans.

"Mum! Daddy Gerry!" Ava's voice was breathless with excitement. "I got it—I've been accepted onto the NASA Cooperative Programme!"

Mei Lin shot upright, her eyes wide with disbelief before laughter bubbled out of her. "My goodness! That's brilliant, Ava!" she exclaimed, leaping to her feet and giving her a big hug. "I knew you could do it!"

"We're so proud of you!"

"This is just the beginning!"

"You're going to change the world, sweetheart."

Ava's smile stretched wide as tears welled in her eyes. In that moment, everything seemed possible.

"Blimey, that's incredible, Ava!" Gerry said, his face alight with genuine delight. "You're going to do great things. You should celebrate with your friends as soon as you are back at university!"

"I will!" Ava beamed. "I must also call Billy—he was the one who secured me the internship that started all this. First, though, I must call Tommy."

She dashed into the hall and, without a moment's hesitation, dialled Tommy. Her excitement spilt into every word.

"Tommy! I got it—I've been accepted onto the NASA Cooperative Programme!"

There was a brief pause, followed by a burst of laughter and cheering on the other end.

"That's brilliant!" he exclaimed. "We must celebrate as soon as you're back in Florida. We'll go out for dinner—my treat!"

In the months that followed, Ava threw herself into preparation. Between her academic workload and the anticipation of the joint programme, her days were brimming with focus. She redoubled her efforts in her science courses, participated in local astronomy events, and volunteered to give talks at nearby schools, sharing her zeal for space exploration and inspiring younger students to dream big.

With each step, Ava was not merely preparing for NASA. She was becoming the woman her father had always believed she could be.

During her summer break in Singapore, when the day finally arrived for Ava to depart for NASA, a whirl of nerves and excitement surged within her as she zipped up her suitcase—carefully packed with essentials, notes, and tools to seize every opportunity of her internship.

As the taxi pulled away from Emerald Hill, she glanced back to see Mei Lin and Gerry standing at the gate, waving. A wave of gratitude warmed her chest for their steadfast support, grounding her in the moment before she stepped into the future.

Upon landing in Florida's vibrant atmosphere, Ava was swept into a realm of innovation and discovery. The NASA facility loomed before her like a beacon of possibility, its corridors and laboratories brimming with opportunities for learning. This far surpassed her previous internship; this was real. Her heart raced, a blend of awe and resolve, as she took her first steps into the unknown.

During the orientation sessions, Ava met fellow students who shared her zeal—bright, inquisitive minds eager to unravel the mysteries of the cosmos. They swiftly bonded over shared aspirations, late-night studies, and the exhilarating thrill of contributing to something far greater than themselves.

As the days unfolded, Ava immersed herself fully in her work. She attended lectures by leading scientists, participated in hands-on experiments, and was surrounded by peers who inspired and challenged her. The environment thrummed with possibility. Every hour brought fresh insights, and every conversation enriched her understanding. In this realm of discovery, Ava felt herself flourishing—her confidence deepening, her joy burgeoning.

One particularly clear evening, the Cooperative Programme students were invited to the rooftop of the facility for a special stargazing event. Blankets were spread beneath the night sky, and the air hummed with quiet anticipation. As they lay back, listening to the soft voices of astronomers identifying constellations and elucidating the physics behind each flicker of light, Ava's heart swelled. This transcended simple stargazing; it was an advanced lesson in the physics of the cosmos.

She gazed up in wonder, the sky stretching infinitely above, feeling both infinitesimally small and profoundly connected. The stars whispered tales of the past, of possibility, of purpose. In that moment, surrounded by peers and aspirations, she sensed her father's spirit in the quiet hush between constellations—a presence woven into the cosmos, watching, proud.

As the lecturer spoke of light years, distances, and the current positions of Voyager 1 and 2, Ava followed their gaze, but her thoughts drifted inward. Her father's presence stirred quietly in her mind, his tales rising like echoes as the stars twinkled above—familiar, timeless. She closed her eyes briefly, transported to those quiet nights with him, lying side by side, his voice brimming with wonder as he named the stars and wove tales from the heavens.

"I'm here," she whispered to the cosmos, a vow uttered into the velvet dark—a silent promise to carry his legacy forward.

Around her, voices murmured in awe, aspirations floating like stardust on the breeze. The sky was boundless, yet Ava had never felt more anchored. In that stillness, she recognised the clarity of her path: she was part of something vast and beautiful, rooted in her past, and drawn forward by purpose.

On the final day of the programme, Ava was unexpectedly summoned to the office of NASA's President of Communications. He greeted her warmly and got straight to the point: they had been thoroughly impressed by her performance over the past few months and wished to offer her a position in the Communications Department upon completion of her degree.

Returning to University after the Co-op programme, Ava carried with her a renewed sense of purpose. The experience had provided far more than access to cutting-edge laboratories or conversations with astronauts—it had crystallised something within her. She no longer merely aspired to work in space medicine; she was determined to shape its future, with her sights set on a role within NASA.

Her days became long and rigorously scheduled. She balanced advanced courses in anatomy, physiology, and neuroscience with specialised electives in aerospace environments and biotechnological systems. When not in lectures, she was in the laboratory or buried deep in the campus library, highlighting passages in dense textbooks or furiously scribbling equations in her ever-present notebook. Space had transformed from a distant dream into her driving purpose.

And then, there was Tommy.

They had met the year before the Co-op Programme, both volunteering with the university's science outreach programme for underprivileged secondary school students. At first, they were merely friends—sparring in study groups, debating ethical dilemmas in medicine over black coffee, and rolling their eyes at lecturers who relied too heavily on PowerPoint slides.

But after Ava returned from NASA, something had shifted.

Tommy was waiting for her at the shuttle stop, holding a homemade sign that read, Welcome back, Space Girl. He wrapped her in a hug that felt different—longer, more assured. And she had leaned in without thinking, her head nestled beneath his chin.

In the weeks that followed, their relationship deepened. They carved out time for each other amidst the chaos of university life—Sunday breakfasts at their favourite diner, late-night walks beneath the stars, and quiet evenings curled up together with data sets and steaming mugs of tea.

One chilly October night, they climbed to the roof of the old observatory. They watched satellites blink overhead and traced constellations with idle fingers.

"I think I love you," Tommy murmured, his eyes fixed on the sky.

Ava turned her head to look at him, startled but certain. "I think I do too," she whispered, then let her hand find his.

"What, love yourself?" Tommy teased, laughing.

"No, I love you too, silly," Ava replied, gently nudging his shoulder with a playful punch and laughing.

It wasn't dramatic. It didn't need to be. Their love grew from a place of mutual respect and quiet understanding. They didn't need to shout it from the rooftops—it was there in the small things: Tommy saving her favourite snacks for long laboratory days, Ava sitting through his basketball matches, even when she barely understood the rules.

As winter drew nearer, so did Lunar New Year—a time Ava traditionally spent in Singapore with her family. She often spoke of it: the scent of incense curling through crowded temples, her mother's sweet pineapple tarts, and the glow of red paper lanterns lining the streets.

This year, she surprised herself by asking Tommy if he wanted to join her.

"You'd meet my parents," Ava said, trying to sound casual but unable to hide the nerves in her voice.

Tommy blinked, then smiled warmly. "I'd love to."

Singapore greeted Tommy with a wall of heat and the sweet scent of citrus blossoms lingering in the air. The city pulsed with life—crimson banners fluttered from windows, vendors hawked sticky rice cakes and glowing paper lanterns, and lion dancers practised to the rhythmic beat of distant drums.

Mei Lin opened the door, arms crossed, her expression unreadable.

"So, you're Tommy."

"Yes, ma'am," he replied, offering a small bow along with a box of gleaming mandarin oranges. "Thank you for having me."

Mei Lin took the oranges with a nod and turned away without another word.

Gerry, ever the warmer of the two, appeared in the hallway with a welcoming grin. "Come on in, son. Don't let her scare you. She grilled me for months when we started courting."

The house was filled with the comforting aromas of sesame oil, fried shallots, and ginger. Ava moved gracefully through the kitchen, working alongside her mother—preparing steamed fish for prosperity, dumplings for wealth, and glutinous rice balls for unity. Tommy tried to help, though his dumplings resembled misshapen moons rather than neatly folded purses of luck.

On New Year's Eve, the family gathered around the round dining table, a symbol of completeness and unity. They lit incense to honour their ancestors, exchanged red packets, and shared stories from years past. Tommy sat quietly, listening more than speaking, absorbing the energy of a culture both unfamiliar and warmly welcoming.

He watched Ava shine in her element—laughing effortlessly with Khian-Seng in Hokkien, gently teasing her mother, and guiding him through the traditions with a blend of ease and pride. In that moment, he realised this trip wasn't merely about meeting her family; it was about truly understanding the roots of the woman he loved. Then, Ava paused, looked at Mei Lin, and said something softly about her father, expressing her longing for him and her wish for his happiness

On New Year's morning, they performed the tea ceremony. Tommy, slightly stiff in his pressed shirt, knelt beside Ava as they carefully served tea to Mei Lin and Gerry, honouring the moment and the bonds it celebrated.

Mei Lin took her cup without a word. She sipped slowly, then finally met Tommy's gaze.

"You make her laugh," she said softly. "You help her study. And you've come all this way just to sit on my floor and serve me hot tea."

Tommy opened his mouth to speak, but Mei Lin raised a hand to silence him.

"She's not easy, my daughter. She dreams with her head in the stars and her feet barely touching the ground. But if you love her—truly love her—ensure she never has to choose between you and the sky."

Tommy nodded, his voice low and steady.

"I don't ever want her to choose. I just want to be the one cheering from the ground when she reaches the stars."

For the first time, Mei Lin smiled—a small, approving curve of her lips. "She was hurt once when she lost her father. Don't ever hurt her again!"

"I would never do that; I love her deeply"

"Oh you big softy" Ava said with a big smile

Later, as firecrackers illuminated the sky and lion dancers brought the streets below to life, Ava and Tommy stood on the balcony of her childhood home, their fingers interlaced as she leaned into him.

"You survived," she teased softly.

He kissed her temple. "I'd survive anything for you," Tommy whispered, his voice low against the hush of the night. "Distance, pressure, time—whatever this world throws at us."

Ava nestled closer, resting her head on his shoulder, their hands still entwined. Above them, the Singapore sky shimmered with the fading glow of fireworks and floating lanterns, drifting out towards the sea like glowing promises.

"You already have," she murmured, gazing up at him. "Through everything—late-night calls, internships, exams, uncertainty—you were always there."

He turned to face her fully, gently brushing a loose strand of hair from her cheek.

"Because I saw the future in you before I even understood my own."

She smiled, the weight of the moment settling in her chest like warmth on a cold night.

"And now it's real."

Then, without hesitation, Tommy knelt on one knee, the city lights flickering behind him like stars drawn down to witness the moment.

Ava's breath caught.

From his pocket, he drew a small velvet box and opened it to reveal a delicate ring—simple, elegant, unmistakably hers.

"Ava," he said, his voice steady but brimming with emotion, "will you marry me?"

Time stilled. The distant sounds of the Lunar New Year celebrations faded into nothing but the pounding of her heart.

"Yes," she gasped, a wide, radiant smile spreading across her face. "Yes! Of course I will!"

She threw her arms around him, laughter bubbling through her excitement. He stood and gently spun her, holding her close as if the moment might drift away if he let go.

Then she pulled back slightly, her eyes softening with joy— and a hint of seriousness.

"But," she said, her voice steady, "you must ask my mum and Gerry first. It's our tradition."

Tommy nodded, his gaze unwavering.

"I wouldn't have it any other way."

They held each other again, wrapped in warmth, love, and the shared promise of all that lay ahead.

The next morning, Tommy stood nervously at the front door of Mei Lin and Gerry's home, adjusting his shirt collar. He'd taken a long walk earlier to gather his thoughts for the big day ahead. The soft buzz of Lunar New Year festivities still lingered in the background, but his focus was unwavering. His hand trembled slightly as he raised it to knock.

From the staircase just inside, Ava leaned on the banister, her eyes sparkling with amusement and love. The smile on her face gave him both courage and a flicker of suspicion—perhaps she had already hinted at what was about to unfold.

The door opened, and Mei Lin greeted him with a warm, knowing expression.

"Tommy," she said gently. "Come in, we should have given you a key."

Gerry looked up from a low seat in the lounge, nodding as Tommy stepped inside. The house was filled with the comforting scents of incense and breakfast, but Tommy scarcely noticed. His palms were clammy, and he cleared his throat.

"I—I wanted to speak with you both," he began, standing taller, though nerves still clung to his posture. Mei Lin and Gerry waited, patient and attentive.

"I love Ava very much," he said, his voice growing steadier with each word. "She is the most extraordinary person I've ever met. And… I'd like to ask for your blessing to marry her."

A brief pause filled the room, though it lasted only moments. Mei Lin's eyes softened as she reached out and gently touched his arm.

"You already have it," she said, her voice tender. "You've made her happy. That's all we could ever wish for."

Gerry gave a small, approving nod. "Welcome to the family, Tommy."

Tommy exhaled with relief, a grin spreading across his face just as Ava descended the stairs to join them.

Later that morning, Ava gently drew Tommy aside, her expression pensive.

"I need to visit the temple," she said. "Alone."

Tommy understood immediately and knew her reasons. He pressed a kiss to her forehead, his hand lingering on hers before letting go.

At the temple, nestled among blooming lantern trees and the lingering scent of incense, Ava knelt quietly before the altar. The flickering glow of candles danced across her face as she lit one with steady hands.

She whispered softly, her words barely louder than the rustling leaves outside the temple.

"Dad, I've met the most wonderful man. You would adore him—I know you would… we all do."

She paused, placing the candle in its holder with careful reverence.

"Wherever you are, please be happy for me. I love you. I miss you more than I could ever express kneeling here."

Tears welled in her eyes, slipping down her cheeks in a gentle stream—tears of joy, tinged with quiet sorrow. This was one of the most significant moments of her life, and the ache of her father's absence pressed deeper than ever.

Yet, in the hush of the temple, wrapped in incense and memory, she felt him.

Not as a sound or a sign—just warmth. Presence. Love.

And in her heart, she knew: he was smiling.

14

The Silent Tears
(Korea)

The late afternoon sun cast a soft, golden glow over the small porch where Daniel and Jung sat side by side—close, yet each immersed in their own thoughts. A gentle breeze stirred the leaves, but the silence between them was heavy with unspoken worries. The impending round of tests loomed, casting long shadows across their hearts.

Daniel gazed out at the horizon, the fields stretching far beyond, his expression unreadable. Beside him, Jung's hands were clasped tightly in her lap, her posture tense, her face etched with concern. Her eyes flicked to him, then quickly darted away—as if she were holding something back, afraid to voice it.

"Jung," Daniel said at last, his voice low and steady, breaking the silence. "Whatever the tests reveal, we'll face it together. We've come through so much, and we're still here. I believe it will be alright."

He reached for her hand, his fingers gently closing around hers—offering warmth, calm, and something solid to hold onto.

"You saved me once," he added, a faint smile tugging at the corner of his lips. "When I was lost, you pulled me back. And if this turns out to be something serious… I know we'll find a way to save me again. We're a team, Jung. Always."

Jung looked down, tears welling, but she swallowed hard and nodded, determined to hold back the flood of fears.

"It's not just about us," she whispered, her voice trembling. "It's Soon Hee, too. What this means for her—her future, our family. I just… I don't want her to grow up lonely or scared, not understanding why her father has to go through this."

Daniel squeezed her hand gently, his eyes warm with unwavering love.

"Whatever the future holds, I'm here. And with you both very much, I believe we can face anything."

The bus ride back to the hospital was quiet, the weight of nerves heavy in the air. Outside the window, winter was drawing near, the landscape shifting with the changing season. Daniel chuckled softly, nudging Jung to break the silence.

"Look at that," Daniel said, pointing towards a row of trees outside the window. "There are far more than last time we came—someone's been busy."

Jung smiled faintly, grateful for the brief distraction. Her mind remained heavy with worry, but she focused on the scenery, trying to set her fears aside.

When they arrived in the bustling town, the familiar hospital where Daniel was to undergo further tests buzzed with activity. Yet, the wait inside their modest room stretched on painfully slowly.

After a while, a nurse appeared and gently called for Daniel.

"He'll be fine, don't worry," she said, offering Jung a reassuring smile as she led him away for the day's tests.

Following the tests, they sat in anxious silence. Jung clasped her hands tightly in her lap, while Daniel stared at his feet, each second stretching unbearably. He kept glancing towards the door, his heart pounding with dread at the unknown news awaiting them.

Finally, a soft knock broke the silence, and the nurse gently ushered them into the doctor's office.

The doctor entered slowly, his expression calm but grave. Daniel and Jung exchanged a tense glance—this was the moment they had dreaded.

The doctor's voice was measured and deliberate, his pause deepening the weight in the room.

"Daniel, Jung," he began, "I've reviewed your results, Daniel, very carefully. As we suspected from the initial tests, it's a serious condition. Your heart is failing, and unfortunately, it's likely to be progressive and terminal. We can't predict exactly how long you have, but it will worsen over time.

"The good news for now, is that we can manage it with medication and close monitoring. We'll begin treatment immediately and collaborate with specialists to provide the best care possible. But I must be honest—this isn't a cure. We can only aim to slow the progression for as long as possible."

Jung's breath caught, her eyes widening with fear. Daniel's composed expression wavered, a flicker of shock crossing his face.

"The course of action now," the doctor continued gently, "is to start medication and keep you under close supervision. We will do everything possible to manage your condition, but I must stress—this is a grave prognosis. Our goal is to prolong your life and maintain its quality as best we can, but I cannot promise a cure. You should prepare for a long, ongoing challenge."

Daniel sank back into his chair, absorbing the weight of the words. Jung's hand trembled as she reached for his, tears pooling in her eyes, though she fought to hold them back. In the silence between them, a fierce, unspoken prayer for strength passed through her.

He looked at her, love and reassurance flowing between them like an unbreakable bond—silent, steadfast, and fiercely protective.

"We'll face it together," Daniel said softly, his voice steady with quiet resolve. "Whatever comes, we do it as a team. We're not giving up hope."

Jung nodded, tears finally slipping free as she gripped his hand tightly. "We're in this—together."

In that room, clinging to hope amid the shadows of uncertainty, Daniel and Jung felt the weight of the diagnosis pressing heavily upon them. They knew this truth would forever alter how Soon Hee saw her father—and reshape their lives.

Later, as the sun dipped low, casting golden hues across the fields, Daniel and Jung sat again on the porch. Jung reached for Daniel's hand, her eyes reflecting a blend of sorrow and quiet determination.

"Daniel," she began softly, her voice trembling, "we need to tell Soon Hee about this. She's growing up, and she's bright—she'll notice if we're hiding something. We must be honest. She's our daughter. She needs to know."

Daniel nodded slowly, the weight of the truth settling in. "She's so lively, so full of energy," he said quietly. "I don't want her to see me as suddenly weak or different from the dad she's always known. But I suppose she needs to understand that I might not be able to run and play with her as much—that I'll need more rest, more care."

Jung gently touched his arm, offering quiet comfort in the heavy moment.

"She loves you, Daniel. She always will; you're her father. And I believe she'll understand. Children are stronger than we think—she'll surprise us."

That evening, bathed in the soft glow of lanterns and surrounded by gentle evening sounds, Daniel and Jung sat Soon Hee down in the cosy living room. Jung took a deep breath, her heart pounding, before speaking softly but firmly.

"Soon Hee," she began, "your daddy has a problem with his heart. It's something we must monitor carefully. The doctors say it might worsen, and he may not be able to run and play as much as before. But that doesn't mean he loves you any less. Daddy will still be here with us—just in a different way."

Soon Hee's bright eyes looked puzzled for a moment. Then she fell silent, digesting the words.

"Will Daddy die?" she asked, her voice trembling slightly.

"He's very ill, but he won't die yet," Jung replied, kneeling beside her. "Daddy will always be your daddy, and he loves you more than anything in the world. Sometimes, he'll need to rest more, but he'll still be here—hugging you, reading to you, playing when he can."

Daniel sat quietly, his heart aching for her innocence, for her guileless trust.

"I might not be able to run about like I used to," he said softly, "but I'll still be here, watching you grow into the girl I know you're meant to be."

Soon Hee nodded slowly, her young face solemn as she absorbed the truth.

"Okay, Daddy," she whispered. "I love you. We still have the radio, too."

Watching her, Daniel felt a bittersweet pang of pride and sorrow. She was so brave—so resilient. And he knew, in that moment, that they had a choice: to let the shadows of his illness darken their lives or to cherish every moment they had, however fleeting.

The days that followed were filled with gentle routines— quiet mornings, storytelling, doctor's visits, and slow, careful play. Daniel learnt to savour these simple moments, knowing each was precious. He and Jung made plans for the future, aware of the limited time they might have but determined to fill it with love and meaning.

Together, amidst the fields and hills of their village, they faced the uncertain journey ahead—holding fast to the truth that love, hope, and the bonds of family can shine brightest even in the deepest shadows.

The morning light filtered gently through the small window of their mountain cabin, casting a soft glow over a simple scene—Daniel slipping quietly out of bed before the sun had fully risen. He moved with deliberate care, knowing how much Soon Hee loved her favourite breakfast—guk with kimchi—and wishing to surprise her. As the aroma of fermented kimchi and simmering broth filled the air, it brought a comforting sense of home, mingled with the fragile hope of returning to normality.

He watched Soon Hee prepare for school, bustling with excitement as she donned her uniform. With a swift hug and a tender kiss on her forehead, he saw her off, her school bag bouncing on her back and eyes bright with curiosity. Sitting quietly on the porch, Daniel watched her vanish down the path towards the school bus stop. The early morning breeze ruffled his hair, and silence settled around him—peaceful, yet heavy with unspoken fears lurking just beneath the surface.

15

Echoes of the Past – Summer 1982
(Florida)

Ava stood in the bustling satellite communications division of NASA's Florida headquarters, enveloped by the steady hum of antennas, screens, and dials pulsing with life. She'd come a long way from Singapore, forging a reputation as a dedicated engineer and scientist— driven by the same insatiable curiosity her father, Daniel, once cherished. Her days were filled with linking satellites, troubleshooting signals, and extending humanity's reach into the cosmos. Yet, amid the ceaseless flow of work and innovation, her thoughts occasionally drifted back to the quiet nights of her childhood—the distant echoes of her past growing fainter but never entirely fading.

Tonight, she and Ryan were celebrating a gruelling week of successful launches. Ryan, originally from San Jose, was her partner on this key project—an animated, kind-hearted man whose passion for space and technology matched her own. They'd met at a conference, and their rapport had blossomed swiftly. She loved how Ryan always made her laugh, how they could talk for hours about exploring the universe or simply about life itself. She called him her "work husband."

Tommy and Ava had planned a night out to unwind and invited Ryan and his wife, Jo, to join them. They often gathered as a foursome, so this was nothing new. They chose to relax at a local Texas-style line dancing bar called The Saddle Rack—a place where the community came together to dance, enjoy live country bands on four stages, admire wall-mounted stuffed bull heads adorning the building, and challenge each other with cowboy hats and broad smiles. The lively atmosphere was precisely what Ava needed to forget, if only briefly, the vastness of space.

Inside, the sound of boots clicking against the wooden floor mingled with laughter and upbeat country music. They grabbed drinks and joined a small crowd, slipping into the line dance. Ava spun with surprising ease, catching even herself off guard. Ryan was right beside her, his playful grin earning cheers from fellow patrons.

Then someone shouted, "Let's try the mechanical bull!" A buzz of excitement rippled through the crowd. Ava, ever eager for a thrill, grinned mischievously. "I'm in," she declared, a gleam of challenge in her eyes.

Tommy laughed. "Alright, but don't say I didn't warn you!"

Ava clambered onto the platform, gripping the leather handles tightly as the mechanical bull roared to life. At first, she moved smoothly, her laughter ringing out above the cheers. But then the machine jerked and bucked fiercely, challenging her every move. The crowd roared louder as her adrenaline surged with each unpredictable lurch.

Just as she was finding her rhythm, disaster struck. The bull spun wildly, and in a flash, Ava was thrown off. She tumbled through the air, her laughter turning to a startled yelp as she hit the ground, sprawling in a heap—yet laughing uncontrollably.

Tommy hurried over, helping her up and ruffling her hair with a grin. "That was brilliant—best crash I've seen all night!"

The crowd erupted in applause, and Ava, shaking her head, grinned despite the bruise on her knee. She turned and gave a playful bow to the cheering crowd.

"Alright, alright," she chuckled, "perhaps I'm better with satellites than bulls."

They spent the rest of the night dancing, laughing, and sharing fleeting moments that made her forget the vast distances she'd travelled from her past. Yet, deep down, the echoes of her childhood—the whisper of her father's stories, the faint thrill of exploration—lingered, an unspoken part of her journey she'd carry into the next chapter of her life.

As the night drew to a close and they strolled home beneath the starry Florida sky, Ava felt a quiet reassurance settle within her. Though the stars above evoked her father's dreams, she knew her own path was just beginning—an echo of her past guiding her towards a future brimming with hope and discovery. Their relationship continued to flourish amid the high-tech corridors of NASA and the warm glow of Miami's sunsets.

Tommy's steadfast presence and playful spirit became a source of comfort for Ava, their bond deepening beyond friendship. Evenings were filled with tales of space, life, and dreams for the future—each conversation drawing them closer together.

"Ava, I reckon it's time we do what we planned a while back. It's time to tie the knot."

"Yes, you're right. I've been so caught up with work. Let's do it—I'm overjoyed."

That night, their wedding plans began to take shape. The ceremony would be an intimate celebration on Sentosa Island, Singapore—a place steeped in childhood memories and the perfect backdrop for a new chapter. Family and friends would gather to witness their union, a symbol of hope, love, and the bridge between past and future.

As the date approached, Ava felt a blend of excitement and longing—her heart swelling with anticipation, yet bearing a gentle ache for her father's presence. She knew, deep down, that his spirit would linger in every embrace, every vow, every star she gazed upon.

On the day, as Ava prepared to walk down the aisle, standing on the sands of Sentosa with the ocean murmuring promises of new horizons, she whispered to herself, "Dad, I know you're with me, right beside me today." She felt this was merely the beginning. Her journey, ignited by discovery and fuelled by hope, was poised to carry her beyond the stars and into a future where love was the greatest adventure of all.

That sentiment echoed softly in her heart as she stood at the altar, the warm ocean breeze mingling with the heartfelt vows she and Tommy exchanged.

The ceremony was exquisite—an intimate gathering beneath the radiant hues of sunset, with friends and family smiling through tears and laughter. Mei Lin watched proudly, her eyes gleaming with love and hope, even as her heart bore a faint ache for Daniel—her brave husband, lost somewhere in the shadows of the past.

Mei Lin rose slowly, a glass held delicately in her hand, her eyes glistening as the room fell into a reverent hush.

"Traditionally, it is the bride's father who gives a speech on a day like this," Mei Lin began, her voice steady yet brimming with emotion. "Gerry has been a father to Ava, doing an excellent job to fill the void left in her life since the day my beloved Daniel—her father—vanished all those years ago. But today, Gerry asked me to speak on Daniel's behalf."

She glanced at Gerry, offering a warm, affectionate smile, mouthing, "I love you."

Taking a deep breath, she continued, "I believe, with all my heart, that somewhere out there, Daniel is watching. He's listening. And I know, deep down, he is with us in spirit. He would have been bursting with pride for his radiant daughter—our Ava."

A pause. A tear slid down Mei Lin's cheek, followed by another.

"Ava," she whispered, her voice trembling with emotion, "you are the greatest gift life has ever given me. In you, I see your father's spirit—his warmth, his curiosity—shining through in everything you do."

She gently dabbed her cheek with a tissue, then glanced around the room, her face softening into a tender smile. As tears welled in many eyes around her, she added with a flicker of mischief and hope, "I hope you find a happiness as deep and enduring as the one I've known. And maybe," she paused, a teasing twinkle in her eye, "it won't take two husbands to get you there."

Laughter rippled through the room—the kind that blossoms from shared memories, deep love, and healing joy.

Mei Lin raised her glass aloft.

"To Ava and Tommy!"

Everyone rose, glasses lifted towards the radiant couple.

"To Ava and Tommy!" the room echoed, voices brimming with love and celebration.

As the ceremony concluded and guests mingled beneath strings of golden lights, Ava spotted a familiar face weaving through the crowd towards her. It was Billy—her father's cherished friend, the man who had always lingered at the edges of her childhood like a quiet guardian, bound to her family by radio waves and memories. The man who had helped spark her NASA journey. A pivotal figure in her life.

His weathered face softened into a tender smile as he reached her.

"Ava," he said, his voice husky with emotion, "I may have the greatest gift for you—something I've been saving for just this moment."

Her heart skipped a beat. There was something in his eyes— a glimmer of nostalgia, of long-held hope—as he reached into his pocket and drew out a small, carefully wrapped package.

"A gift?" she asked, her voice barely above a whisper. "For me?"

He nodded, offering the package to her.

"Yes. Something your father would've wanted you to have. I reckon… it's time."

She took the package, feeling its unexpected weight and the coarse texture of the paper beneath her fingertips. Her hands trembled as she glanced up at Billy. He had stepped back now—hesitant, almost uncertain—but there was something in his expression that suggested he'd waited years for this moment.

Later that night, as the celebration drew to a close and the stars blanketed the sky, Billy gathered a small group in the soft glow of the garden—Mei Lin, Tommy, Gerry, and Ava. Lanterns flickered nearby, casting a warm light over their expectant faces.

Billy stood for a moment in silence, his posture tense, his hands clasped tightly. Then he exhaled and spoke.

"I have something to tell you," he said, his voice low but carrying the weight of something long buried. "It's going to come as a shock. So… please—just let me explain before you say anything."

The soft murmur of the remaining guests faded into the background. Mei Lin's expression grew taut. Ava leaned forward, her gaze fixed on Billy, eyes searching his face for answers. Tommy reached for her hand, his grip firm. No one spoke.

The night was still—waiting.

Billy took a deep breath, steadying himself. "Over the past few months, I've been in contact with someone… in Korea. It began over a ham radio frequency—nothing unusual at first. Just a curious signal I picked up one night."

He paused, glancing briefly at the group before continuing, his voice softer now, laced with emotion.

"But then… something about his voice—it caught me off guard. The tone. The way he hesitated. Like he was searching for words or memories. Like he was… trying to reach someone."

Billy's throat tightened, and he looked directly at Mei Lin, then Ava. His eyes glistened.

"I didn't want to believe it—not at first. I thought perhaps I was hearing what I longed to hear. That my mind was playing tricks on me." He swallowed hard. "But the more we spoke, the more certain I became."

He let the silence linger for a moment before uttering the words that would change everything.

"I'm certain it was him. It's Daniel."

A stunned silence settled over the group like falling snow. The flickering lanterns cast soft shadows across Mei Lin's face as she raised a trembling hand to her lips.

"Oh, Billy…" she whispered, her voice barely steady. "Please, don't say that unless you're certain. I—I couldn't bear it if…"

"I know," Billy said gently, taking her hand in his. "That's why I kept silent until now. He never called himself Daniel. He said his name was Eun Soo. Then, after a few months… silence. As if he'd vanished again."

Mei Lin's eyes brimmed with years of grief, the ache of hope daring to blossom. "You truly believe it's him?"

Billy nodded gently. "With all my heart, I do."

Ava's breath caught. Her heart pounded in her chest—loud, fierce, undeniable.

"It's him," she whispered, her voice trembling. "I feel it. I know it. Dad's out there… somewhere. And he's trying to come back."

Tommy squeezed her hand. "Then we'll find him. Whatever it takes."

Billy nodded, his expression turning more resolute.

"I'll keep listening. But if we truly want to reach him, we'll need to try everything. I believe the greatest gift"—he looked directly at Ava—"is still awaiting you."

Ava turned to Mei Lin, her eyes bright with urgency.

"Mum… do we still have Dad's old radio?"

Mei Lin blinked, momentarily startled.

"Yes. It's in the attic. But, darling, it's so old—who knows if it still works?"

Ava turned back to Billy, her voice firm, alight with a new fire.

"Uncle Billy, you can fix it, can't you? You and I… we can try. Please."

Billy's eyes softened. He held her gaze for a long moment, then gave a quiet, resolute nod.

"Alright. I'll come by tomorrow. We'll see what we can do."

And in that moment—beneath the velvet night sky, with wedding lights flickering and distant music fading—hope stirred anew. Not loud, not certain, but real. A fragile thread across time, stretching between what was lost and what might yet be found.

Ava clutched Tommy's hand, tears gliding down her cheeks.

"This is too important," she whispered. "We can't let go. We owe it to him… to all of us."

The next day, in their modest kitchen, the atmosphere was charged with anticipation. Everyone gathered around the dusty, battered radio—an old relic that had once belonged to her father. Though scratched and worn, it was priceless, a bridge to the past that still resonated with meaning.

Billy placed it carefully on the table, his movements precise. He adjusted wires, tested the antenna, tuned the dials with a steady hand, and checked each connection. The soft clicks and static of the radio filled the silence, each sound a heartbeat.

Ava stood close, her face pale yet resolute, her eyes fixed on the radio as if willing it to spring to life.

"Alright," Billy said softly, the weight of the moment in his voice. "I'm going to try."

He leaned in, his fingers hovering over the microphone, then pressed the button.

"Eun Soo, are you there?" he said, his voice firm yet gentle. "If you can hear me… please. You must answer."

He took a deep breath, tuned the radio to a clear frequency, and spoke into the microphone with a blend of trepidation and hope.

"Eun Soo… this is Billy. I'm here, and I believe you're out there. If you can hear me, please—say something. We're waiting. We're here for you."

The room fell silent, save for the crackle of static and the faint hum of the radio. Billy's voice echoed into the stillness, repeating his plea.

"Eun Soo, it's Billy. I know you're out there. We've been searching for you for so long. Please, if you're listening—say something. Just let us know you're safe."

Minutes stretched on, each heavy with tension. The hope that perhaps—just perhaps—Daniel was listening wasn't enough to coax him from the shadows. The static persisted, cold and unrelenting.

Meanwhile, in Korea, Daniel sat alone in a dimly lit room, hunched over a small, ancient radio. Billy's voice crackled through the speakers—familiar yet distant—calling out across the miles. He listened intently, every fibre of his being tense, every nerve raw with longing to respond.

But fear gripped him tighter than hope. The voice was unmistakable now. What if he answered—and it was merely a mirage? What if the truth haunted him?

Tears streamed down his face as he clenched his fists, trembling in the dark. He rose and paced the room, yearning to seize the microphone and shout,

"I'm here! I'm here!"

But he didn't. The words on the radio went unanswered, and his heart ached under the weight of silence.

Needing to hide, to shield himself, he could not speak. Instead, he listened, tears falling silently like rain—caught between longing and fear, helpless yet desperately yearning.

Time dragged on, slow and heavy. Billy's voice repeated the call, steady and pleading,

"Eun Soo… if you can hear us, please. We're waiting for you."

But no answer came. Only static filled the air—the vast distance unbridgeable.

At last, Billy sighed softly, the weight of disappointment settling over him. His gaze met Ava's, her eyes glistening and streaked with tears.

Gently, he reached out and rested a hand on her shoulder.

"I'm sorry," Billy said softly, his voice thick with emotion. "But we'll keep trying. I know he's out there. I believe that with all my heart. We'll keep listening, keep reaching—because somewhere out there, Daniel is still striving to find his way back."

Ava nodded through her tears, clutching her father's old radio close to her heart. The hope was faint but glimmering. Deep down, they all knew that, even if shadows of doubt lingered, the connection—the bond—was never truly broken.

Their belief in Daniel's strength and love was what would keep their hope alive, no matter how long the night's shadows stretched.

Mei Lin looked at Billy and said softly,

"As you're leaving to go back home tomorrow evening, please come by for lunch before you go. I know Daniel would have loved to be here too."

Billy nodded, thanked everyone, then walked over to Ava and embraced her warmly.

"I'm sorry, Ava. I didn't mean to upset you on your wedding day, but I thought… well, you know."

Ava stood, and hugged Billy. "Uncle Billy, this is the best present anyone could have given me, we will keep trying"

With that, Billy turned and stepped out into the cool night air, closing the door gently behind him.

As the night wore on, the house grew quiet and still. The soft hum of crickets outside and the faint glimmer of moonlight streaming through the windows created an atmosphere both serene and heavy with unspoken longing.

In the dim silence, Mei Lin gently touched Ava's shoulder.

"It's late," she whispered softly, her voice gentle yet weary. "We're all exhausted. You and Tommy should stay here tonight, and not go to the hotel. Rest—just for a little while."

Ava looked up at her mother, eyes red and glistening with unshed tears. Nodding gently, she squeezed Tommy's hand, and together they ascended the stairs, retreating to their room, each grappling with the restless tide of emotions within.

But as the house settled into a hush of peaceful slumber, Ava lay awake, her thoughts tangled and heavy with longing.

Sleep eluded her, chased away by the fragile ember of hope that still glowed from the night before.

Quietly, she slipped from beneath the covers, careful not to wake Tommy, and crept softly down the stairs into the dim, still living room.

Moonlight streamed through the curtains, casting silvery shadows across the floor. Ava approached the old ham radio—her father's radio. Once merely a timeworn relic, it had become something more: a lifeline to the past, a beacon for the future.

Her fingers hovered over it, hesitant yet reverent. The dials were cold to her touch. The device was silent… until she switched it on.

A crackle. Then soft static.

She swallowed hard, her hands trembling as she adjusted the knobs. A surge of emotion welled in her chest as she leaned towards the microphone.

"Dad? This is Ava," she whispered, her voice barely more than a breath. "I'm alone now. I… I don't know where you are, but I'm here. I'm waiting. Please… talk to me. Please." Her voice faltered, thick with grief.

"Dad, it's Ava—your daughter. Please answer me."

She paused, then added with urgency, "Eun Soo… I know you've been speaking to Uncle Billy. Please… if you can hear me, say something."

Far away, deep in the mist-veiled mountains of Korea, Daniel sat hunched in a small, dimly lit room. The soft orange glow of the radio illuminated his face. Jung and Soon Hee had long since gone to sleep, leaving him alone with the static. Then—faintly—her voice.

Daniel's breath caught. His pulse thundered in his ears. It couldn't be. Could it?

Her words stirred something deep and wild within him—something long locked away. Fear clutched at him, memories flashing like sparks—uncertain, painful, unresolved.

He hesitated, his heart pounding.

Then, with a trembling hand, he pressed the receiver. His voice cracked through the static like a ghost.

"Hello… this is Eun Soo. Do I know you?"

To Ava, the voice was unmistakable. Though strained and uncertain, it struck her heart like lightning. She gasped, tears springing instantly to her eyes. Her fingers trembled against the mic.

"Oh my God," she choked out. "I've waited so long to hear your voice." Her sobs broke free before she could stop them. Still, she pressed on, summoning the courage she'd been building for years.

"Eun Soo… this might sound impossible, but I think you're my dad."

Back in Korea, Daniel reeled. The name—Ava—sliced through the fog like a blade. His chest tightened. His vision blurred. The world spun.

"Ava?" he murmured, the name fragile on his lips. "Do I… do I know you?"

"Dad! Yes, it's me," Ava whispered urgently. "I'm here. Please… talk to me. I miss you. I've always missed you. Just say something… anything. I love you."

The line crackled. The signal faltered, stuttering in and out like a dream teetering on the edge of fading. Ava gripped the mic tighter, every fibre of her being pouring into her voice.

"Dad, please… I need to hear you again."

Then, faintly, a sound. A name repeated—soft, disbelieving, brimming with tremor and wonder.

"Ava… Ava… Ava…"

Daniel's hands flew to his head. The room spun wildly. He stumbled backward, and then, like a marionette with its strings severed, he collapsed onto the sofa.

The static returned, steady and hollow.

Ava leaned closer, desperately straining for more. "Dad? Dad?!"

But there was nothing.

Miles away, Daniel lay unconscious. Yet in his mind, something extraordinary was unfolding. It was like tumbling through time—memories rushing past like stardust on a current of light. He saw Singapore: warm skies, golden beaches, bustling streets alive with laughter. Mei Lin's eyes. Their wedding day. The first time he held Ava. The joy in her tiny face. Her first steps. Her voice calling him "Daddy" from the sand.

It all came back—clear, vivid, unstoppable.

The sound of her voice had shattered the dam.

It had called him home.

All this time, Ava kept talking—whispering into the void, clinging to hope that somehow, somewhere, her father would hear her. Her words drifted across the static, carrying her love and longing into the shadows, waiting for light to pierce the darkness once again.

Again and again, Ava tried to reconnect, unaware that thousands of miles away, in a remote mountain cabin in Korea, she had finally reached him—only for him to collapse before he could respond.

She didn't know. She couldn't have known.

Just as she was about to switch off the radio, the weight of disappointment pressing heavily against her chest, a faint crackle pierced the silence. A voice—barely a whisper—trembled through the static.

"Ava…? Is that you?"

Ava's breath caught in her throat. The world stilled.

The voice was fragile, hesitant, barely clinging to the moment, but unmistakably his.

"I think… I might be your dad. You sound familiar…" Daniel's voice broke, every word strained and laden with emotion—as if it pained him to speak, to believe, to hope.

Ava's knees buckled, her body folding as she gripped the edge of the table. Tears streamed down her face as the moment she had dreamt of finally arrived.

"Daddy?" she gasped, barely able to form the word. "My God… is it really you?"

A sob escaped her lips.

"I've missed you so much. I never stopped looking. I never stopped hoping. Why did you leave? Why didn't you come back to me and Mum here in Singapore?"

She was sobbing now—loud, unrestrained, her heart breaking wide open. "Wait—wait—I need to get Mum. She has to hear this. I need to get her, don't leave, please—"

But on the other end of the line, Daniel was unravelling.

In the dim, flickering light of the cabin, he gripped the edge of the table to steady himself. The weight of Ava's voice—the memories it stirred—was too much, too sudden. His chest heaved with confusion. Her name echoed in his mind, reverberating through fragile, newly awakened memories that felt too vast to contain.

"Ava…" he whispered, the name a question and a prayer entwined. "I… I need to go. I can't… I'm not sure what's real. I'm sorry. I need time."

His voice cracked. "We'll talk again, I promise. But I need to go."

And then—silence.

The static returned, then faded to a hollow hush.

Ava stared at the radio, stricken.

"No, no—don't leave—please—"

But it was too late.

The voice, so fleeting, was gone. The connection severed. Her chest pounded, her breath catching in her throat. The moment had slipped through her grasp.

Without thinking, she bolted up the stairs, the wooden steps cold against her bare feet. Her heart raced, each beat pulsing with urgency. She reached the landing and tore down the corridor, her hand trembling as she flung open her mother's bedroom door.

"Mum!" she cried. "Mum, wake up!"

Mei Lin stirred, blinking in confusion as she fumbled for the lamp. The soft glow bathed the room, casting light on Ava's tear-streaked face and quivering frame.

"Ava?" Mei Lin murmured, her voice heavy with sleep. "What is it? What's wrong?"

Ava drew a ragged breath, her voice trembling. "It's him," she whispered, eyes wide and glistening. "It's Dad. I heard him. I spoke to him. He's alive."

Mei Lin's eyes widened, her mind reeling between hope and disbelief. For a moment, she simply stared, her body trembling as her heart grappled with Ava's words.

Then, slowly, still trembling, Mei Lin rose from the bed, slipping into her dressing gown. She enveloped Ava in a fierce embrace, holding her tightly as tears blurred her vision. For a long moment, neither spoke—they clung to each other, overwhelmed by the possibility that, after all these years, her husband was alive and calling to them across the distance.

"Is it really him?" Mei Lin whispered, her voice thick with tears. "Are you certain?" She glanced at her stepfather, who smiled back and nodded.

Ava nodded fervently, clutching her mother close. "Yes, I'm certain. I spoke to him, Mum. It was his voice—just as it was before. We shared everything—I know he's out there. I just know it."

In that moment, the shadows of doubt and despair gave way to something brighter—hope, fierce and unyielding. The future brimmed with new possibilities. Her heart pounding, Ava whispered again, "He's alive, Mum. Dad is alive."

Gerry looked on, drawing his robe about himself. "I'll make us some tea, and you can tell us everything."

Ava and Mei Lin nodded. As she clung to her mother, Ava felt an almost surreal sense that fate had finally begun to turn in their favour.

The next morning, as the sun cast its first golden rays over the horizon, the doorbell rang. Ava rushed to answer it, her spirit alight with anticipation. Standing on the doorstep was Billy—her father's old ham radio friend—wearing his familiar hat and carrying a small, battered bag. His face was weathered, but his eyes gleamed with quiet hope.

"After your call, I thought I'd come by early," Billy said softly, stepping inside. "Mei Lin told me to come over later today before I left for the airport, but this couldn't wait. I needed to hear everything."

Ava practically glowed as she led him into the living room.

"Billy, you won't believe what happened last night. I was down here, trying to reach him… and then, I heard it. His voice. Dad's voice. He answered me. I spoke to him—he's out there, Billy. I'm certain of it!"

Billy's eyes widened in disbelief, a slow smile spreading across his face.

"You're telling me… you actually spoke to him?" He leaned closer, almost afraid to believe it. "That's incredible. That's—well, that's a miracle."

Ava nodded fervently, clasping her hands together. "We're not certain exactly where he is, but he knows I'm here. He answered, and his voice was so clear… I could hardly believe it." Her voice trembled with emotion. "He said it was overwhelming and he needed time to process it all."

Billy sat back, visibly overwhelmed, nodding slowly. "That's astonishing, Ava. Truly astonishing. This changes everything. If he's out there listening, he's still fighting— that means there's still hope. I understand he needs time; he has a whole life and now one he didn't know existed."

Billy regarded her with a careful, searching gaze. "So, what's next? We keep trying, keep the connection alive. Perhaps, if fortune favours us, we'll hear him again—the right way this time. We'll keep calling until he can respond."

Ava's eyes gleamed with fierce determination. "Yes! We keep trying, Billy. I shan't give up. I know he's out there. I feel it in my heart. I believe I'll hear him again. And next time, I'll ensure he knows it's me—his little girl—waiting for him."

Billy nodded solemnly, gently resting his hand on her shoulder. "I promise, Ava, we'll do everything we can. I'll keep listening—every day, every night. Your father's spirit is strong, and I believe he's reaching out to us. We must be patient—and never lose hope."

Khian-Seng, who had been sitting in the corner, jumped to his feet.

"I must go to Korea again and get him!" he exclaimed.

Mei Lin placed an arm around him. "We must wait a little longer. He needs time to adjust to what he's just been told. If you show up unexpectedly, assuming you can even find him, it could have a serious effect on him. Let's wait until he's ready."

In their eyes, amidst the tears and trembling smiles, burned a renewed fire—an unbreakable vow that, no matter how long the shadows lingered, they would keep reaching out. For in their hearts, they knew Daniel was somewhere in Korea, though his precise whereabouts remained a mystery.

16

The Life I No Longer Know
(Korea)

Daniel woke that morning with a sense of disorientation, as if everything in his mind were a flickering shadow—faint images and voices he couldn't quite grasp. His eyes fluttered open, and the room gradually came into focus. It was his familiar space in the village, yet everything felt distant, like a life he no longer recognised.

Gently, he reached out and shook Jung's shoulder. "Jung," he whispered, his voice trembling, "I need to tell you something… I had a strange conversation last night. It's about my past—about someone named Ava."

She stirred slowly, her eyes fluttering open, filled with soft concern. "What? What did you hear?" Her voice was husky from sleep, but her expression sharpened as she sensed his unease.

He sat up, struggling to piece together the words. "There was a voice… I heard it clearly, though I don't fully understand. It sounded like someone calling to me. They mentioned… a girl's name—Ava, she said I was her father. And… well, I passed out, and in a dream, things came flooding back— images and faces. I saw fleeting glimpses—a little girl I don't quite recognise, and a woman who seemed… familiar. I know I was married. But the details elude me. I don't know who I am now. She said I was from Singapore!"

Jung listened, gently squeezing his trembling hands. Her heart ached for him, for the struggle to hold together the fragments of his fractured memory. "It's alright," she said softly, her voice brimming with reassurance. "You're trying to make sense of something long buried. That's why it's confusing. But we'll take this one step at a time. You're not alone. I'm here, and we'll uncover what's real—together."

His eyes searched hers, filled with fear but tinged with a fragile glimmer of hope. "I don't want to rush," he whispered. "I'm afraid to reach out again. I don't know what's real anymore—what this life is, what came before. I need to understand what's true, what's merely echoes in my mind. I need time!"

Jung nodded, her emotions entwined with empathy. "Take your time. We'll go at your pace. Whatever you recall, whatever you feel, we'll face it step by step," she said softly, gently brushing his hair. "We'll rebuild as best we can, even if the pieces seem shattered now."

Daniel closed his eyes, striving to steady the chaos within. The life he thought he knew—the one he dared to hope still existed—was slipping further away with each passing moment. Yet, amidst the confusion, within the shadows of his lost memories, a faint thread of love and hope endured. For now, that was enough: to move forward cautiously, seeking a path back—towards a life he no longer recognised, yet still carried within him. The weight of a thousand memories—some vivid, many confounding—pressed heavily on his chest.

The room was silent, thick with unspoken emotions, as Jung gently clasped his trembling hand. Her eyes searched his face, brimming with love, longing, and deep concern. She saw him struggling, caught between two worlds: the life he lived now with her and Soon Hee in Korea, and the daughter he lost in 1963, Ava, when the accident tore their family apart.

"Daniel," Jung whispered softly, her voice trembling with emotion, "it's alright. You're grappling with years of buried memories, some hidden deep within your mind. Don't rush it—this will take time, and the faster you try to go, the more muddled you'll feel. Let's take it slowly. Your mind is stubborn—you do recall her, don't you? Your little girl in Singapore, Ava. The one you had to leave behind. I know you love Soon Hee, and she's your daughter here, but you're still tied to a girl named Ava in Singapore—she remains part of you, even if your memories of her are jumbled and distant. We knew you had a past life; we just never uncovered it. Now it seems you have."

He looked into her eyes, pain and confusion flickering in his own. "I… I recall her," he whispered, his voice cracking. "But… it's like remembering a half-forgotten dream. I hear her laugh, see her face, but I don't know her anymore. I feel her love… but I don't know how to reach her again. I don't know which life is real and which isn't."

Tears shimmered in Jung's eyes as she gently supported him. "That girl—Ava—is your daughter, too. I'm certain she loved you more than anything in the world. She's waiting for you to find her—still hoping, still loving. But I'm worried, Daniel. I love Soon Hee. She's our daughter here, in Korea, right beside us. Ava, though, is the daughter you knew, the girl you had in Singapore before the accident. We need to learn more before we tell her she may have a sister—for her sake, and for ours."

His shoulders trembled as tears spilled, unrestrained and raw. "I feel… I know I loved Ava. I hear her voice, see her smile, but I don't recall everything. My mind is a puzzle missing countless pieces, and I fear I'll never piece it together. I want to believe this is true. I've waited so long to discover who I truly was—to the point where I forgot, and it ceased to matter. This life with you and Soon Hee is one I cherish, a life I don't want to change, despite the unanswered questions I must resolve. But I'm afraid, Jung, so very afraid of what I'll uncover. I don't know how to move forward—I don't know if I ever will."

Daniel's voice trembled with doubt. Jung reached out, her hand gently stroking his hair, her eyes brimming with compassion and unwavering support. She brushed a few strands from his forehead, her touch soothing.

"We'll uncover this together," Jung whispered softly, her voice a quiet promise. "Step by step, we'll find a path that you—and everyone else—can embrace."

He closed his eyes, enveloped by her warmth and comfort. The steady cadence of her voice and the gentle caress of her hand gradually soothed him, and soon, exhaustion overtook him. Daniel drifted into sleep, the tension eased for now by her presence.

But suddenly, he awoke with a start—something had jolted him from that fragile peace. The room was silent, yet a strange urgency lingered, as if a whisper of hope still hovered in the ether.

Jung sat beside him, her eyes soft yet hopeful. "I've prepared something to eat," she said gently. "Come, let's sit at the table. A bit of food might help clear your mind."

Daniel nodded slowly, rising from the bed, and made his way to the small, humble table. The aroma of warm rice and simple soup filled the air, offering a rare moment of grounding.

Just as he settled into the chair, Soon Hee bounded into the room, her face alight with concern. "Are you alright,

Daddy?" she asked softly, sitting beside him, her small hand reaching out to clasp his.

He gazed at her, weary but touched by her tenderness. "I'm alright, sweetheart," he murmured. "Just… trying to sort everything out in my mind."

Soon Hee looked at him with wide, curious eyes. "It's a lot, isn't it? Do what I do—take your time."

He managed a faint smile. "Yes, I will. Good advice, as always."

Jung watched quietly, a gentle smile touching her lips. She hesitated for a moment before speaking. "I've been thinking," she said softly. "I have an idea. Perhaps… I could try reaching out to Ava on the radio. We could see if she can hear us, and perhaps, just perhaps, we could unravel this to help you."

Daniel looked up, initially uncertain, then vulnerable. "I don't know," he whispered, his voice trembling. "I'm scared. What if I can't recall everything? What if I can't understand?"

Jung reached across and clasped his hand, offering reassurance. "We don't have to do anything you're not ready for. But perhaps speaking to Ava—hearing her voice—might help you discern what's real and what isn't. It might bring some answers. What do you think?"

He hesitated, his mind torn between hope and fear. "I don't know, Jung," he said quietly. "I'm frightened. What if hearing her again… makes everything worse? What if I become even more lost within myself?"

Jung offered a gentle smile. "Whatever you decide, it was merely a suggestion. Take your time, and when you're ready, we'll do what you choose."

Over the subsequent weeks and months, Daniel grappled constantly with thoughts of what lay beyond the radio. His heart yearned to reconnect with the life he'd lost—with Ava, the girl waiting for him in Singapore. Yet another part of him faltered, haunted by fear—what if he couldn't bear what he discovered? What if the past he recalled was but a fragile illusion, unlike the real life he lived now?

He often wandered into the mountains alone, treading narrow, winding paths, his mind adrift in memories and doubts. At times, he spent hours with Soon Hee, playing quietly in the yard or hiding in the woods, her bright laughter ringing out as she chased butterflies or climbed trees. When she searched for him, he would hide gently, his heart aching, watching her grow and smile, striving to hold onto the love they shared. Those precious moments grounded him, reminding him of the family he still held—the daughter in Korea, Soon Hee, and the love enduring beyond the shadows of his lost memories.

The torment—those restless nights filled with voices and static—began to erode his spirit. Unanswered questions gnawed at his core, twisting deep within his soul, until even he questioned whether he could bear the uncertainty any longer.

Witnessing his anguish, Jung resolved to act. One tranquil evening, when Daniel had slipped into a peaceful sleep after a day wandering the hills, she approached the radio. Her hands trembled slightly as she switched it on, her heart pounding with hope and trepidation. Carefully, she adjusted the dials, her mind racing—what if this was his chance? What if she could reach Ava and, somehow, draw her father back from the shadows?

She took a deep breath, her voice soft yet steady as she pressed the button. "Ava, if you can hear me," she whispered into the silence, "this is Jung, Eun Soo's friend. My name is Jung." She deemed it prudent to establish a connection before revealing the full truth about Daniel's new life.

The static sputtered and hissed. For long moments, silence. Then, faintly—almost like a whisper carried on the wind— an answer emerged. The radio crackled as a distant voice broke through, fragile and trembling, yet unmistakably recognising: "This is Ava… Oh, thank you, Jung, thank you for this. Is my dad with you? Is he alright? It's so good to speak to someone. I've waited every evening for months, hoping against hope."

Tears blurred Jung's vision as she listened, her heart pounding like a drum. She scarcely dared to believe it, yet hope flickered alive in her chest. "Ava…" she whispered softly, her voice thick with emotion. "Can you hear me? Your father is striving to find his way back. He needs time to adjust. Please be patient—everything will be alright."

And so, in that tranquil night, when the world seemed to pause, Jung reached out across the distance. Her voice, trembling yet resolute, echoed into the static, calling her husband's lost spirit home.

Jung spoke gently to Ava, her voice tender and laden with emotion. "Sweetheart," she whispered softly, "I understand you want answers—why your father left, whether he'll return. I know he longs for that too. But we must remember—your father has lived a different life for many years, one he believed was his only life, the only one he knew—until now."

Ava's voice trembled with a mix of confusion and longing, her questions echoing through the static.

Jung continued gently, "Since you spoke, he's been searching within himself, striving to discern what's real and what isn't. Learning he had another family, someone waiting for him—it's all new to him. It's like discovering a world he never knew existed. That takes time and patience. He needs time to process everything—to recall what he's lost and to shape what his new life might be."

"So… I just have to be patient?" Ava's voice wavered, heavy with emotion.

"I know it's hard," Jung replied softly, "but sometimes the greatest love is shown in waiting—waiting for someone to return, to remember who they are, and to realise that love never truly fades, even when things seem shattered."

Ava took a deep breath, clutching her mother's hand tightly. "I want him to come home," she whispered, her voice quivering. "I miss him so much."

"We all do, sweetheart. But the most important thing is to hold on to hope—hope that one day your father will remember everything. And when he does, he'll return to us. Until then, we must believe and wait with all our hearts."

17

The Confession
(Korea)

For months, Jung had been speaking with Ava, their conversations weaving a fragile bridge across time and distance—a delicate thread of hope binding two hearts. Each night, as Daniel slept, Jung tuned the old radio with trembling hands, seeking the distant voice of the daughter he no longer remembered. Ava's words carried longing, love, and desperation; the ache in every syllable pierced Jung's heart deeply.

She understood how profoundly Ava missed her father—how vast and deep the void was. Though decades of silence had stretched between them, Jung believed it wasn't too late to mend the broken bonds. Quietly and patiently, she poured all her compassion into those crackling conversations, forging something new—something stronger than memory.

One morning, as the first soft rays of light filtered through the thin curtains, Jung leaned in and gently shook Daniel awake.

He blinked slowly, his eyes clouded at first, then settling on her with quiet tenderness.

"Daniel," she said softly, brushing a lock of hair from his forehead, "will you come for a walk with me? Just to our spot—the one overlooking the valley."

He hesitated for a moment, sensing something unusual in her tone, then nodded.

The morning air was crisp, birdsong dancing across the sky as they stepped onto the dewy grass. Their walk began in silence, the only sound the soft crunch of footsteps along the worn path.

When they reached the familiar overlook, a gentle breeze stirred through the trees, rustling the leaves and brushing against Daniel's skin like a whispered memory.

Below, the valley stretched endlessly, bathed in golden light. Daniel stood still, his gaze lost in the horizon, a flicker of thought tugging at the edges of his expression.

Jung drew a steadying breath.

"Daniel… I need to tell you something," she said quietly. "Please, just listen before you react. This won't be easy, but I've kept it from you long enough."

He turned towards her, concern tightening his brow.

"What is it?"

She clasped her hands tightly, steadying herself.

"I've been talking to Ava on the radio," Jung said, her voice barely above a whisper. "The girl from Singapore… she's your daughter, Daniel. I'm certain of it."

He didn't move.

"We've spoken many times now," she went on, her words gentle yet urgent. "She's been searching for you—desperate to reconnect. She fears she'll never see you again."

Daniel's body stiffened. His gaze fell to the earth at his feet.

"She's held on all these years," Jung continued, her voice quivering. "She still loves you. She never stopped. She's grown into a strong, beautiful woman—and all she wants is a chance to reclaim what was taken from you both."

Still, he said nothing. His jaw tightened, the tendons in his neck taut. Slowly, he turned his face back towards the valley.

A storm passed through his features—grief, disbelief, guilt, confusion. Emotions too vast for words, too deep for reason.

"You've been speaking to her?" he asked at last, his voice hoarse and fragile. "And you're certain?"

"I am," Jung said, her eyes glistening with tears. "There's no doubt. Her words… her stories… her heart. It's Ava, your daughter, and she's never stopped believing you were alive."

Daniel's knees buckled beneath the weight of it all. The years lost—the birthdays missed, the nights she must have cried alone—crashed over him like a tidal wave.

His breath hitched, hands trembling as they clutched the edge of the railing.

"I want to see her," he whispered, his voice breaking. "I need to. I need to tell her… I didn't choose to disappear. That I never stopped loving her. I want to make this right."

Jung reached for his hand, holding it tightly, her touch steady and reassuring.

"We'll get there, Daniel. It won't be easy—but she's waiting. She's ready. And I'll help you remember, piece by piece, until you're whole again."

He nodded slowly, tears slipping down his cheeks as his gaze remained fixed on the distant horizon.

"There's something else, too. Your wife, Mei Lin. Do you remember her?"

"It's painful to admit this, but yes, I've been thinking of her. Over the past few weeks, I've had vivid dreams as I process this," he said.

"Well, she waited many years for you, but when you were declared dead by the Koreans, as you'd been missing for so long, she remarried."

There was a silent pause as Daniel processed the information he'd been given.

"Well, that seems only fair, especially if she thought I was dead," he said.

They sat in silence, contemplating this profound change in their lives.

Finally, Jung's voice broke the quiet. "We need to tell Soon Hee."

Daniel's nod was firm this time. "Yes. When we return."

They walked home slowly, the cabin rising ahead like a quiet promise. The air around them hummed with unspoken tension—a delicate balance of fear and hope.

Inside, Daniel called out, his voice calm yet resolute.

"Soon Hee? Could you come here a moment, please?"

She paddled into the room, brushing a loose strand of hair from her face. Her brow furrowed as she registered their serious expressions.

"Hello, my darling," Daniel said gently. "Come sit down. Your mum and I have something important to tell you."

Soon Hee's face fell, worry clouding her eyes.

"Are you… getting a divorce?" she asked.

Jung smiled softly, shaking her head.

"No, nothing like that."

Daniel reached out, taking Soon Hee's hand as she settled between them. He drew a deep breath, steadying himself.

"When I first met your mum," he began slowly, "it was after an accident. I had lost my memory. Your mum helped me recover—helped me become the man I am now."

"I know, Dad," Soon Hee said quietly, her voice steady yet cautious. "You've told me that story many times."

He nodded slowly, then met her gaze with a vulnerability she had never seen before.

"But what I didn't know… what I couldn't remember… was that I had another life before this one."

Soon Hee's eyes widened, hanging on his every word.

"Only recently have I begun to uncover who I truly was," he continued.

Soon Hee tilted her head, half-teasing to ease the tension. "So… who are you, Dad? Anything exciting? A secret agent, perhaps?"

Daniel managed a faint smile, shaking his head.

"No, nothing that thrilling. I'm originally from Singapore. My real name is Daniel Walker-Chung. And the biggest part of the story is… I have a daughter from a marriage before I met your mum."

Soon Hee blinked, confusion and surprise flickering across her face.

"What do you mean?" she asked.

Daniel swallowed hard. "You have a sister, Soon Hee. Her name is Ava. She's my daughter. I lost her… when I lost myself. But she's found me again."

For a long moment, silence hung between them.

Soon Hee stared at them, her mouth slightly open. Then she whispered, "I have a sister?"

Daniel's heart clenched. "Yes. And she wants to meet you. She wants to meet us all."

There was a beat—a breathless pause—then Soon Hee's eyes lit up.

"Wait… a sister?" she said again, disbelief melting into wonder. "A real one?"

Jung laughed softly through her tears. "Yes, a real one."

Soon Hee's face broke into a wide grin. "That's brilliant! I've always wanted a sister! When can I talk to her?"

Daniel exhaled deeply, moved beyond words. His lips curved into a gentle, grateful smile.

"Soon," he said softly. "Very soon."

"Brilliant! I have a big sister!" she exclaimed, again.

"Yes, you do," Daniel said, smiling gently.

"I'm so excited! Hopefully I can meet her soon? This is so brilliant, Dad! Anyway, I'm off to meet my friends—I can't wait to tell them all about it."

With that, Soon Hee dashed out the door and down the road.

"Well, that was rather easier than I expected," Jung said with a soft laugh, heading towards the kitchen. "Shall we try to reach Ava on the radio this evening?"

Daniel glanced at Jung and nodded. "Yes, let's do that."

That evening, Daniel approached the old radio, his hands trembling slightly as he switched it on. Jung and Soon Hee sat close beside him, their fingers intertwined, drawing strength from their shared hope.

"Now," Daniel said softly, his voice thick with emotion, "Ava, this is Dad. Are you there? It's me—your father."

He repeated the message into the crackling static, his voice wavering yet fervent, desperate to reach the daughter he scarcely remembered but loved more fiercely than words could express.

Far away in Singapore, the faint hum of the radio crackled through the speakers, carrying the fragile hope that Ava might be listening.

"Hello, Ava," Daniel said again, his voice breaking with emotion. "This is Dad. If you can hear me, please… answer. Please."

His words vanished into the static, unanswered but heavy with longing. He drew a deep breath, his eyes fixed on the faint glow of the radio's dial.

"Let's not fret," Jung said softly, striving to steady her voice. "I told her to listen today—I knew we'd be speaking soon."

A long silence stretched, then suddenly, through the crackling static, a fragile yet unmistakable voice broke through.

"Hello, Dad… this is Ava."

The room brimmed with tears—raw, uncontainable tears of hearts stretched across distance yet bound by love. Ava's voice quivered with emotion, a fragile beacon of hope and love that transcended years and silence.

"Dad," Ava choked out, her voice trembling with pain and longing, "I'm so sorry. So very sorry… for everything. I wish I could tell you how much I've missed you."

"Please—stop," Daniel replied, his voice breaking. "It's not your fault, nor mine. What matters now is that we make up for the time we've lost. So much has happened, but I want to see you. I want to finally see you. Ava… what about Mum? How is she?"

"She's here, Dad. She's listening."

There was a pause, then the soft rustle of movement on the other side.

Mei Lin stepped forward, her hands trembling slightly as she took the microphone and pressed the button gently.

"Hello, Daniel. This is Mei Lin." Her voice was tender yet brimming with emotion. "You'll never know how long I've waited to hear your voice again. I never lost hope that you were still alive."

Tears streamed down Mei Lin's cheeks as Gerry stood beside her, his arm gently around her shoulders. She glanced up at him, her expression caught between relief and heartbreak.

"Daniel, there are so many things to say—so much has happened in our lives," she said.

Mei Lin's words spilled out in a rush, tears flowing as she poured her heart across the miles.

Daniel's eyes brimmed with tears, his voice thick with emotion.

Then Mei Lin turned slightly to Gerry and said softly, "Daniel, I'll put Ava back on. She wishes to speak with you."

Before Ava could speak, Daniel leaned closer to the microphone, his voice quivering.

"Ava… my girl. I love you more than words can express. I've missed you every single day. I'm so sorry I wasn't there. I wish I could turn back time."

"Dad, stop," Ava interrupted gently yet firmly. "We need to talk… and we need to meet in person."

There was a brief pause. Then her voice returned, steadier now.

"I'm sending you three tickets to Singapore. We'll meet here—and from that moment, we'll begin the rest of our lives together. Plus, I want to meet my little sister Jung has told me about all these months."

In that moment, the world seemed to pause—the tears, the hope, the love converging into a single, unbreakable wave across the distance. For the first time in years, the shadows melted away, replaced by the promise of a future—one built on love, healing, and the courage to face whatever lay ahead.

Daniel's mind swirled with anticipation, love, and fear. Each heartbeat echoed with the possibility of finally holding his daughter—of seeing her face, hearing her voice, and telling her how deeply he loved her. Yet beneath the excitement ran a quiet undercurrent of doubt.

What if he had forgotten too much?

What if he wasn't the father she remembered?

Could he truly begin again… or were the lost years lost forever?

In the days that followed, the cabin hummed with quiet urgency. Bags were packed, tickets arranged, documents double-checked—each task infused with the weight of something long hoped for and now within reach. Jung moved through the flurry with steady hands and a trembling heart. Her eyes shimmered with hope, though traces of worry lingered. She understood how much this moment meant—especially to Ava, whose voice still echoed through their nights like a distant lullaby. Everything had to be perfect.

Half a world away, Ava was a bundle of nerves and anticipation. Her heart raced with each passing day, each tick of the clock bringing her closer. She spent hours rehearsing what she'd say when they met—how she'd express through tears how deeply she had missed him.

Beside her bed stood a small suitcase, ever ready. Inside were carefully chosen treasures: faded drawings, old photographs, messages—all fragments of a love that had lingered in the shadows for far too long.

On the morning before their departure, Ava and Mei Lin sat together in quiet stillness, drawing comfort from their closeness. No one needed to fill the silence—it was enough to share the space, to breathe the air heavy with anticipation.

Ava wrapped her arms tightly around her mother, holding on for a long moment. Then she turned to Gerry.

"How are you feeling about all this, Gerry?" she asked.

He smiled, his eyes soft with affection. "To be honest, I'm simply happy to see you happy. That's more than enough for me."

Ava's eyes welled up as she leaned forward and kissed Gerry gently on the cheek. "I'm so lucky," she said softly. "I've had two remarkable fathers."

Back in the cabin, the time had come to leave Korea and embark on their journey to Singapore. The house hummed with last-minute activity—zippers pulled shut, bags lifted, lights switched off. Every step carried profound meaning, each heartbeat a drum of hope and fear.

As they made their way towards the waiting bus, the world outside seemed to pause—still and breathless, as if it, too, sensed everything was about to change.

"Do we have the passports?" Daniel asked, his voice taut as he glanced at the pile of luggage near the door.

Jung reached out and touched his arm, her voice calm yet reassuring. "Yes, we've got everything. It's all going to be fine. Just breathe."

He nodded, though the flutter in his chest wouldn't ease. It wasn't merely travel nerves—it was the weight of returning to a place he couldn't recall, yet deep down, he knew had once been home.

The bus rumbled to life beneath them, jolting slightly as it rolled onto the uneven road. Through the windows, the city flashed by—familiar sights tinged with distant memories, softened by time and longing.

Inside, a quiet tide of nervous energy swelled.

Daniel sat still, clutching the tickets as though they anchored him to this new reality. His gaze remained fixed on the passing streets, but his thoughts raced—fears and hopes colliding, each more vivid than the last.

In that moment, as the bus shook and rattled towards the airport, they all understood—whatever lay ahead, this was the start of the greatest journey their family had ever undertaken. At last, the path to hope had opened, winding steadily towards the future they had longed to find.

18

The Arrival, Summer 1985
(Singapore)

At the airport, the whirl of movement, noise, and lights stirred a heady mix of excitement and apprehension. Soon Hee clutched her small carry-on tightly, her eyes wide with wonder as they approached the check-in desk.

"This is my first time on a plane," she told the attendant proudly, her voice a blend of pride and nerves.

The attendant smiled warmly. "You're going to love it. Window seat?"

"Yes, please!"

As the plane soared into the sky, Daniel sat beside Soon Hee, gazing out the window as clouds drifted by like fragments of forgotten memories. His mind raced with thoughts of what awaited in Singapore—Ava, Mei Lin, answers, the past.

Hours later, as the plane descended steadily towards Changi Airport, the cabin hummed with soft announcements and the quiet shuffle of passengers preparing for landing. Flight attendants moved gracefully through the aisles, checking seat belts, straightening trays, and offering final reminders.

Daniel sat silently, the new Korean passport heavy in his hands. Bark Eun Soo. The name stared back at him like a ghost. He had studied this passport countless times before, but now—now it felt strange. Alien. False.

This isn't me. The thought surged through him like a tidal wave breaching a dam. The name, the nationality, the life he'd built in Korea—all began to blur and unravel. It was like waking from a long, deep sleep, only to realise the dream had never been his at all.

He glanced out the window again, though Soon Hee was claiming most of it as she gazed. Yet, as the familiar skyline of Singapore emerged through the morning haze, a flood of memories returned. A sudden wave of clarity washed over him. I belong here. I always have.

His fingers trembled as he pressed the passport shut. A tightness gripped his chest—not quite fear, but the heavy weight of truth. Reaching into his coat pocket, he slipped a small tablet beneath his tongue, waiting for the pressure to ease. Eyes closed, he drew a deep, steadying breath.

Who am I? What is real?

The questions churned like storm clouds in his mind, threatening to overwhelm him. Then a warm hand found his arm—steady, reassuring.

"Daniel," Jung murmured, her voice soft and laden with quiet wisdom, "it's alright. You're here now. You're home. We'll uncover the answers together. Just breathe."

He opened his eyes, meeting Jung's serene, steadfast gaze beside him.

"It feels peculiar to be called Daniel after all these years," he whispered.

Jung offered a gentle smile, her hand lightly brushing his. "Then we'll call you whatever feels right. There's no hurry. We have time."

Beyond the window, Singapore sprawled beneath them—a memory poised to be reclaimed.

The plane descended steadily towards Changi Airport's tarmac. Within the cabin, a hushed anticipation thrummed. Flight attendants glided through the aisles, conducting final checks—securing harnesses, adjusting tray tables, and gently reminding passengers to keep their seatbelts fastened.

His heart thudded fiercely against his ribs—heavy, oppressive, yet strangely liberating. Sensing the familiar tightness creeping in, he slipped a tablet beneath his tongue to ease the angina and closed his eyes briefly.

The doubts—the questions—surged through his mind once more: Who am I? What is real? The boundaries between past and present blurred, intertwining like fleeting shadows. Was this why he had always felt like a stranger in his own mind? Why he roamed through memories that never quite belonged?

Just then, Jung's hand rested on his arm, warm and steadfast. Her voice, soft and brimming with gentle reassurance, broke through his thoughts. "Daniel," she whispered, "You will soon be seeing the daughter you haven't seen for many years, it's alright. I'm know she is as nervous as you are. One step at a time, you'll work it out together, at your own pace"

At that moment, the captain's voice crackled over the cabin speakers—steady, calm, grounding.

"Ladies and gentlemen, this is your captain speaking. Please ensure your seatbelts are fastened as we commence our descent into Changi Airport."

Almost at once, the seatbelt sign illuminated, and the cabin lights dimmed. Passengers settled into their seats—some with nervous glances, others with eager anticipation. The plane shuddered as it sliced through the thinning atmosphere, the familiar yet now strangely profound roar of the engines filling the cabin.

When the wheels touched the runway, gentle jolts propelled them forward. The warm, humid air of Singapore seeped in as the aircraft slowed, the city's skyline gleaming beneath the brilliant sun.

The doors creaked open, and the crew began preparing for disembarkation. With bags in hand and hearts thudding, passengers moved towards the bustling terminal. For Daniel, however, each step felt surreal—each one drawing him closer to an identity he was only now beginning to comprehend.

He took a deep breath, clasping Jung's hand tightly, and together they advanced towards the exit. The moment they stepped onto the tarmac, the warm humidity enveloped them like a familiar embrace—a poignant reminder of home. They pressed onward into the shimmering expanse of Changi Airport, where a long, emotional journey was drawing to a close—and a new chapter was dawning.

Their bags arrived swiftly, and they loaded them onto the trolley before setting off.

Hand in hand, Daniel and Jung walked with Soon Hee skipping beside them. They faced the crowd, hearts pounding with anticipation, standing on the threshold of the family reunion they had waited for so many years.

As Daniel wove through the bustling crowd, the world around him seemed to slow. The clamour and movement faded to a distant hum, as if time itself held its breath. The crowd parted gradually, clearing a path until, at last, he stood in stunned silence—face to face with the daughter he had yearned to see.

And there she was—the woman she had become. Ava. His Ava. Now fully grown, yet her face still echoed the little girl he knew, her radiant smile aglow with love and longing carried through the years. Tears streamed down her cheeks unbidden, catching the sunlight as she gazed at him, her eyes wide with awe and emotion.

Daniel's body felt suddenly heavy. Leaner now, weathered by time, he bore little resemblance to the young father she once knew. His face was etched with lines of age and experience, his hair streaked with grey, his eyes brimming with memories—once lost, now resurfacing. His breath caught as he looked at her, tears welling in his own eyes.

Without hesitation, Ava broke into a run, closing the distance with desperate urgency. Overwhelmed, Daniel found his footing and stepped forward. Now face to face, they stood still—eyes searching—hers filled with love, his with longing. In that silence, they laughed—a tearful, joyful sound that shattered the years of separation.

Leaning into each other, they embraced—clinging tightly, as if to reclaim every moment missed, every second lost to the shadows of the past. Their arms encircled one another, holding fast to hope, forgiveness, and a vow to never again let love slip away.

In that moment, amid the cheers and bustling crowd, a new chapter dawned—one paved with tears, courage, and an unbreakable bond that time and distance could never erase.

That love had never truly faded. It had lain dormant, veiled in shadows, awaiting the moment to be rekindled. Now, it blazed brighter than ever, illuminating the space with a warmth no words could fully capture.

"Oh, my Daddy… my Daddy," Ava whispered, her voice quivering with emotion. Tears streamed down her face.

In that moment, Daniel realised—she was still his baby, his child—and he held her tightly.

"It's alright now, Ava. I'm here. We're together at last."

Then Ava turned gently to Soon Hee, now a teenager, standing quietly in the background with a soft smile.

"Soon Hee," Ava said softly, "I'm so happy to meet you at last, I've always wanted a little sister."

Soon Hee stepped forward, her eyes aglow with a blend of joy and awe. She reached out and embraced Ava, holding her tightly. "Me too, this is so cool"

Turning back to Daniel, Ava smiled through her tears.

"It's alright, Dad. These are tears of joy, not sadness. Mum couldn't face the airport," she explained gently. "It was all too much for her. She'll meet you later at the house for dinner—my stepfather will be there too."

She turned slightly. "This is my husband, Tommy."

"Pleased to meet you. My, a lot has changed," Daniel said, extending his hand to shake Tommy's.

"But… there's someone else eager to meet you," Ava added, glancing back.

From behind her, a small figure emerged—hesitant at first, shy yet eager. A little boy, no more than three years old, peeked out from behind Ava's skirt. His wide eyes gazed up at Daniel nervously, tiny hands clutching her clothes as if seeking reassurance.

"Dad, this is Daniel. Daniel, this is your grandfather."

Ava's voice quavered with emotion, her eyes glistening. "Say hello."

The little boy hesitated, then gazed up at Daniel with bright, curious eyes.

"Hello," he said shyly, his voice barely a whisper. "I'm… very happy to meet you, sir."

Daniel's knees buckled as a flood of emotion overwhelmed him. Tears streamed down his face uncontrollably—a blend of joy, sorrow, and longing. The realisation of how much he had missed was more profound than words could capture. His chest heaved with sobs, all the pain and hope spilling out in waves, as he reached out with trembling hands and drew the boy into a gentle embrace.

In that tearful, sacred moment, Daniel understood—no matter the years lost, the shadows of doubt, or the secrets buried deep in time—they could all be overcome. For love— true and unbreakable—had found its way back to him. And now, he was truly home.

They made their way to Ava's car, anticipation hanging heavy in the air. The drive through the city was slow and winding, the streets alive with movement, lights, and clamour. Daniel sat quietly, gazing out the window at the unfamiliar skyline stretching before him. Skyscrapers soared skyward, their shimmering glass reflecting the brilliant sunlight—a stark contrast to the city he once knew.

"I can't believe how much this place has changed since I was last here," Daniel said softly, his voice tinged with awe. His eyes roamed over the modern buildings and bustling streets, feeling both overwhelmed and astonished. "It's so different... so much more vibrant. It almost doesn't feel real."

Ava gazed at him, her expression softened by compassion. "A lot has changed," she said gently. "But at its heart, it's still the same city—brimming with hope and dreams. We're merely in a new chapter now."

Upon arriving at the hotel, Ava stepped out first, her face aglow with a blend of excitement and tenderness. She assisted with their check-in at the front desk, her voice warm and reassuring.

"Get some rest," Ava said softly, offering a gentle smile. "I'll return to collect you at seven thirty."

She waved before turning and vanishing back towards the car, little Daniel jr. clasping her hand. Daniel watched her depart, feeling the weight of it all—the long-separated father reunited with his family, slowly piecing together the fragments of their lives.

Inside their room, Daniel paused before settling on the edge of the bed. Jung sat beside him, her hand resting lightly on his shoulder.

"How are you feeling?" she asked softly, concern flickering in her eyes.

"I'm alright," Daniel replied, striving to steady his voice. "It's a lot—so much to catch up on in so little time. And I'm nervous about meeting Mei Lin and her husband. I'm sure he's a fine chap—he's done a splendid job raising Ava, far better than I could have."

Jung regarded him with a gentle smile, her expression soft yet candid.

"I don't believe that's true," she said softly. "Look at Soon Hee. She's wonderful—so kind and bright. You've done an amazing job there. Ava has built a fulfilling life, brimming with love. That's because she has a loving family, which includes you, Daniel. You've made a difference in her life, even if the memories aren't all clear yet."

Daniel returned her smile, a blend of gratitude and hope spreading across his face. "You're right," he murmured. "I suppose I must take it one step at a time. But I'm here now, and I want to make things right."

Jung squeezed his hand gently, her heart swelling with love and determination. "We will," she whispered. "Together, we'll do this. Step by step. Now, get some rest—we've a big evening ahead."

Daniel sat quietly in his finest suit, tailored especially for this journey. He hadn't worn a suit in decades, and though it felt faintly unfamiliar, it was like an old friend returning. The fabric, neat and pressed, draped comfortably as his hands rested on his knees, waiting at the desk in their room. The soft glow of the lamp cast gentle shadows across his face. Jung carefully arranged her hair, her hands trembling with anticipation and nerves. Her reflection shimmered in the mirror, but her eyes held quiet resolve as she prepared for this moment.

"You look beautiful, Jung," Daniel said softly, a genuine smile spreading across his face. His gaze lingered on her, brimming with love and longing.

"You clean up rather well yourself," she replied, her smile warm despite the quaver in her voice.

"Soon Hee, are you ready?" Jung called to the adjoining room.

Soon Hee glided in, giving a little twirl as she entered. "How do I look?" she asked with a beaming smile.

"Beauitful. I'm so very proud of you," Daniel said, rising to give her a gentle peck on the cheek.

Suddenly, a soft knock at the door sent Daniel's heart racing.

Jung paused, took a deep breath, and moved to open the door. There stood Ava, smiling softly. She embraced Jung warmly.

"You look beautiful, Jung," Ava said from the doorway. "Shall we go?"

They descended together, the air thick with emotion. Outside, the night was dark and serene, the street lit only by the moon and a few lingering streetlights. As Daniel gazed out the window during the drive, the scenery felt familiar— the winding roads, the ancient trees—and he murmured,

"Yes, I recall this. It hasn't changed much here."

The car turned into Emerald Hill, a tranquil street compared to most of what he had seen thus far, and Daniel's heart thudded with the weight of what lay ahead. He glanced at Ava, her face aglow—expectant and brimming with hope.

As they stepped out and approached the front door, Ava gently touched his arm.

"You knock," Ava said softly, her smile encouraging. "This is your moment."

Daniel raised his hand, pausing briefly before knocking with quiet resolve. Moments later, the door opened slowly, revealing Mei Lin. Her hair, now streaked with silver, framed a face radiant with warmth. Her smile—brighter than ever—melted his heart. Tears welled in Daniel's eyes as he gazed at her. Her face was more familiar than he recalled… and more beautiful than he'd dared to hope.

She stood there, tears streaming down her cheeks, her smile quivering with emotion. Behind her, her husband stood quietly, his expression gentle and understanding. The room seemed to hold its breath, capturing a moment suspended in time—the instant when past and present collided.

Daniel's voice, thick with emotion, broke the silence.

"Mei Lin," he whispered, eyes glistening, "it's you… it's truly you."

She rushed to him, arms outstretched, and they embraced—two souls reunited after decades apart. The air brimmed with unspoken words, with love pouring through tears and trembling hands. In that embrace, in that long-awaited collision of hearts, they both knew—they had truly come home.

Daniel stepped back, his eyes glistening with emotion as he turned to Mei Lin. His voice quavered as he gazed into her face, brimming with tenderness and gratitude.

"Mei Lin," he said softly, "I'd like you to meet the woman who saved my life—my dearest friend… and my wife."

Jung's eyes widened, a blend of surprise and warmth softening her expression. Without hesitation, she stepped forward and gently embraced Mei Lin, her arms encircling her in a quiet, heartfelt hug.

"Hello," Jung said warmly, her voice rich with sincerity. "It's truly wonderful to meet you at last."

From behind, a hand rested lightly on Daniel's shoulder. A calm, steady voice followed—low, yet imbued with quiet resolve.

"Greetings. I'm Gerry—Mei Lin's husband." His smile was genuine, laced with quiet pride and warmth. "It's a privilege to meet you both at last. I've heard so much about you over the years, Daniel—stories I never imagined I'd one day hear confirmed in person."

Daniel gazed at Gerry, his eyes glistening with emotion. Gratitude and awe welled within his chest.

"It's an honour to meet you, Gerry," he said softly. "Thank you—for everything. For caring for Mei Lin… for raising Ava… and for sharing this moment. I don't take it lightly."

Gerry gave a humble nod, his eyes kind. "We've all been awaiting this for a long time," he said gently. "And I'm grateful it's here at last—together, as it should be."

He stepped aside, gesturing towards the warm glow within the house. "Come in. Dinner's nearly ready. Let me fetch you both a drink."

As they stepped into the house, a familiar face awaited them at the foot of the stairs. Nur's eyes shimmered with tears, her voice trembling as she greeted him.

"Oh, Mr. Daniel, sir… welcome home."

Daniel stepped forward, pulling Nur into a gentle, grounding hug, feeling her tremble in his arms. Then he turned and walked through the familiar space until he stood before his big brother. Without a word, he opened his arms wide in an unspoken plea, a quiet sign of the unbreakable bond they shared.

In that powerful embrace, everything else faded: the years, the distance, the silences. They said what words could never capture, a silent testament to love and brotherhood rooted deep beneath the surface. No words were needed, only the raw, honest connection of two souls finally reunited.

The golden light from the garden lanterns bathed the table, flickering softly with the evening breeze. Crickets chirped gently in the background, weaving their song into the tranquil night as the family gathered around the meal, each face reflecting the weight and wonder of the day.

Daniel cleared his throat softly, emotion thick in his chest as he gazed from face to face. His eyes lingered on each person—Jung, Soon Hee, Ava, Tommy, Gerry, Khian-Seng and finally, Mei Lin—each a thread in the tapestry of his story, anchoring him through time and silence.

"I haven't the words," he began, his voice low yet steady, "for how does one thank those who've restored their life?"

He paused, gazing skyward at the stars, as if seeking something beyond himself.

"I lost many years… and I've made peace with that. But tonight—gazing at all of you—I realise something. I didn't merely survive. I was found. I was loved. Even when I didn't know it, even when I was lost… I was never truly alone."

Ava wiped a tear from her cheek. Soon Hee reached over to clasp his hand.

Daniel continued, his eyes glistening. "I may not recall every detail yet. But what I do know is this: I have a second chance. And I'll spend every day earning it—loving better, listening more, being present."

He turned to Jung, then Mei Lin.

"Thank you—for waiting, for forgiving, for believing. I cherish each of you."

A soft, reverent silence fell, and then Mei Lin reached across the table, her hand resting over his.

"We're here," she said simply. "That's all that matters now."

And for the first time in a very long time, Daniel felt whole.

"You all deserve to know what happened—how it nearly cost me everything," Daniel said, his eyes distant as memories stirred. "When I crashed in Korea in 1963, I was on the brink of death. Flung from the wreckage, bleeding and broken, I recall the flames, feeling myself slipping away… I thought I was done. But it was Jung who found me, who pulled me to safety. If she hadn't come, I wouldn't be here today. She saved my life. She risked everything for me—a debt I can never repay."

He paused, swallowing hard as emotion threatened to overwhelm him.

"I nearly lost it all—my past, my family, my future. But she fought for me, carried me when I couldn't walk, and nursed me back from the edge. That's the kind of love that saves lives—true, steadfast, unbreakable. I'm forever grateful she never gave up on me."

The table fell silent, the weight of his words settling over them—sacrifice, pain, and hope interwoven.

Daniel turned to Mei Lin, his gaze softening. "And what of your story? Tell me—how did you two meet?"

"Well, it was about five years after you vanished," Mei Lin said. "Bo introduced us at her dinner party. It was that simple, really. We've been fortunate."

"Ava, tell me more about your life—there's so much to catch up on," Daniel said softly.

Ava's face brightened, and she began eagerly.

"I've been living in Florida, working at NASA now," she said with pride. "I took a sabbatical to stay here in Singapore. I still conduct research, and little Daniel came along. I've built my career in satellite communications. It's been a thrilling journey, and I love it. I get to work with the stars— quite literally—helping send signals across space. That's thanks to you, Dad. I still cherish those bedtime stories about the stars.

I'm also completed my PhD in physics, alongside a medical degree, exploring ways to keep astronauts healthy in space. I missed you terribly, Dad, but I'm truly happy. I've forged a new life, and I hope you'd be proud of me."

Her words spilled out, brimming with excitement and a touch of longing.

"Little Daniel is growing up fast—he's so smart and kind. He just started pre-school, and every day he asks about you. I tell him stories about the stars and space, and he loves them. It's strange—I feel like I've finally found a piece of you, even if you're not here to see it."

Daniel's eyes shimmered with tears as he listened, every word filling the emptiness with a little more hope.

"You're amazing," he whispered, voice thick with emotion. "I wish I could be there to see it all—your dreams, your family, your life. But I promise, I'm trying… trying to find my way back to you, to all of you. And I won't stop."

They all sat quietly, the night wrapping them in a gentle embrace. Amid the stars, the shadows of the past grew a little lighter, and the weight of decades of longing began to lift— if only for this one moment.

The stars above twinkled gently, quiet witnesses to a reunion long overdue. Daniel gazed at the faces lit by warm lanterns and the soft glow of the night sky. The heartbreak, the confusion, the doubt—they were gradually yielding to hope.

Gerry reached across the table, his voice soft yet resolute.

"Tonight, we cherish this moment," he said gently. "Whatever the future holds, you're all finally together—and that's what truly matters. Shadows cannot conceal the love here—love that time, distance, and pain could never wholly erase."

Jung clasped Daniel's hand, her eyes glistening with tears of relief and joy.

"We've waited so very long," Mei Lin whispered, "but now we know—he's alive, and he's come home, if only for a spell. That's what counts."

As they sat around the table, that fragile hope blossomed brighter than ever—poised to guide them into a future where love, forgiveness, and the promise of reunion would at last dawn after all the darkness.

Blimey, this has been a wonderful evening, but all this excitement has quite worn me out. I need a bit of beauty sleep," Daniel said, rising slowly and clasping Jung's hand.

"Shall we see you tomorrow?" he asked, glancing at Ava.

"Try to stop me," she replied with a grin. "Now that I've found you, I shan't let you slip away again."

As they approached the door, Mei Lin paused briefly.

"Wait here a tick," she whispered. Without awaiting a reply, she dashed upstairs. Daniel watched her go, a question lingering in his gaze.

Moments later, she returned with a bundle of old, weathered letters. She looked at Daniel with tender reassurance.

"I hope you don't mind," she said softly, tears streaming down her cheeks, "but these are the letters I wrote to you after you vanished. I wanted you to have them."

She paused, her eyes glistening with emotion. "They span about five years—everything about our lives, about Ava growing up. I never sent them, as I had no address to send them to. I never reopened them, but now I wish for you to have them. They're yours."

She passed the bundle to Daniel, her gaze flickering between him and Jung.

"Please, I hope that's all right."

Jung reached out and clasped Mei Lin's hand tenderly, offering a warm, reassuring smile.

"Of course. How lovely," she said softly. "It's a treasure—something to help you grasp all you've missed."

Daniel's eyes brimmed with tears. Gently, he took the letters, kissed Mei Lin softly on the cheek, then nodded at Gerry. With a subdued smile, he turned towards the door. Without a word, he stepped into the waning light, clutching the bundle tightly—feeling the burden of the past and the hope of what yet lay ahead.

19

A New Dawn

Daniel stirred slowly, the world still shrouded in darkness. Outside, the air was crisp and heavy, the earliest whispers of dawn faintly tinting the sky with a soft blue-grey hue. The hotel stood silent, serene in its stillness—but Daniel knew the night had passed, carrying away a long, turbulent chapter of his life.

He showered and dressed, craving a moment's solitude before the others rose. Stepping outside, he hailed a taxi.

"East Coast beach, please," he said. The driver nodded and drove off.

Upon arriving, the sun was rising above the water. Daniel strolled towards the shore, a ritual he hadn't performed in over twenty years.

Now, standing at the sea's edge, Daniel confronted that peculiar, uncertain moment that follows great change—the space where the old begins to fade, yet the new has not fully taken form.

He sat quietly on the soft sand, gentle waves lapping at his feet. In his hands, he clasped a bundle of weathered letters—messages that had traversed time and silence.

Slowly, he unfolded one, recognising Mei Lin's familiar handwriting—her heartache and love spilled onto the page two decades past.

He read her words in the dappled sunlight, feeling the raw emotion etched in every line. Her voice seemed to resonate across the years, her pain and yearning stirring his senses anew. This was the day she had poured her soul into the letter—when hope and despair vied for her heart. Smudged ink blurred the words, and tear stains marked the paper.

"My darling Pip,

I pray you're safe, wherever you may be, my dearest boy. My heart aches beyond measure. I weep myself to sleep each night, awaiting any word, hoping you're still alive. Even the smallest scrap of news would mean everything.

Ava misses you terribly—she weeps constantly. I try to assure her it'll be soon, but when might that be?

We've tried every means to reach you. The British authorities have contacted officals in Korea, but to no avail.

My darling, my heart shatters each time I hear your name. Suddenly, tears well in my eyes, and I feel daft as strangers stare at me in the street.

Just the other day, I found myself weeping in the kitchen corner. I'd brewed your favourite teh for breakfast, even called up the stairs for you. What a fool I am! Something as simple as a cup of teh can undo me.

Our families have been ever so supportive—they've ensured we never fret about money, and you always saw to it we were provided for. They pop round for dinner each week to check on Ava and me. Nur is splendid too—you truly chose well in her.

I must stop now, as Ava awaits her bedtime story—something you once did, and now it's my turn.

I miss you dearly. I love you beyond what words can express, and I pray you return to us soon.

My love, as ever.

Mei Lin"

Daniel clasped the letter tightly, pressing it to his chest. Tears streamed freely as he longed to have been there—to have eased the pain. Yet, despite the anguish, he knew he must continue reading. He needed to grasp what Mei Lin had endured, what he had missed as Ava grew and changed. His head bowed gently as he opened the next letter.

"Dearest Pip,

I sit in our bedroom, gazing out across the street. Rain lashes down—I recall how you loved such days. I think of us running wild in the rain as children, and how I'd give anything to clasp your hand once more.

It's been twelve months since you stepped out the door and never returned. Khian Seng travelled to Korea again to search for you, spending a week in villages along the roads you might have taken. Once, he thought he'd glimpsed you, chasing into the woods, but found nothing—only the wind whispering through the trees. He'll return to search again; we shan't give up.

How can someone simply vanish into thin air? I cannot fathom it. Did you choose this? Did you deliberately turn away from your family's love? Why have you done this to us, Pip? Why?

I had to pause to finish this letter, my darling—I'm so terribly sorry. I miss you beyond measure.

We shall never abandon hope of finding you, whether you wish to be found or not.

I can't write more now; I must stop here.

I pray you're safe and well, my dearest. We love and miss you more than words can express. Please come home.

Your Mei Lin"

Tears streamed down Daniel's face as he whimpered, then suddenly cried out,

"No, please God, no! How could you do this to us?"

His face sank into the sand as he pounded his right fist in anguish. Clasping the letters tightly, he rose with effort and opened another.

Despite the anguish, he pressed on with reading.

The words told of a heart broken in two, of a quiet house now empty without him. Ava—then just a child—lay nestled in her bed, immersed in her world of books and drawings.

Each night, she read aloud from her favourite tales and sketched pictures of her daddy, her innocence radiant through the pain of yearning.

Mei Lin wrote of watching Ava—her tiny hands colouring, her eyes aglow with hope—sketching pictures of Daniel's face, her young heart yearning to bring him back. She longed for him to read her bedtime tales, to hold her close, to make them whole again. Yet the anguish was heavy—the anguish of loss, of waiting, of yearning across the empty years.

Her words, brimming with love and yearning, seemed to rise gently from the page:

"Wherever you may be, my darling, I pray you're safe and content. I hope you can sense how deeply I love you, even from so far away. Please return to us. Please come home."

Daniel traced the lines with trembling fingers, feeling Mei Lin's voice in every word, knowing her love had sustained them through two long decades. She had penned these words in moments of hope and despair, clinging on silently, praying he would one day read them and grasp how profoundly she had always loved him—and how much they all still yearned for his return.

Now, twenty years on, he clasped her words tightly. For a moment, he closed his eyes, letting her love envelop him once more.

After painstakingly reading through the letters, he reached the final two.

"My dear Daniel,

It's now been four years since you left us, and with each passing year, we've grown stronger. We light a candle on your birthday and share a slice of your favourite chocolate cake. Ava is now in secondary school, and you'd be ever so proud of her. She's top of her class—she truly takes after her father's wit.

I'm sorry to tell you that your mother passed away last weekend. She missed you dearly every day and always asked after you. In the end, we told her you'd been found and would return soon, but work was keeping you occupied. We knew she had only a few days left, and I hope you don't mind that I told her that small fib. I only wished for her to find peace before she passed.

She had a beautiful farewell, surrounded by family and friends. Everyone still asks after you and wonders if we've any news.

I must go now—I'm meeting friends at the café. I've begun to venture out more lately. Ava's older now, and I find I've more time to do things for myself.

Your Mei Lin

Brushing away his tears and finding solace in the letters, he gently unfolded the final one Mei Lin had given him. His hands quivered as he began to read the last fragment of her heart laid bare on the page:

"Dear Daniel,

This letter has been difficult to pen, and it's taken me ages to find the words. For years, I grappled with what to say and how to express it. But now, I must put my feelings into words, however painful the truth may be. It's been over five years since you vanished, and each day I clung to hope of seeing you again. Yet life moves on, whether we're ready or not.

I want you to know I've found a path forward. I've met someone—his name is Gerry—and he's been a loving presence in my life. I never imagined I'd find happiness again, but with him, I have. It's different, though, and I cannot wait forever. I've accepted you're not returning.

You were ever so wonderful with Ava—so loving, so patient—helping with her studies and sharing tales that made her smile. She still speaks of you, sketching pictures of her Daddy and cherishing the moments you shared. You left a mark on her heart no one can replace.

I hope you don't mind that I've moved on. I wish to be honest—I've loved and lost, and now I've found happiness anew. Gerry isn't a replacement; he's a new chapter in my life. Yet you'll always be the one I loved first, the father she adored, and the man who filled my life with dreams and hope. No one can take that away.

Gerry proposed, and I accepted. I want you to know I carry you with me always. Wherever you may be, I pray you're content—and I hope, somehow, you're glad for me too.

Take care of yourself, Pip.

Yours forever,

Mei Lin"

Daniel watched in silence as the sun rose higher, casting warmth across the still, dark waters. The sight was breathtaking—both beautiful and heartrending. Within him, a torrent of thoughts surged fiercely, a tempest of emotions he could scarcely comprehend. This wasn't merely the dawn of another day; it felt like the dawn of a new life—though he knew it could never be the same. He sat, pondering what that life might truly hold.

Memories of lost love, fractured identity, and unanswered questions haunted the edges of his mind—flickering shadows that refused to fade. Yet, beneath it all, a faint glimmer of hope burned startlingly bright.

He thought of the past—of the life he'd lived for decades before the accident, the family he had loved and lost: Jung, his daughter Soon Hee, and Ava—the daughter whose voice still echoed in his thoughts.

The words resonated softly in Daniel's mind as he rose slowly from the damp sand, feeling the cool earth beneath his feet. The horizon stretched endlessly before him—the vast, shimmering sea blending with the sky, a symbol of infinite possibilities and long-lost dreams. The light climbed higher now, casting a golden glow that illuminated a path forward. It was as if the universe itself whispered that the darkness of night was yielding at last—the shadows receding to make way for a new dawn.

Daniel paused, drawing a deep, shuddering breath, savouring the fresh air that filled his lungs. The ocean's rhythmic roar beckoned him home—back to himself, yet not to the life he once knew. He had a new life now, as did Mei Lin.

Quietly, he turned from the water and began walking—each step tentative yet purposeful, as if every movement were a surrender to the possibility of healing.

Drawn by the rich aroma drifting on the gentle breeze, Daniel approached a modest hawker stall near the beach. The stall was unassuming—wooden tables beneath a makeshift canopy, shaded by a cluster of trees—but the scent of fragrant spices, fried foods, and steaming congee was unmistakable. It summoned memories of mornings after dawn, when he and Ava had come here years ago—simple moments brimming with laughter and love.

The stallholder looked up from his sizzling wok, his eyes crinkling with a warm smile.

"Good morning," he greeted, his voice hearty and kind. "Anything I can get for you, sir?"

Daniel nodded, a faint smile touching his lips.

"Yes… congee and roti prata, please."

"Take a seat, it'll be ready in a moment," the stallholder said, gesturing to the nearest table.

Daniel settled onto a nearby bench, the warm bowl steaming gently in his hands. Around him, the city was stirring, but within, a tempest of memories began to swell. He closed his eyes briefly, letting the familiar comfort of the food anchor him.

Then, vivid memories flooded back—so potent it was as if he were reliving them.

He recalled Ava, how they had sat together on this very beach, her tiny fingers splashing in the shallow water, her face alight with joy as she mastered swimming. How she'd giggled uncontrollably, splashing him back, her laughter echoing across the waves like a song of innocence and hope. He saw her pushing herself, trembling with nervousness, then conquering her fears—her face radiant, outshining the sun. The fierce, pure pride he'd felt surged through him once more.

"This is some of the finest congee I've ever tasted," he said softly, savouring the words as if they summoned a quiet memory from mornings long past. "Thank you. Truly."

The stallholder chuckled, pride gleaming in his eyes.

"Fresh every morning, for friends like you. Come again."

"Thank you, I shall—and I'll bring the entire family next time."

Daniel lingered on the bench a while longer, watching birds flutter in a nearby tree, a faint smile playing on his lips.

In that serene moment, he made a silent vow: he would find a way to reclaim the time lost with Ava. He owed that to them both—for his past, his daughter, and the family he'd fought so fiercely to recall.

For deep in his heart, he knew that no matter how long the shadows lingered, they could never dim the love that endured—waiting to be rekindled at the dawn of a new day.

20

Acceptance and Beginnings

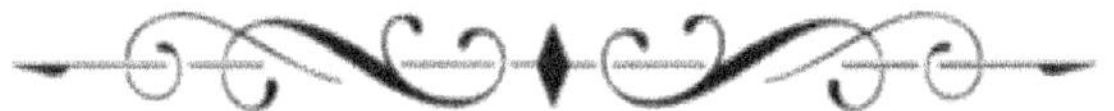

aniel stepped into a taxi, the engine purring softly as he headed back to the hotel. The early morning light was soft, casting long shadows across the city skyline. His mind grappled with a curious blend of peace and unease—the quiet hope that he was beginning to recall more, and the lingering fear of what else he might unearth.

When the taxi arrived, its doors glided open, and Daniel stepped out. The hotel lobby felt both familiar and foreign—as if a place he once knew but now had to rediscover.

He found Jung and Soon Hee awake in their room, morning sun streaming through the windows. Soon Hee looked up and rushed over with open arms, her face alight with curiosity and concern.

"Dad!" she exclaimed. "Where have you been? We were worried!"

Daniel knelt, a faint smile playing on his lips as he reached out to her. In his hand, he held a brief note left on the dresser. It read simply:

"I took a walk to the beach. I needed to think. I'll be back soon."

The words, concise yet poignant, carried an unspoken message of love and hope.

Jung stepped closer, her eyes soft with relief. She gently brushed his arm.

"We're glad you're back," she said softly, her voice thick with emotion. "We missed you."

Daniel gazed at both of them, a wave of gratitude washing over him.

"I read the letters Mei Lin gave me. Everything's going to be alright. Please don't worry about me. Let's take a walk into the city," he suggested gently. "Before we meet Ava for lunch at the Raffles Bar and Billiard Room. I want to see it all—see how much it's changed."

They dressed quickly and stepped out into the bustling streets. The air was warm and vibrant—the hum of activity on Orchard Road, the chatter of shoppers, and the subtle pulse of a city that had grown even more lively since he'd left all those years ago.

They strolled past Tangs shopping centre, where high-end boutiques displayed their wares, windows gleaming with the latest fashion and jewellery. Neon signs flickered overhead, advertisements flashing bold promises, while street performers and vendors enlivened the scene. They wove through crowds of tourists and locals alike, breathing in the heady blend of cultures and modern life.

Daniel paused briefly, marvelling at a towering shopping centre whose glass façade mirrored the sunlight—a reflection of past and present.

"It's different," he said with awe, "yet somehow… still the same. This city has a heartbeat of its own."

Soon Hee walked ahead, eyes wide with excitement as she pointed towards a street performer juggling glowing orbs. Jung smiled, drawing them both close.

Together, they wandered through the vibrant streets, soaking in the energy, the sights, the sounds—each moment a piece of the new life they were forging and a bridge to the memories they all cherished.

As they approached the iconic Raffles Hotel, its colonial architecture rising majestically above the street, Daniel drew a deep breath. The hotel was more than a mere building—it was a symbol of history, where past and present intertwined. Just ahead, they would meet Ava, and in that moment, the long, uncertain journey towards reunion and understanding felt tantalisingly close.

They stepped into the grand, elegant lobby of the Raffles Hotel. The polished marble floors gleamed softly beneath the warm glow of chandeliers, and the rich scent of mahogany, jasmine, and fragrant tea gently pervaded the air. Daniel inhaled deeply, absorbing the atmosphere—familiar, yet altered by the years. The bustling street outside thrummed with energy, a city that had evolved and transformed, yet still clung to its cherished history.

Ava guided them around the corner into the Bar and Billiard Room, a charming annexe beside the main hotel, encircled by verdant gardens. She gave her name, and they were ushered to a quiet corner by the window, where sunlight streamed in, casting a golden shimmer across the table. They settled into their seats, gazing out over the lush surroundings as the world outside pulsed in a vibrant dance of colours and sounds.

Ava drew out her diary and began sharing her plans—an itinerary she'd meticulously crafted, listing all the places they would visit to reconnect with the past and forge new memories as two families.

Her excitement was understated, her eyes shimmering with hope and anticipation.

"I thought we should start here," she said softly, "then visit all the places we used to frequent—the old park, the bookshop, the cafés… all those little corners that hold our memories." Her voice glowed with warmth and enthusiasm. "I've even arranged a few surprises. I want this trip to be the finest yet—for all of us."

Daniel gazed at her, a quiet smile playing on his lips. His eyes held a glimmer of relief—like someone finally finding their footing.

"Last night," he said softly, "I was reflecting on everything—that night, after the accident. On how you and your mother must have felt, losing me like that. I've spent years searching for who I was, longing to turn back time, to do more, to be better. I want to reclaim the time lost, Ava. I want to see everything—those streets, those places we cherished. I want to feel I belong here again, with you, with her, and with this city holding our memories. I also want to share with Jung and Soon Hee the life I had before, while embracing the life I have now."

Ava reached across the table, gently squeezing his hand. Her smile was warm, understanding, brimming with love.

"We know we can't turn back time, but we can move forward—as a family. We'll do it," she whispered. "We'll visit all those places—the ones you recall, and some new ones too. We'll take our time. I've planned every detail. It's going to be extraordinary. New memories to weave with the old, and I promise, it'll be perfect."

He gazed into her eyes, feeling a spark of hope kindle within him.

"That sounds perfect," he murmured, his voice thick with emotion. "More than I could ever have hoped for. I know now I can begin to forge a new life—here, with you, with my family. I just need to take it day by day. What do you say, Soon Hee?"

"It sounds cool," Soon Hee said, clasping Jung's hand and smiling.

Ava leaned in, her voice soft and hopeful.

"And we'll create new memories—beyond mere sightseeing. We'll shape a future that belongs to all of us. Together. Now, let's eat!"

After lunch, Daniel glanced at his watch, a gentle weariness washing over him. His eyes shimmered with a longing for rest, and he reached out to gently squeeze Ava's hand.

"I think I'd best return to the hotel now," he said softly. "I need some rest—we've a big day tomorrow."

Ava nodded, sensing the weariness behind his words. She glanced at Jung and Soon Hee. As Daniel rose, Ava clasped Jung's hand.

"Jung, Soon Hee—fancy visiting the Long Bar? Perhaps try a Singapore Sling? It is full of charm. And you get to throw peanuts on the floor" she said winking at Soon Hee

Jung hesitated briefly, then smiled warmly, glancing at Daniel.

"Go ahead, you two. I'll rest a bit. See you later." Daniel said smiling back at them.

"Very well, that sounds lovely," Jung said. "Let's go. It'll be pleasant to sit and unwind. No Singapore Sling for Soon Hee, though—she'll have orange juice."

Soon Hee laughed and nodded eagerly, her eyes alight with curiosity.

"Yes! I want to see where Dad used to visit. It sounds amazing, especially if you can throw peanuts on the floor!"

Daniel watched them depart, a gentle smile spreading across his lips.

"Have a splendid time," he said, waving softly. "I'll see you later. Enjoy yourselves—and don't forget, you're weaving new memories too."

With that, they walked along the corridor, up the stairs and stepped into the iconic Long Bar. The long wooden counter stretched out like a ribbon of history, lined with stools and bathed in warm light. The atmosphere was vibrant yet relaxed, filled with the murmur of conversation and laughter, and the distinctive scent of roasted peanuts. Heaps of empty shells littered the floor beneath their seats, a charming quirk that added to the bar's allure.

They found a cosy nook on the balcony, overlooking the bustling street below. A soft drizzle had begun, transforming the city lights into shimmering reflections on the wet pavement. The group settled in, ordering their drinks—Jung and Soon Hee sharing a vibrant, alcohol-free fruity cocktail, while Ava, feeling adventurous, chose a classic Singapore Sling. The tang of the drink was sharp yet sweet, perfectly balanced.

The rain fell steadily now, each drop tapping softly yet insistently on the windows, weaving a rhythmic, almost hypnotic symphony. Outside, the street gleamed slick and shadowed, headlights casting faint glimmers through the veil of rain. The gentle roar of the storm seeped into the room, blending with the quiet murmur of their conversation and lending a layer of sombre reflection.

Soon Hee gazed out over the rain-slicked street, her face serene but her eyes clouded with unspoken worry. The wet pavement mirrored the flickering streetlights, distorting the scene into a swirling watercolour of movement and shadow. It was as if the weather, like her thoughts, sought to wash away her fears—yet only sharpened them, rendering them more persistent.

Jung reached over and gently clasped her hand, her fingers cool but comforting. She offered a quiet, reassuring squeeze as they sat in a heavy silence, broken only by the tap-tap of the rain, the distant rumble of thunder, and the faint creak of the balcony railing swaying slightly in the wind.

After a moment, Soon Hee rose and stepped away from the table, drawing closer to the balcony railing for a clearer view of the rain-soaked street below.

Ava, seated nearby, observed her quietly for a moment before her soft voice broke the stillness—hesitant yet earnest.

"Is Dad alright?" she asked, gazing gently at Jung.

"Your dad had a serious accident, and it took a long time for him to recover. He has a heart condition that makes him tired, which the doctors are monitoring and treating."

Ava absorbed Jung's words silently, her brow furrowing with concern. She looked down at her hands clasped around the glass, a blend of worry and determination stirring within her.

"I just want to ensure we don't lose him again," she whispered, her voice trembling slightly. "I don't want him to endure anything like that again."

Jung reached over and gently clasped Ava's hand, her expression soft yet resolute.

"We're all here now," Jung said softly. "We'll care for him, and for each other. You're not alone in this."

Outside, the rain maintained its steady rhythm, a gentle reminder that even the heaviest storms eventually pass—and that new growth often follows the darkest times.

Ava's gaze fell to her hands, clasped tightly around her glass. Then she looked up at Jung.

"Is he in danger? Will he be alright?"

Jung leaned closer, her voice as gentle as the rain pattering steadily outside.

"Ava, we cherish each day as a gift. Try not to worry too much. Now that I've told you, please don't ask your dad about it—he prefers not to discuss his health. Let's simply be here, in this moment. The rain is soothing, and so are we. Sometimes, that's enough."

Ava's voice quivered, tears welling in her eyes.

"It's just… I have him back now, and this…" Ava trailed off.

"I understand," Jung said softly. "But let's cherish these moments."

Ava nodded silently, her worry lingering beneath a quiet resolve, drawing strength from Jung's steadfast support.

"The last thing I want," Jung added gently, "is to distress your dad further. He's been away too long already, and he needs our strength."

The three sat in quiet contemplation, the steady rain drumming against the roof and windows like a lullaby echoing their hopes and fears. Outside, the storm blurred the streetlights, softening their glow behind veils of falling water. Yet within the silence, a fragile peace settled—a quiet acceptance that some things were beyond control, and all they could do was hold fast to each other and await calmer days.

After a while, the rain eased, fading into a soft murmur. The storm's fury subsided, leaving the world cleansed and glistening beneath the muted streetlight glow. Soon Hee and Jung savoured their drinks slowly, enveloped in the cool serenity of the evening.

Ava looked up, her face still slightly weary but touched with quiet resolve.

"I think I should take you back to the hotel now," she said gently. "You'll need rest before tomorrow. I'll come to fetch you at ten."

Jung nodded, her smile warm and reassuring.

"That's a good idea, sweetheart. Rest is vital—especially after today." She reached out and tenderly brushed Ava's hair.

"It's been a long day for all of us. Just get some rest—you and your dad both need to recharge. Tomorrow's a fresh day."

Ava nodded, a gentle smile settling on her face. She knew the rain wouldn't last forever, nor would the worries weighing on their hearts. As they gathered their belongings, a quiet promise of brighter days lingered in the air—calmer days when hope could flourish anew.

They moved slowly towards the door, the rain still softly pattering on the windows as they stepped out into the cool night. The air, scented with damp earth and fresh rain, brushed their cheeks as they strolled down the quiet street, the distant glow of the hotel guiding them home.

Inside the car, Ava drove in silence. As they pulled into the hotel drive, the porter opened the door and glanced at Jung.

"Sleep well tonight, alright?" she said with a warm smile. "And perhaps tomorrow, With that, the car slipped away into the night. The rain eased into a soft drizzle, carrying the promise of rest and renewal—an end to one chapter and the quiet hope of what tomorrow might bring.

Ava hesitated briefly before stepping through the front door. The house was still, the warm glow of the living room lamp casting gentle shadows across the floor. She moved cautiously, her heart pounding with a blend of nerves and hope. When she finally settled beside Mei Lin, her voice was barely a whisper.

"Mum," she said softly, "I have news about Dad."

Mei Lin looked up, her eyes glistening with unshed tears, a faint smile flickering across her face.

"What is it, dear?"

Ava took a deep breath, her voice quivering.

"Dad has a heart condition. He doesn't wish to discuss it, so… let's not press him, alright?"

Mei Lin's shoulders trembled as she absorbed the words. Tears welled in her eyes again, but she blinked them back. Her hand quivered as she reached out to clasp Ava's.

"Fate is truly against us," she whispered, her voice laden with sorrow and frustration. "But we must hold on—for him, for all of us."

They sat in heavy, hushed stillness, the weight of the night pressing upon them. Mei Lin ran a gentle hand through Ava's hair, seeking solace in her presence. At last, she mustered a faint, weary smile.

"Sleep well tonight, alright?" she said softly, her voice soothing despite the ache in her heart. "And perhaps tomorrow, Dad will feel better."

Ava nodded, resting her head against her mother's shoulder. Outside, the night was tranquil—no rain, no wind—just a serene calm that enveloped them like a shield. The world beyond glimmered with hope, a whisper of renewal—a close to one chapter and the fragile dawn of another, brimming with quiet hope for what tomorrow might hold.

And so, they sat together in loving silence, holding each other beneath a tranquil, starlit sky, quietly awaiting the dawn.

21

A Bridge Across Time

Daniel's voice was tentative yet steady as he dialled Mei Lin's number. When she answered, a familiar warmth flowed through the line, though a trace of nervousness lingered beneath his words.

"Mei Lin," he began softly, "could we meet at East Coast for breakfast? Just the two of us. I'd truly like to see you… if that's alright."

There was a pause, then a gentle, breathless reply.

"Of course, Daniel. I'd like that too."

Daniel waited at the taxi rank by East Coast Park as Mei Lin arrived.

"Shall we take a stroll?" he asked, and together they headed towards the beach.

"Shall we sit here?" Daniel suggested, gesturing to the sand.

They settled side by side on the tranquil sands of East Coast Beach, the early morning light casting a soft glow over the calm sea. The air was crisp, and the gentle lapping of waves against the shore wove a serene backdrop—yet within, Daniel's emotions churned.

He gazed out over the water, memories flooding in like a tide. Slowly, he turned to her, his voice quivering with vulnerability.

"I read your letters," he said quietly, almost fearful of what might follow. "All of them. Every single word. And honestly… it was more than I expected."

Mei Lin's eyes brimmed with tears as she met his gaze, her voice catching.

"You didn't have to read them… I kept them all these years because I hoped—perhaps someday…" Her voice faltered, her hands trembling as she tugged at her sleeve. "I wanted to believe you'd read what I wrote, that somehow you'd grasp how much I loved you—how much I still do."

Daniel's face tightened with anguish, a deep ache settling into his bones.

"I didn't realise how much the words… the pain they held. It felt as though I were buried alive in them. As if I'd been gone so long that everything I thought I knew, everything I believed about myself, was torn apart when I finally read what you'd written. The heartache, Mei Lin—it was like wandering through a fog, lost in my own absence, my own silence, afraid of what I might uncover if I looked too closely."

Her tears spilled over as she reached out, trembling.

"I thought I was being brave, writing all those things, hoping somehow you'd find your way back to me. But I was hurting so deeply—terrified I'd lost you forever."

He looked down, his voice breaking with emotion.

"It was an agony I'd never known before. The pain of being apart, of knowing I'd left you and Ava behind—all those years of silence. I read those letters and realised how much time had slipped away from us… how much we'd lost. And yet, in those words, I saw your love—how fiercely you fought for us, for me. Even in my absence, you kept a part of me alive."

They sat in silence, broken only by the distant cry of seagulls and the rhythmic ebb and flow of the tide. The sun rose slowly, casting a golden glow over the water, as if seeking to mend what words alone could not.

Daniel finally met her gaze, his eyes glistening with tears.

"I know I can never make up for those lost years, Mei Lin. We've both moved on with our lives. We have families now. We can never be as we were, but I want to try. I want to understand. And I want… I want us to find a way to forge new memories—as two families, becoming one—no matter how long it takes."

Mei Lin reached out, her hand trembling yet steady as she clasped his. In that moment, beneath the vast, boundless sky, they both sensed that the bridge between their past and future was beginning to mend—woven with tears, pain, and fragile threads of hope.

The breeze stirred slightly, carrying the salty tang of the sea and the weight of their tangled emotions. They sat close, silent for a long moment, overwhelmed by the depth of their feelings—the ache of separation, the hope of healing, and the raw honesty that had finally pierced the wall of silence.

Daniel reached out, gently brushing his fingertips across her hand, as if to reaffirm her presence—to hold fast to the delicate thread connecting them. His voice was thick with emotion.

"All these years, I thought I was lost—adrift in my own guilt and regret. I carried such confusion, unsure of who I was or where I belonged. I had settled on being Korean, and that was my life. Then, suddenly, Ava found me."

Mei Lin gazed at him, her eyes glistening with unshed tears.

"I knew you couldn't simply leave and forget us. But the pain… Daniel, the pain of waiting, of wondering whether you were alive, whether you still loved us—that never truly faded. Every moment I kept those letters, every night I pored over Ava's drawings, I clung to the hope that someday, somehow, we'd be reunited."

He squeezed her hand gently.

"And I'm here now. Perhaps late, far too late—but I'm here. Finally. And I want us to move forward, not as a married couple, but as friends, and parents of a wonderful daughter— and grandparents, who would have thought!" He gave a soft chuckle. "Even if it's just step by step. I can't undo the years we lost, but I can start forging new memories. I want you to know I'm sorry for all I missed, but I'm also grateful—for this second chance I never realised I was holding onto."

Mei Lin's breath caught, her chest tightening as she fought to maintain her composure.

"It's been a long journey," she whispered, her voice quivering. "But perhaps... it's not too late for us to reconnect—not as husband and wife, but as friends. We've both carried such pain, yet so much love. And we have Ava. We lost our way in the silence. Now, perhaps, we can find it again—one step at a time. Do you agree?"

"I do."

The sky brightened as the sun climbed higher, casting a warm, golden glow over the boundless ocean stretching before them. The storm had long passed, leaving a renewed sense of hope—born from honesty, pain, and an unyielding desire to find each other again.

They sat in silence, sensing the fragile bridge between them taking shape—not through grand gestures, but through the quiet, unspoken understanding that they would tread it together, no matter how long it took.

After a while, the gentle wave of emotion settled in their hearts. Daniel and Mei Lin rose, deciding to head to a nearby hawker stall for a simple breakfast. The lively air buzzed with morning chatter, sizzling pans, and the aroma of freshly cooked dishes.

"I know a great place," Daniel said.

As they approached the hawker stall, a cheerful man with a broad smile and twinkling eyes greeted them warmly.

"Good morning! Back so soon, and you've brought a lovely wife with you too," he said, giving Daniel a friendly nod as he began preparing their order.

Daniel returned the smile, his expression relaxed and genuine.

"Yes, I've brought my"—he paused, then added softly—"very dear friend to try your splendid congee. Thank you."

The hawker grinned as he handed them steaming plates of congee, kaya toast, soft-boiled eggs, and teh tarik.

"Good friends are always welcome here."

As they settled at the stall's small table, the sun's rays gently warmed their backs, and the world seemed to ease into a tranquil rhythm—cleansed of the stormy conflict from before, replaced by a quiet, tentative hope.

They ate slowly, side by side, each bite a small step forward, a reminder that healing came not all at once but through gentle, simple moments—savoured deliberately, one day at a time.

In those quiet minutes, steeped in the aroma of breakfast and the soft hum of the morning crowd, an unspoken promise lingered: whatever the past held, there was still a chance for new beginnings—slow, steady, and brimming with hope.

As they finished their meal, the soft hum of the morning enveloped them. Daniel leaned back slightly, a gentle smile playing on his lips, and glanced at Mei Lin.

"Shall we go? I'm sure everyone's wondering where we've got to."

Mei Lin nodded, her eyes warm with quiet hope. "Yes, let's."

They rose from the stall and strolled back to the house. At the gate, Ava, Jung, Soon Hee, and Gerry awaited, their faces alight with anticipation. A calm surrounded them—an unspoken understanding that they were here to forge something new, rooted in kindness and respect.

Jung stepped forward, her gaze soft yet steady. She looked at Daniel with quiet concern.

"Are you alright?" she asked gently.

Daniel offered a reassuring smile, his eyes serene.

"Perfect," he replied. "We're fine. Everything's perfect."

Jung nodded, her smile soft as she sensed the peace within him.

"That's good to hear," she said, her voice hushed. "It's heartening to see you like this."

With spirits lifted and smiles shared, they set off together towards Seletar. The open spaces welcomed them—bathed in sunlight and filled with the scent of fresh air. Daniel held little Daniel's hand as they strolled, the boy gazing up with wide, curious eyes, quietly absorbing the journey as it unfolded.

As they moved forward—surrounded by laughter, plans, and memories yet to be forged—it was clear that kindness and a willingness to embrace one another were the true compass guiding them towards a brighter future. Whatever the past had held, they were here now, together, stepping into a new chapter brimming with hope, understanding, and the quiet promise of countless adventures to come.

22

Paths of Uncertainty

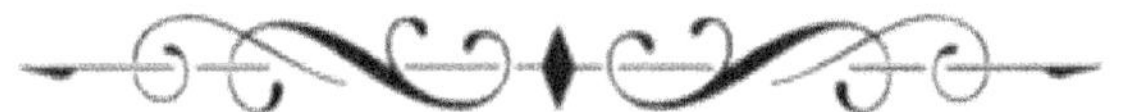

The end of the trip drew near. It had been a remarkable three weeks—filled with discovery, reconnection, and a slow, steady healing. These days had woven new threads through old wounds, crafting a tapestry of hope and forgiveness. Every walk, every shared meal, every quiet moment had drawn them closer to understanding—not only of the past but of the path ahead for their separate yet deeply intertwined lives.

This was their final day in Seletar—a place etched in their hearts, where boundaries had softened and new beginnings gently beckoned. The late afternoon sun filtered through the canopy, casting dappled gold along the winding trail. The air was rich with the scent of earth and the faint fragrance of blooming flowers—a soothing balm after days of emotional reckoning. The trip was ending, but what lay ahead was not an end at all. It was a beginning—a chapter shaped by acceptance, respect, and the quiet hope of forging an honest future together.

Daniel and Mei Lin had shared long conversations during their walks—moments of reflection that seemed to stretch into eternity yet passed in a breath. They never spoke openly of a future together; that chapter had long closed. Both had accepted that their marriage was over. They had gone their separate ways, each now devoted to another—Daniel to Jung, and Mei Lin to a life with Gerry.

What remained between them had transformed into something quieter, steadier—a bond rooted in friendship, understanding, and mutual respect. Love, in its purest form, now meant championing one another's happiness, even when that happiness lay in separate lives. It meant honouring the new ties that shaped their families today.

A few steps behind, Ava paused, gazing up at the towering trees. The leaves rustled softly above, whispering secrets into the breeze. For the first time in days, she felt a flicker of hope—tinged with trepidation. A quiet thrill of possibility stirred within her, tempered by an unease she couldn't quite name. She wondered what her father truly felt—whether he was finding peace with the past and what the future might hold for them all.

Suddenly, Ava slipped away from the others, her feet nimble on the uneven terrain. Quietly, she approached Daniel, hesitating as she looked up at him. Her eyes glistened with unspoken worries—a tempest of emotions she'd held within. Brave yet uncertain, she stood there, a devoted daughter seeking to navigate the new world unfolding around her.

"Dad," she said softly, her voice quivering, "what are your plans now? I mean… now that you know who you are. Will you move back to Singapore?"

Daniel paused, caught off guard. For a moment, he said nothing, letting her words linger in the space between them, heavy with meaning.

The truth was, he hadn't looked that far ahead. His mind still reeled from all that had surfaced—the past he had buried, the present he was striving to shape, and a future that remained uncharted.

He looked at her then, truly looked—saw the courage beneath her concern—and felt his heart tighten.

"I… I haven't really thought about that," he admitted softly, running a hand through his hair, the weight of unresolved questions pressing upon him. "There's so much to process, sweetheart. All these years—I've been searching for myself, trying to grasp what's real, what's possible. Honestly, I just need time to decide what's next. Whether to stay here or return… I truly don't know yet."

Ava's fingers curled gently around his, her grip anchoring her resolve. Her eyes searched his face, seeking a glimmer of reassurance.

"But… do you want to come back? Stay here?" Ava asked quietly. "Because I worry about you, Dad. You looked so scared that day at Raffles. Are you okay?"

Daniel gazed at her, cradling her face in his hands. She trembled beneath his touch, and his usually warm, lively eyes were now shadowed with uncertainty.

"Hey now," he said, his voice thick with emotion. "I don't really know what I want right now. I've been lost for so long—confused, unsure. But I'm grateful—so grateful for these days, for you, for everything we've shared. What I do know is that any decision will be made with Jung and me deciding what's best for us all. We're together now, Ava, and we'll never lose each other again, no matter what's decided. I just need some time. I promise I'll figure it out—the future, you, us. It'll take a while, but I will."

He paused, his expression softening. "We'll have more time together—I promise you that. We have so much to make up for. And I'll talk to Jung about our plans… perhaps about moving here. I know Soon Hee loves it and adores having a big sister."

Ava's eyes brimmed with tears, but her smile was steadfast.

"Dad, I'm moving back to Singapore too. I want to be closer—to you, to Mum, and to my new family. If I've learnt one thing… it's that you mustn't waste time. Money can't buy it."

Daniel paused, his gaze drifting to the small hand clasped in his own—the hand of a grandson he scarcely knew yet loved with a depth he couldn't fathom. The boy gazed up at him with wide, curious eyes, brimming with the same innocence and quiet hope Daniel sought within himself.

"No one knows that better than we do. That's certain."

In that fleeting moment, emotion surged through him. He was holding the future—the laughter of a child, the promise of a fresh start. Daniel knelt, and little Daniel reached up to touch his face, a tiny hand pressing gently against his cheek. Daniel smiled, tears welling once more.

This little boy—so full of wonder—reminded him that beyond the heartbreak and guilt, there was still love. Still patience. Still the chance to begin anew. For him. For them all.

He gazed at Ava, then at Soon Hee and Jung. Each had forged their own life. Their paths no longer ran side by side, yet an unspoken bond connected them—a recognition that love had evolved. It was no longer about missed chances. It was about honouring the present, respecting each other's journeys, and embracing joy in new forms.

Daniel gently caressed his grandson's tiny hand, then turned to Ava, meeting her gaze. His voice was soft yet resolute.

"I haven't all the answers yet. But I promise—I shan't waste another moment. We've lost too much already. I want to find my way, to be the grandfather and father I ought to be. This little one"—he glanced down at his grandson—"deserves the best. And I want to be there for him. Not just today, but every day henceforth."

A faint, hesitant smile curved Ava's lips.

"I want that too, Dad," she whispered, a flicker of hope gently rising within her.

Daniel rose slowly, carefully setting little Daniel down before reaching out to rest a hand on Ava's shoulder.

"We're all learning, my dear. It's alright to take our time. No rushing, no pushing. We're simply walking this path as honestly as we can, with kindness guiding each step."

They walked on—side by side—each bearing their hopes and uncertainties, yet hopeful that this newfound understanding might herald something quietly beautiful.

As the golden light of the sun bathed the sky in hues of amber and rose, Daniel realised that while the past could not be altered, the future was theirs to shape—one gentle step at a time, with love, patience, and the quiet trust that all would unfold as it should.

Daniel gazed down at his grandson and gently squeezed little Daniel's tiny hand. "Let's go," he said softly, his voice warm. "Let's go fishing on the pier whilst the others have their picnic. Just you and me—for a bit."

The boy's face lit up with excitement, and he nodded eagerly. Together, they strolled to the wooden pier. The others watched quietly as Daniel and little Daniel found a tranquil spot, casting their lines into the shimmering water. Sunlight danced on the surface, and the gentle lapping of waves wove a soothing melody. Nearby, the family shared food and stories, their gazes often drifting to the bond blossoming between the two.

Daniel sat beside his grandson, guiding him with the fishing rod. Their shared silence held a simple, unspoken understanding. After a moment, Daniel smiled and said, "You're doing a splendid job. The finest fisherman in all of Singapore."

Daniel then eased himself up from the pier's edge and turned towards the group seated on a rug, chatting amiably. A soft smile spread across his face as he glanced at Jung nearby—a silent thank you, a quiet hope for what lay ahead—as he waved gently.

But in an instant, everything changed. Without warning, Daniel's knees buckled, and he staggered forward, clutching his chest. His body tensed, then lost all balance. With a splash, he plunged into the water, sinking beneath the surface. His hand remained pressed to his chest, his face frozen in shock and confusion as he vanished into the gentle ripples.

The family on the rug froze, stunned as the water's ripples spread, shattering the tranquil scene in a heartbeat. A heavy silence fell, broken only as they scrambled to their feet, eyes wide with dread.

Jung was the first to react, her voice quavering as she cried out,

"Daniel! Oh, heavens—Daniel!"

Ava's scream pierced the air, sharp and laden with terror. She sprinted to the pier's edge, legs moving swifter than ever, heart pounding fiercely. Tears blurred her vision as she shouted desperately,

"Dad! Dad, no! Please!"

Little Daniel, nearby and bewildered, began to wail. His small face twisted in fear, tears streaming down his cheeks as he clutched his chest, unable to grasp the chaos unfolding around him.

Without hesitation, Gerry sprang into action. He dove into the water, swimming swiftly towards Daniel, arms reaching desperately as he battled the current and shock. His face was set with fierce determination as he gripped Daniel's shoulders and hauled him to the surface.

"Call an ambulance!" Gerry shouted, straining to lift Daniel onto the pier's edge, fighting the water's resistance. With all his strength, he dragged him onto the wooden planks and swiftly checked for signs of life. Daniel lay still—pale, chest unmoving.

Gerry didn't falter. He took a steadying breath, pressed his hands firmly on Daniel's chest, and began CPR. He tilted Daniel's head back, sealed his mouth over his, and delivered rescue breaths. Every second was a struggle—each compression, each breath, a fervent plea for life.

"Keep fighting," Gerry urged, his voice urgent yet steady. "Come on, you'll be alright. Just breathe, damn it…"

On the pier, the family stood frozen in helpless dread. Ava clung to Soon Hee, sobbing uncontrollably, her hands clawing at the air. Jung's face was ashen, tears streaming silently as she prayed in hushed tones.

The seconds stretched into an eternity—ragged breaths and distant sirens piercing the heavy silence. Gerry's hands never faltered, relentless on Daniel's chest, his gaze fixed on his face.

Suddenly, beneath his hands, Daniel's chest twitched—a faint, quivering shudder. Gerry leaned back slightly, keeping his mouth pressed firmly to Daniel's, whispering fiercely, his voice taut with hope and effort.

"That's it… come on… breathe, give me a sign."

His hands pressed harder, urging the weary body to respond.

Seconds dragged on like hours until, at last, a faint twitch—Daniel's chest rose in a shallow gasp. A collective breath caught in the throats of those watching, relief washing over them, yet tempered by the urgency still lingering.

In the distance, sirens grew louder, cutting through the tranquil afternoon. Flashing lights emerged as an ambulance skidded into view, paramedics leaping out with swift precision. They moved like a well-oiled machine—checking Daniel's carotid pulse, attaching monitors, their voices calm yet urgent.

Gerry stepped back, tension etched on his face as they stabilised Daniel—securely bound and carefully strapped to a stretcher.

"He's got a pulse now," a paramedic confirmed.

The siren's wail crescendoed—a desperate, hopeful cry that this fragile spark of life might yet burn brightly.

As the paramedics hurried to load Daniel into the ambulance, the family stood frozen in stunned silence. Ava clung tightly to Soon Hee, tears streaming down her cheeks. Mei Lin's eyes were wide, her hands quavering as she watched the paramedics work. Jung's face was taut with worry, her voice barely a whisper.

"We must get him to hospital. He's strong—he'll be alright."

Gerry approached, gently lifting little Daniel into his arms.

"I'll look after him," he said softly. "You lot need to get to hospital. Ensure Daniel's with the finest doctors. I'll follow once he's safely settled."

Without hesitation, they nodded. Fear and hope mingled as they piled into the car and sped towards the hospital. The ambulance siren's wail faded into the distance behind them—each heartbeat echoing their fragile hope that Daniel would survive, and that, perhaps, their lives might begin to mend.

23

Tomorrow's Dreams

T he sterile hum of the hospital corridors felt deafening as they hastened through the sliding doors, hearts pounding with a frantic blend of fear and hope. The ambulance team had already rushed Daniel into the emergency theatre—lifeless one moment, then fighting for every breath the next. Ava, Jung, Mei Lin, and Soon Hee followed swiftly, their steps urgent and uneven.

At the reception desk, Jung spoke first.

"Excuse me, do you know where Daniel Walker-Chung is? He was just brought in by ambulance—"

"No, wait. It'll be Back Eun Soo," Jung corrected herself, biting her lip.

The nurse checked her system, then replied softly, "He's been taken straight to surgery."

The words struck them like a wave. Now all they could do was wait—quavering and powerless—as the seconds stretched into an unbearable eternity.

In the crowded waiting area, Ava clasped her hands tightly, tears streaming down her cheeks, refusing to wipe them away. Her stomach twisted into knots, nerves frayed and raw.

I only just got him back," Ava whispered, her voice cracking with anguish. "And now… I don't know what to do. What if I lose him again? I can't—oh, heavens, please don't take him from me."

Her sobs grew louder, her eyes red and bright with desperation.

Jung sat beside Ava, her face pale, eyes red-rimmed from stifling tears. She tried to be strong—for Soon Hee and Ava—but the weight of the moment bore heavily upon her. Gently, she took Ava's quavering hand in hers.

"He'll be alright," Jung whispered softly, her voice fragile. "He's strong… a fighter."

Tears slipped down her cheeks despite her efforts to restrain them. Deep within, she bore the heavy knowledge that Daniel's heart condition was far graver than he had ever revealed to Ava or Mei Lin.

They sat in heavy silence, the burden of their worry nearly unbearable. Each second stretched endlessly as they waited for any news from the doctors.

Beyond those heavy doors, deep in the sterile labyrinth of hospital corridors, Daniel's body was a battlefield. Surgeons and nurses fought with relentless resolve against time and fate. They worked frantically, aware of the narrow window, praying their efforts would suffice to save him.

The line between hope and despair was razor-thin—each ticking minute a stark reminder of life's fragility.

In the waiting room, Ava broke the silence, her voice quavering.

"I only just got him back," she whispered, her voice a fragile breath. "I've lost so much time already… I can't lose him again. Please, someone, tell me he'll be alright."

Jung squeezed her hand gently, tears streaming down her cheeks.

"We must believe," she said softly. "We must cling to hope. That's all we can do now."

In that cold, tense waiting room, no words could capture what they truly felt—only the silent, relentless hope that, against all odds, Daniel would survive, that this nightmare, this heartache, would end. That the man who was more than a father, more than a husband, would awaken and find his way back to the family he cherished.

Later, in the quiet hours of the night, Daniel had been in surgery for hours. The family gathered anxiously in the dimly lit waiting area, hearts pounding with a blend of hope and dread. The sterile silence was thick with anticipation—each passing minute an eternity. Finally, a calm-faced surgeon emerged from the operating theatre, his expression sombre yet reassuring. The surgeon approached them gently, his gaze meeting each worried face.

"The operation went as well as we could have hoped," he said softly. "Daniel is still sedated, but his vitals are stable. It'll be a few hours before he wakes, and we'll need to monitor him closely. For now, I suggest you all go home and rest. He's in good hands—but he's not out of danger yet."

Relief washed over them in quiet waves, tempered by exhaustion. They absorbed his words in silence, clinging to the fragile hope that the fighting chance they'd prayed for remained alive. Tears welled in their eyes, and each murmured a quiet thank you—grateful, yet keenly aware the long night of waiting was far from over.

Jung gently drew Ava into her arms, the younger woman's face etched with fear and worry.

"He's strong," Jung whispered. "He's come this far, and he'll keep fighting."

"I'll stay here with him. You lot need to rest. We'll get through this—one step at a time."

"If you don't mind, I'd like to stay with you," Ava said quietly.

"Ava, you'll be more help to your father if you rest. You can return in a few hours. I'll ring if anything changes."

Ava hesitated, then nodded. "Alright, you're right. But let's all go home—you need rest too."

Jung gave a weary nod in agreement.

The others moved quietly towards the doors, each step heavy with unspoken prayers and fragile hopes that morning would bring better tidings.

After a brief taxi ride, they reached home, gathering in the sitting room. The atmosphere was calm yet thick with the residue of recent days. Soft golden light spilled across the space, casting gentle shadows as they shared memories— each tale coaxing a faint smile or a tear.

Jung rested her hand on her cup, her gaze drifting, her thoughts far away.

"You know," she began softly, "Daniel loved the radio. He'd spend hours tinkering with it, chasing the clearest signal, always dreaming of reaching someone far off. He was so passionate—it was as though he found a voice in those static-laden signals, a way to stay connected, even when all else seemed lost. And that's how he found you all again."

Ava smiled wistfully, nodding.

"He used to listen to the radio constantly… and he taught me to grow rice and vegetables in the garden. Said it was vital to know how to care for the land—to nurture things so they grow strong." Her voice warmed with the memory, and the others chuckled when she added, "He even tried to teach me to plant carrots, but I reckon I mostly just dug holes for fun."

The room filled with gentle laughter—the kind that springs from cherished memories. Even amidst the pain, those tales reminded them of Daniel's resilience and humour—his dreams rooted in small, simple joys.

Gerry grinned, leaning back, savouring the warmth of the moment.

"I knew he loved the radio and had crafted some rather clever things, but I never realised he was such a techie," he said with a smile. "No wonder he loved those faint radio signals."

"He always believed we could reach anyone, anywhere in the world, with hope… and a bit of patience," Mei Lin said.

"Let's hope there are many more chances for him to tinker with the radio and those sounds that sometimes drive you a bit mad," Jung said, mindful that Daniel's condition was grave.

They laughed again, and for a fleeting moment, peace settled over them. In sharing these memories, they held him close a little longer—keeping his spirit alive through each tale told. They treasured those quiet moments, woven from fragments of the past, bound by the love and resilience Daniel had inspired in them all.

Bearing the weight of uncertainty, they eventually retired to bed, seeking solace in sleep. Ava, though exhausted, lay awake for hours, gazing at the ceiling. Her mind replayed every moment with her father—the laughter, the lessons, the quiet, comforting presence she missed more than words could convey. Sleep eluded her, her thoughts tangled in a restless knot of hope and dread.

By 8:00 a.m., they were all awake. Faces drawn but resolute, they mustered their strength and prepared to return to hospital. The long night had only deepened their yearning for answers. They needed to be there when Daniel awoke.

The drive was quiet and tense, the air thick with unspoken worries. Upon arriving, they glimpsed the surgeon beside Daniel's bed, speaking softly to someone in the room. Their steps slowed, instinctively pausing just outside the doorway. Shoulders taut, they watched in silence.

The surgeon moved with purpose, his expression calm yet compassionate. As he stepped into the corridor and caught sight of their anxious faces, he offered a gentle smile.

"I'll return in an hour to speak with you," the surgeon said, his tone reassuring yet professional. "You may see him now—but please, no excitement. He's gravely ill."

The family exchanged glances—anxiously hopeful, yet keenly aware of how fragile each moment was. Without a word, they stepped forward, entering the room where Daniel lay.

He rested quietly beneath neatly tucked linens, his chest rising and falling in a steady rhythm. As they gathered round his bed, a faint smile touched his lips. Each person, in their own quiet way, offered silent prayers—words of hope, love, and yearning—for the man who meant so much to them. They willed him to keep fighting, to stay with them a little longer.

Daniel's eyes fluttered closed as he drew a deep, quavering breath. The room seemed to still with him, holding its breath in tandem. His face, pale and lined with the weight of all he'd endured, revealed the effort it took to remain present. Then, slowly, his eyes opened again, and he looked directly at Jung.

"Jung," he whispered, his voice hoarse and thick with emotion. "I need to speak with you... alone. Please, everyone, give us a moment."

The others hesitated, sensing the gravity in his tone. Yet with quiet understanding, they stepped away, granting the couple space—an unspoken acknowledgment of the moment's weight and all it might mean.

The hospital room was dim, sunlight slipping through half-closed blinds, casting long stripes across the floor. The others had gone, as Daniel had requested. Now it was only Jung—the woman who had once pulled him from wreckage and taught him to live again.

She sat at his bedside, her expression composed yet taut, as though she already knew.

Daniel reached for her hand. Even now, with barely the strength, her touch steadied him.

"I spoke to the surgeon this morning," he began, his voice low, words measured but heavy. "It's time, Jung. The damage… it's too far gone."

Jung didn't flinch. Her gaze held his—strong, brave, yet not unbroken.

"We knew this might come," she said softly.

Daniel nodded. "We did. But hearing it… makes it real. There's not much time left. Days, perhaps."

Silence fell between them, laden with all that needed no words. Then, slowly, Daniel reached for her hand with both of his.

"I need you to know something before they return. Before time runs out."

She leaned closer, listening, her tears held just behind her eyes.

"You saved me, Jung. Not just from that crash. From the emptiness. From the silence in my mind. I had no name, no memory… but you gave me a life nonetheless. You taught me to laugh again, to trust… to love. I wouldn't have survived without you."

Jung looked down, tears slipping silently onto his hand.

"You healed a man with nothing to offer. And then… you gave me everything. A home. A life. Soon Hee." His voice broke on her name. "Another daughter. A chance to be a father again, even without the memories of before."

Jung closed her eyes, her lips quavering.

"I need you to be strong now," Daniel continued, his voice steadier despite the pain. "Not just for yourself. For Soon Hee. For Ava and Mei Lin. They're all part of this now. One family, somehow."

Jung gazed at him, her eyes shining yet fierce.

"I don't know how I'll do this without you."

"You do," he said gently. "You've always known. You were the strong one. You'll be the bridge between the families— between the past and the future, between all I was… and all we became."

She leaned in, resting her forehead against his, her breath catching as she stifled a sob.

"You're not leaving alone," she whispered. "Not truly."

Daniel gave a faint smile, his eyes damp.

"No. For I'll carry you with me. And you—you'll carry me forward."

A soft knock sounded at the door—a gentle rhythm signalling the others were waiting.

Daniel reached up, slowly, and brushed a strand of hair from Jung's face. His fingers lingered, tenderly smoothing her hair back in a final, loving gesture.

Jung looked at Daniel and reached into her bag pulling out an old book. "Daniel, I know you planned to give this to Ava at the airport when we were leaving. But I figured you actually want to give it to her now"

Daniel took the book from Jung's hand. "I don't know what I would do without you"

"Go now," he whispered, his voice thin but resolute. "And let the others in."

Jung kissed his hand, steadied herself with a deep breath, and turned to the door. Her spine was straight, her heart full.

"Ava, Soon Hee, your father wishes to speak with you alone," Jung said, embracing Mei Lin as she passed.

Soon Hee and Ava clasped hands as they stepped closer to Daniel's bedside. Daniel gazed at them both and smiled.

"Seeing you two like this—friends and sisters—makes me the happiest man in the world. What I'm about to tell you requires courage. You have each other now—something I never thought possible. But I'm afraid the surgeon has informed me the prognosis is not good."

Both Soon Hee and Ava gripped Daniel's hands tightly, tears streaming down their faces.

"Soon Hee, I want to say—I love you so much. You're incredible, and you make your mum and me so proud," Daniel whispered softly. "Keep studying; you can achieve all your dreams, and I'll be watching you every step of the way."

"Ava, I'm overwhelmed with joy that we've been given this second chance — to see each other again, to hold what was almost lost. Please, don't be sad. That's not how it's meant to be. We've been given an incredible gift, a rare moment to reconnect and make up for the time we lost. I'm so proud of you, more than words can say. Gerry has been a wonderful father, stepping into my place when you needed him most. He has done a splendid job.

Be happy, Ava. I love you. That is something I've always been fortunate enough to tell you. Now, stay strong, girls. You will need to lean on each other and look after your mother. Please call Mei Lin and Gerry in. I want to speak with them alone."

 Daniel's gaze drifted to the book on the desk beside his bed. His voice grew soft and tender.

"Ava, can you take this for me? There's something inside I've kept hidden for a very long time, something I want you to have."

She gently opened the book, and there it was — the pressed flower she had given him, the one he had carried as a fragile symbol of hope and protection.

"You see," he whispered, his voice thick with emotion, "this flower kept me safe on my journey. It helped Jung find me and bring me back from the edge of death."

Tears welled in Ava's eyes. "Oh, Daddy, you kept this all these years."

He nodded, his voice trembling with love and regret. "Jung found it in my pocket. We both knew it was something special, though I didn't remember why at the time. Now I do. That's why I want you to have it."

This moment, this second chance to be together, carried the weight of everything they had lost and everything they still had to hold onto. Love, hope, and the promise of new beginnings filled the space between them, wrapped in a silent and profound connection that nothing could take away.

Mei Lin and Gerry entered the room.

"Mei Lin, as you now know, the surgeon's news is grim. There's nothing we can do about that, but let's be grateful we've come together again as a large, new family. We have the chance to say our goodbyes, to leave nothing unsaid—for that, we must be thankful. Gerry, I can't thank you enough for caring for my family, for being a father to Ava and a devoted husband to Mei Lin. You two are perfect for each other. I need you to be strong and look after the girls. I'm an incredibly fortunate man to have you all in my life."

"Not to worry," said Mei Lin. "We'll also care for Jung—she's like a sister to me now."

"We certainly will," said Gerry, placing an arm around Mei Lin's shoulder. Mei Lin then beckoned the others back in.

Daniel smiled at them both. "Thank you." His voice faltered on those words, tears clouding his vision, but he fought to hold on, struggling to voice the words his heart had held for so long. Then, softly, he gestured to them all, calling them into the room.

He gazed at everyone gathered there, his eyes lingering on each face with quiet affection.

"Love doesn't end with death," he whispered, his voice trembling yet resolute. "It lives within us, in everything we do. I carried that love for all of you—even when I was lost in the darkness."

A heavy silence settled over the room, so profound it weighed on their hearts—an unspoken farewell, a prayer that hope might yet endure. Jung nodded silently, tears streaming down her face, fully aware that the hardest part lay ahead— accepting the inevitable while clinging to the love that had always bound them.

Just then, the surgeon entered quietly. Daniel met his gaze with a weary, knowing look and nodded.

The surgeon hesitated briefly before speaking.

"Ah, so he's told you all," the surgeon said softly. "Be prepared. This won't last more than a couple of days. We'll do everything we can to keep him comfortable and ensure he's not in pain. Please spend as much time as you need with him. I'm terribly sorry—it's not better news."

Ava looked at the doctor, her voice steady yet tinged with hope.

"Could we take him home to pass away? I'm certain he'd prefer to be in his own home rather than a hospital bed."

"Yes," the surgeon nodded. "We can arrange that. I'll organise the ambulance now. If you can prepare a bed in the sitting room, I'll ensure he has sufficient pain medication."

With that, Ava phoned Gerry to make the necessary arrangements.

Within a few hours, Daniel lay in the ambulance with Jung beside him, the steady hum of the vehicle mingling with their quiet breaths. The city blurred past outside as they hastened towards the old shophouse, where Gerry had prepared a bed downstairs. The familiar place, steeped in memories of simpler days, now bore the weight of the moments to come.

Upon their arrival, Gerry was already there, offering gentle reassurance. He assisted in carefully transferring Daniel to the prepared bed. Each soft breath Daniel took seemed to carry both relief and fragility. The room was filled with those he loved—Jung, Ava, Soon Hee, and Gerry—all gathered close, their faces etched with worry and deep affection.

They spoke softly, sharing memories of days gone by. Ava chuckled as she recalled the times Daniel had taken her fishing at Seletar, his patient attempts to teach her how to grow vegetables, and the countless nights he'd spent tinkering with radios, striving to connect with the world beyond.

"Dad," Ava said softly, "remember how we loved fireworks? We've got some for you now in the back garden. Let me prop you up so you can see out the window."

Daniel smiled faintly, a glimmer of warmth piercing his weariness. As Jung adjusted his pillows, Ava drew back the curtains, letting the soft light of early evening flood the room—carrying the quiet comfort of home and the flickering promise of light even in the darkest hours.

The room was still, save for the faint crackle of spent fireworks outside and the gentle rhythm of Daniel's breathing. Ava and Soon Hee sat close, their hands entwined, sharing a fragile yet unspoken bond of strength. Gerry quietly brushed a tear from his cheek, the weight of the moment settling deep within him.

Jung rested her forehead against Daniel's hand, her voice barely a whisper. "We'll carry you with us always—in every laugh, every memory, every step forward."

Daniel's eyes closed slowly, a serene calm washing over his face. Though his body was frail, the love that filled the room lent him quiet strength in those final moments. The family remained close, enveloped in the warmth of their shared love and the gentle glow of the fireworks fading in the sky.

The family drew closer, their hands finding one another, sharing a warmth that words could not fully convey. Outside, the night deepened, but within that small room, time seemed to pause, cradling them in a fragile bubble of love and remembrance.

Jung leaned back slightly, her eyes brimming with tears yet touched by a quiet peace. "He's still with us," she said softly, "in every breath, every heartbeat, every story we share."

Ava nodded, her voice steady despite the ache in her chest. "We'll carry him in our hearts always. Together, we'll ensure his love never fades."

As Daniel's breaths grew fainter, the room held its collective breath—honouring a life fiercely lived, a love deeply felt, and the unbreakable bonds that would guide them forward.

Ava watched silently, the weight of the moment settling around her like a delicate veil. The room seemed to hold its breath once more, the only sound the faint rhythm of Daniel's waning heartbeat.

Jung lingered close, whispering words meant only for Daniel. "You'll always be with me, in every breath, every step."

Daniel's eyelids fluttered shut, his hand tightening once before slowly relaxing in hers.

The stillness deepened, and the family's shared love filled the silence — a quiet, unspoken promise that though his body would rest, his spirit would live on in each of them, forever.

Jung stayed close, her forehead resting softly against his, her tears falling like quiet rain. The room felt suspended in time — wrapped in the stillness of love and loss.

One by one, the family wiped away their tears, drawing strength from the bond they shared. Ava's fingers found Soon Hee's, their hands clasped tightly, a silent promise to carry Daniel's love forward.

Gerry's voice broke the silence softly. "He's finally free now. Free to rest."

Outside, the last embers of the fireworks flickered faintly in the night sky, a final, shimmering tribute to a life fiercely lived.

And though Daniel was gone, the love he left behind would never fade.

24

The Last Goodbye

The house stirred slowly, as if holding its breath. Ava rose next, roused from fitful sleep by the soft morning light filtering through the curtains. They dressed in muted tones, their movements careful and deliberate, as though wary of disturbing the fragile peace enveloping them. Outside, the first drops of rain began to fall, tapping gently against the windowpanes like a solemn hymn—a reminder that, even in sorrow, life pressed on, and they would carry Daniel's memory with them always.

Downstairs, Gerry busied himself quietly, preparing tea and breakfast, the familiar routines a small anchor against the swelling tide of grief. He glanced up as Mei Lin joined him, her hands clasped tightly in her lap.

"We'll get through this," he said softly, offering a weary smile.

She nodded, grateful for the steadiness in his voice.

Outside, the city's life pressed on—unaware, relentless—but within this modest home, time seemed to linger, marked only by soft footsteps, whispered prayers, and the steady, shared heartbeat of a family holding fast.

Soon Hee slept on, curled beneath soft blankets, oblivious to the quiet rituals unfolding around her. Jung paused at her door, hesitating briefly before brushing a stray lock of hair from her daughter's face. The tender gesture was both an act of comfort and a silent vow—that no matter what lay ahead, she would shield her family.

"Come, my darling, it's time to get ready. We need to be at Seletar soon—it was your dad's favourite place," she said softly.

In the kitchen, the faint aroma of brewing tea mingled with the soft morning light. Mei Lin and Gerry exchanged a glance—a shared understanding passing between them. Today would be difficult, but they would face it together.

The soft ticking of the clock resonated through the stillness, marking the steady passage of time—a reminder that soon, they would step beyond the shelter of these walls.

"Are we all ready?" Gerry asked. Mei Lin nodded, and they headed out the door to the cars waiting outside. The journey was silent, each lost in their thoughts.

They walked towards Seletar, where Jung gathered the family at a row of tables, their faces pale yet resolute. Mei Lin placed a small bouquet of jasmine and orchids on the low table, their fragrance delicate and comforting.

Soon Hee's voice broke the silence as she spoke softly. "Let's say a prayer together, for strength, for peace, and for Dad's journey ahead." Hands joined, eyes closed, breaths mingling in unison—a quiet circle of love and support.

Ava stepped forward first, her voice barely above a whisper yet steadfast with conviction.

"Dad, you taught me to be strong, even when the world seemed to crumble around me. I promise to carry your strength with me every day." She placed a small folded paper boat beside the urn, a symbol of the many fishing trips and quiet moments by the water they had shared.

Soon Hee followed, her eyes glistening with tears.

"Your kindness and patience have shaped who I am. I'll hold onto your love and the lessons you taught me—always." She gently laid a sprig of jasmine next to the boat, its fragrance rising like a silent prayer.

Jung's hand trembled as she touched the urn, her voice thick with emotion.

"You were my hope, my heart. Even in your silence, you spoke to me—of love, of courage, of never giving up. I'll carry you with me forever. Rest well, my darling."

Mei Lin lingered a moment longer, her fingers brushing the fabric of Daniel's jacket once more.

"We grew up together as children and later as husband and wife. We faced everything together, just as you said. I'll find you in the sunrise, in quiet moments, in every breath." She folded the jacket carefully, placing it beside the urn.

Gerry, steadfast and quiet, stood with his hand on Jung's shoulder, sharing the weight and solace of the moment.

As their final words faded, Khian Seng and Billy stepped forward, lifting the urn with care. The group moved together towards the water's edge, where gentle waves lapped against the shore, ready to receive the spirit of the man they all loved.

As their words drifted into the hush of the morning air, a soft breeze stirred the lake's surface, as though nature itself bowed in reverence.

Jung stepped forward one last time, clasping Soon Hee's hand tightly in hers. Her gaze lingered on the urn, the water, and then the faces of those who had shared this sacred journey.

"He once told me," she said, her voice faltering slightly, "that if he could no longer be here, I should find him in the stars, the warmth of the sun, the signal that never fades. That love, once sent into the world, always finds its way back."

She reached into her pocket and drew out a small piece of folded paper—a page from Daniel's journal. With trembling fingers, she released it into the lake, watching it float briefly before softening and sinking.

"Goodbye, my love," she whispered. "May you ride the frequencies of the universe, free and eternal."

Together, family and friends approached the water's edge, each releasing flowers—white frangipanis, jasmine, and hibiscus—into the gentle current. The blossoms swirled around the urn as it was lowered carefully into the lake, where it floated for a moment before the water embraced it into its depths.

A profound silence followed, filled with breath, tears, and memory. Then, from somewhere behind them, a small radio—one of Daniel's cherished relics—crackled to life. A soft melody played, faint yet familiar—a love song, a message from the past, a final signal piercing the static.

They stood, arms entwined, watching the last of the morning light dance across the water.

Even in farewell, Daniel's presence lingered—carried in the waves, in the hearts of those he touched, in the quiet hum of a connection that never truly ends.

The group drew closer, sharing stories, laughter, and tears— each word a tribute to the man who had been their guide, their inspiration, their friend.

Finally, Mei Lin stepped forward, her voice trembling yet resolute.

"Daniel, you were my anchor, my strength, my love. I hope you're at peace, free from pain and worry. I promise we'll carry your dreams forward—your love will never fade. You are already an eternal star in our hearts."

Quietly, they lifted the urn, hand in hand, and walked to the water's edge. The gentle ripples lapped at the shore, as though welcoming him, as they prepared to bid their final farewell.

As the ashes slipped from their hands, scattering into the serene depths of Seletar, a profound peace settled over them. In the hush of the moment, their tears shimmered like tiny droplets of hope, mingling with the water—a symbol of love's eternal journey.

In that moment, they understood: Daniel was not truly gone.

His spirit flowed on—carried by the waters, held in their memories, dwelling quietly in their hearts—an eternal vow of love that no tide, no time, could ever erase.

The ripples glimmered softly in the sunlight, as though honouring the quiet beauty of a life well-lived—one rooted in love, dreams, and connection.

Mei Lin's voice broke the silence, tender yet serene, carried on the breeze like a benediction.

"Daniel always believed in hope," she whispered. "In the power of connection, no matter how faint the signals. He found beauty in the smallest things—the hum of static, a fleeting voice, a star shining brightly in a dark sky. To him, love was the greatest broadcast of all."

Khian Seng stepped forward, his expression brimming with emotion.

"He was a man who saw possibilities where others saw only limits," he said softly.

"A dreamer who reached for the stars in his quiet way. I recall those late nights beside him, the radio crackling with life, voices dancing across the void—each a testament to his belief that love, and hope could bridge any divide."

Billy nodded, brushing a hand across his face, his voice low and heartfelt.

"He was the one who believed in the impossible. The kind of man who never stopped trusting that kindness and friendship could transform the world. I still hear his laugh—deep, warm, true—and I know his spirit lingers, reaching us through the invisible signals of life."

They stood in reverent silence, the stillness enveloping them like a gentle embrace. Then Jung stepped forward, her voice steady yet laced with profound emotion.

"Daniel, you gave us so much—your love, your dreams, your courage. We'll carry those onward. Your light. Your hopes. I know you can hear us. We'll keep your dreams alive, just as you kindled them in us."

She paused, a tear tracing down her cheek, and gazed across the water.

"You're not gone," she whispered. "You're in every star that shines, every story told, every heartbeat shared. You're part of the eternal sky now, and the boundless sea. And someday, we'll meet again—whether in this life or beyond. You are my eternal love."

With that, they gently placed a small, handcrafted wreath of flowers on the water's surface—a tender, symbolic tribute. The group stood in silence a moment longer, letting the love and memories wash over them like waves lapping gently ashore.

Gradually, the gathering began to disperse, leaving the tranquil waters to cradle their silent farewell. The sky darkened slowly as dusk settled, tinged with the soft promise of hope and renewal. Though their hearts remained heavy, there was an undeniable sense that Daniel's spirit endured— woven into the fabric of their lives, guiding them onward with a love as vast and eternal as the sea.

As they turned away, treading softly through the lush landscape, their steps remained quiet yet steadfast. In their hearts, they bore the peace of knowing: love's broadcast is never truly lost. It echoes on—etched forever in memory, shimmering in every star, rippling through each wave, and pulsing within every silent heartbeat.

As evening settled gently over Singapore, the sky deepened into a vast, velvety canvas strewn with stars. A soft coolness drifted through the air—a soothing balm after the day's warmth—carrying the faint fragrance of jasmine and dew-kissed grass. The rustle of leaves in the night breeze whispered like memory itself—quiet, comforting, eternal.

Ava and Daniel Jr. stepped into the garden, their footsteps softened by the yielding earth beneath them. Around them, the world stilled, bathed in serene tranquillity, broken only by the distant croak of crickets and the gentle lullaby of the night. The moon began its ascent, a pale silver disc casting its glow across the garden, blending with the stars in a quiet, celestial dance that stretched endlessly into the heavens.

They stood side by side, gazes lifted to the night sky—a quiet reverence binding them. In that moment, time seemed suspended, past and present woven together by love's unbreakable thread. The stars glimmered softly above, like tiny beads of light stitched into the dark fabric of the cosmos, each one echoing Daniel's spirit—his dreams, his laughter, his boundless love—shining down from the heavens.

Ava tilted her head, her voice a mere breath, eyes shimmering in the moonlight. "Look," she murmured. "A new star shines in the sky tonight." And in that delicate whisper, brimming with awe and wonder, lay a truth beyond words: Love endures. Always.

Daniel Jr. turned to her, his face gently lit by the starlight. His small chest rose and fell, heart thrumming with emotion. Then, almost instinctively, he reached out and clasped her hand—tiny fingers closing firmly around hers. His voice, pure and heartfelt, resonated with the love that had sustained him, even in his young heart. "I love you, Grandpa," he whispered into the cool night air, his words quivering yet true.

His voice carried a quiet, unyielding bond—death might claim someone from the world, but never the love sown deep within him by Mum, Dad, and Grandpa. That love had taken root, steadfast and enduring, like something no loss could ever sever.

In that tranquil moment, beneath an endless sky strewn with stars, they sensed Daniel's presence—his love shining brighter than any constellation. It dwelt in every glimmer, every breeze that caressed their cheeks, and every heartbeat resonating in their open hearts. Though he had faded from sight, his spirit was woven into the vastness above, murmuring messages of love that would never fade.

They stood in silence—an eternity of love and sorrow folded into a single breath—knowing, with quiet certainty, that Daniel's story was etched across the night sky.

His love was no longer confined to memory or words; it was celestial now—guiding them, inspiring them, and forever radiant in the tapestry of their lives.

Together, in the tranquillity of the night, they watched the stars wheel—hearts aching, yet brimming with hope. A gentle breeze stirred the treetops, carrying a murmur of Daniel's love—an unyielding bond that no tide or time could ever erase. And in that sacred moment, they felt something within them begin to heal—knowing the greatest gift of love is never lost, only transformed into eternity among the stars.